# ROYAL BLOOD

## TEMPLAR SERIES, BOOK 5

## DEBRA DUNBAR

debra dunbar
FIENDISHLY FUN FICTION

# CHAPTER 1

*I*t felt like every cell in my body was alive, tensing, hovering right on the edge of ecstasy as Dario worked his way along my skin with his hands and mouth. I shivered, enjoying every bit of this torturous anticipation while he skillfully tormented me, bringing me right to the brink of orgasm.

"Beg me, Aria." Fangs scraped against my skin. "Beg."

Something drifted in the back of my mind—something that said this was wrong, that his voice, those words weren't right. But his tongue teased up my inner thigh, and I suddenly could think of nothing else.

"Please. Please, please, please," I chanted.

"Please what? What do you want, Aria?"

His voice was velvety smooth. I tried to wrangle my thoughts, to articulate what I wanted only to feel the scrape of those teeth again. They triggered a yearning, a craving so sharp I could barely stand it.

"Bite me," I gasped, shoving aside that alarmed worry in the back of my mind. "Take my blood. Bite me."

He kissed my thigh, my waist, between my breasts, then dragged his fangs across the pulse in my neck.

"No." That worry was getting louder, more insistent. "My thigh. Inside my thigh where it won't show."

"But I want it to show, Aria. I want the world to know you're mine, that I have a Templar begging me to take her every night, begging for me to drink from her."

I wasn't in my bed. That voice wasn't Dario's.

I tried to roll away, to pull free, but it was too late. The vampire bit. Hard. Pain shot through me, quickly combined with a rush of pleasure. The two feelings battled for dominance, pain winning out as he ripped savagely into my throat.

I screamed, and he laughed. I wasn't in my bedroom, I was in a cage, naked on a cold cement floor. There were bite marks all over my skin along with the bruises. The symbol I'd painted on my neck hadn't worked. He'd taken me. He'd killed the entire *Balaj*. He'd killed Dario.

My family hadn't come for me.

With another scream I jolted upright in bed, covered in sweat. A dog whined by my side, a cat stared at me in concern from the edge of my bed.

Another nightmare. I glanced over at the clock. Outside of the two animals, I was alone in bed. It was a few hours before dawn, but Dario had left. That had been happening a lot in the last few weeks. He'd had so much to do trying to pick up the pieces of his decimated family and step into his new role as Master of the *Balaj* that our evenings together had turned into little more than booty calls.

And when he wasn't here, that's when the nightmares crept in.

Reaching up a hand, I touched the scar on my neck and shivered. It was a dream. It was just a dream. Simon was dead. I'd killed him. And Dario would never do something like that. Never.

Shaking off the memories, I jumped out of bed and pulled on some workout clothes. Clearly I wouldn't be able to go back to sleep again. Might as well get my morning run in early and have time for a leisurely breakfast before heading in to my shift.

The first six months I'd lived in Baltimore I hadn't practiced regularly with my sword. I hadn't lifted or jogged, or much of anything beyond work at the coffee shop and, I hated to admit it, sulk. But now I had purpose, and had realized with painful clarity that six months of relative inactivity had seriously put a dent in my skills. Wolfram had nearly beaten me at that reenactment tourney. I'd been taken out by beanbag-wielding mages three times at LARPs. My cardio and strength weren't what they used to be. And worse, I'd been disarmed twice by that asshole Simon. Yes, he was a vampire with greater speed and strength than I had, but Templars had been taking down vampires single-handedly since the Crusades. Keeping my sword against a Master might have been a stretch, but at the very least I should have been able to keep the sword for all of ten damned minutes.

So now I got up at an ungodly hour every morning, did calisthenics and jogged three to five miles. Every evening I did strength training and sword practice.

Fulk, my newly adopted bull terrier stood at the edge of my bed, his tail wagging with a sort of begging anticipation as I got my clothes on. Gaia, my cat, watched me for a few seconds, then curled back up to sleep, realizing food wouldn't be appearing in her bowl for at least another hour.

Dressed, I eyed the flak jacket beside my bed and with a sigh put it on. The thing weighed a friggin' ton. If it hadn't been November, I would have come up with all sorts of excuses, not the least of which would have been potential heat stroke, to avoid exercising while wearing it.

The jacket wasn't for protection, although in my neighborhood, a vest was probably a good thing to have. No, jogging with this thing on, with my sword across my back, was the equivalent of working out in plate mail. I needed to build my strength, and adding this weight to my daily runs was just as important as the deadlifts and pushups I did in the evenings.

I sat down to lace up my shoes and Fulk snuffled in my ear. "Yes, I'll take you. I'm doing five miles today, though. You better keep up."

He always kept up. For a solid ball of muscle with somewhat stubby legs, the bull terrier could really move. And I got the impression he could run far longer than I could at this time. The only real issue I had running with him was that with one hand on a leash, it wouldn't be particularly easy to draw and use my sword. Although the chances that I'd need my consecrated Templar weapon while jogging down the street with a bull terrier were pretty slim.

I headed downstairs, the dog right at my heels. "You ready to go boy?"

Fulk darted past me, then ran back and forth between his food bowl and the leash, not sure which option he wanted the most.

Yeah, I'd named him Fulk. It was in honor of the Count of Anjou who was a famous Templar in the twelfth century. Unfortunately I hadn't realized that Fulk sounded an awful lot like that other F-word, so when I was calling my dog in the park, people thought I was shouting obscenities at him.

It was too late to change the name now. I would just have to enunciate more carefully, and hope that no one started calling my dog Fuck.

Whistling the pooch over to me, I did what I did every

morning, every time I came back from work, every time I settled in for the night. I took his blocky, wedge-shaped head in my hands, and looked deep into the mischievous little eyes.

"Raven?" I whispered.

Fulk stilled, staring back at me in that way dogs do, as if he were trying to read my very soul. Then his tongue shot out and slurped across my chin.

I kissed the top of his head and gave his ears another scratch, disappointed, but happy I'd adopted him even if there was no sign of my friend's spirit in those dark eyes.

Putting the coffee on to brew, I looked down and muttered a choice word at the small puddle of water around my refrigerator. Yesterday the ice maker had gone on the fritz. I'd cleaned it all up and turned the thing off, but it seemed the leak was somewhere in the line before it got to the fridge.

It was too early to call the property management company, so I threw an old towel on the floor, made a mental note to call them later today, then hooked the leash onto the collar of my very excited dog and headed out. We'd had a cold snap this week, the daytime temps dropping from their usual mid-forties down to just below freezing. That meant the pre-dawn readings were in the low teens and twenties— not at all what my Virginia self was used to and not really typical in Baltimore this time of year from what the others at the coffee shop had told me.

My breath clouding before me, I took off down the street and shook away the remnants of the nightmare with the rhythm of my stride. Within a few blocks I was sweating, more because of the extra weight of the vest and my sword than any speedy pace. My mind wandered as I ran, thinking about the Thanksgiving holiday in two days, about my increased hours at work, about the next reenactment thingy where I'd be expected to wear a dress and not my armor. I thought about my grocery list, the next oil change for my car, and how I needed to call the property management about the broken ice maker in the fridge.

I thought about Dario. Had I made a mistake moving our relationship to a physical one? Would it be possible to sustain something long term with him without involving my blood? Would either of us have the strength to hold back on that?

We each had duties and responsibilities which occasionally conflicted. How would we handle that? Did he expect I'd give the *Balaj* preferential treatment if one of those conflicts occurred? I grimaced, realizing that I already had given them preferential treatment. And Dario had certainly gone to bat for me with Leonora in the past. Would he continue to do that now as the Master, or would he need to take more of a hard line as the head of his family?

And would he ever have time for more than dinner and sex two or three times a week?

I was so engrossed in my thoughts that I tripped over something and went flying. My hands flew out as I landed belly-first on the pavement, skidding forward and nearly taking out a parking meter with my head.

I let out a few very un-Templar-like words and eyed my hands, which were stinging and sore, covered with sidewalk rash, dirt embedded in the scrapes. I grimaced at the tear in my coat as I stood and brushed my hands on my pants. I'd need to fix that with my less-than-stellar seamstress skills. Maybe I should ask for a coat for Christmas, given that this one now looked like I'd dug it out of a garbage can.

Fulk waited patiently as I took inventory of my cuts and scrapes. Satisfied that I hadn't torn my ACL or sprained my wrist, I turned around to see what the heck I'd fallen over.

It was a man with his legs outstretched. A guy bundled up

against the cold and propped up against a parking meter as he sat on the sidewalk.

"Shit! I'm so sorry!" I brushed my hands on my coat once more, then approached to further apologize. Life on the streets had to be bad enough without early morning joggers tripping over your legs.

The man remained motionless, a blanket wrapped around him and a knit cap pulled low on his head. I hesitated, not wanting to disturb some dude who might be still drunk from last night, or who had managed to sleep through my almost stepping on him, but I felt as if I should check and make sure he was okay.

"Sir?" I stepped close to him, bending down a bit to see his face. Was this even a guy? Wrapped in a blanket with that hat, I couldn't really tell.

Fulk sniffed the man, then looked up at me as if for guidance on what to do next.

"Sir?" A puff of air clouded before me, making me realize that I wasn't seeing the same from this man... woman...whoever.

It had probably dropped below twenty last night and although he had a blanket, he was out here on the street with no shelter. Malnourished. Maybe drunk. Maybe ill. Had he succumbed to the cold?

"Sir?" I went to tap him with my foot only to realize how horribly rude that would be. So instead I knelt down farther and reached out a hand to gently shake him.

The man, or woman, was cold. Stiff. As frozen as the sidewalk he was sitting on.

I scrambled backward. Fulk gave a startled bark and stared at me in alarm. Dead. I'd tripped over a dead person— some homeless man...or woman. I'd been pretty darned poor since moving to Baltimore, sometimes going without a meal or eating the cheapest thing I could find in the grocery store, but I'd never faced this. Even poor I'd had the bank account my parents regularly contributed to as an emergency option. Even poor I'd had an apartment to go home to, heat, hot water for a shower, a bed with a warm down comforter and squishy pillows.

I'd never really known poverty. Until six months ago, I'd lived the sort of wealthy, privileged life that most people only dream about—and I'd never once realized that was out of the ordinary. Yes, I knew some people went without. I knew there were places in the world, places a short drive from my family's insanely luxurious estate, where people lived in abject poverty. But it had all seemed so remote, something to contribute to a few times a year, feeling smug and self-right-eous as we mailed off our check. But since I'd moved to Baltimore, I'd realized how many people lived right on the edge of homelessness—and realized how many people toppled over that edge.

And although I'd seen more dead bodies than I ever imag-ined in the last few months, this one at my feet hit me hard.

Yanking my phone out of my pocket, I dialed 911, sat down on the cold sidewalk next to my dog and a dead person, and waited.

The police and the paramedics arrived at the same time. And right behind them a man I hadn't expected to see at five o'clock in the morning on, what had to have been in this city, a fairly common call.

"Don't you ever sleep?" I called out to Detective Justin Tremelay. I was pretty sure the clothing under the long wool coat was wrinkled as always, and that his socks didn't match. He was hatless and without gloves, although the cup of coffee he carried in his hand was most likely keeping his fingers warm.

"I was awake and out of the shower when the call came over the radio. I figured you were the only woman crazy enough to jog in this neighborhood before dawn, so I came out to see what trouble you'd gotten yourself into this time."

I held up my scraped palms to show him. "I tripped over a dead man."

Tremelay looked over at the paramedics who were checking to make sure the man was, in fact, dead, while a few people I assumed were from the medical examiner's office waited nearby. The paramedics gave the other guys the nod and they began removing a gurney from a nondescript van in an unhurried fashion.

"This isn't exactly noteworthy compared to everything else you've been embroiled in the last few months," Tremelay commented with a quick sip of his coffee.

I shivered, wishing *I* had a cup of coffee. Now that I wasn't running, I was feeling the chill, my sweat probably starting to turn to ice on my skin. "Did he freeze out here? What do you think happened? Why didn't he go to a shelter?"

I'd volunteered at a cold weather shelter last month and couldn't imagine why someone would choose to take their chances on the street as cold as it had been last night. The man hadn't even tried to get out of the wind under a porch or between two row houses. He must have been miserable exposed to the elements like this, even with the blanket.

Tremelay took another sip of coffee. "A lot of the homeless are mentally ill, and they either don't want to be in a shelter, or their behavior gets them kicked out. And some users would rather take their chances on the street than not have access to their drugs for the night."

As the officer walked over to us to take my very brief and not very enlightening statement, I couldn't help myself from watching as the two EMTs straightened the man out as best they could, unwrapping the blanket from him and removing his hat.

Yes, it was a man. Yes, he was dead from the blank staring

eyes, and the abnormal pallor that I could clearly see from ten feet away. I frowned, noting that the man wasn't dressed in what I assumed a homeless person would be wearing. I'd imagined a dozen layers of thrift-store, cast-off clothing, but this man had on a decent pair of khaki pants and what looked to be a designer brand knit shirt. What he didn't have was a coat.

How had a middle-class suburb guy ended up without a coat in a sketchy area of Baltimore, wrapped in a cheap fleece blanket on the sidewalk in below-freezing temps?

"He doesn't look like he's living on the streets," I commented to Tremelay.

The detective glanced over at the body being zipped into a bag and loaded onto a stretcher. "We've got lots of working poor in this city, Ainsworth. Could be he got off his shift too late to get to a shelter. Could be he was using and either dozed off and froze, or overdosed. We've lost a lot of homeless people this week with the cold snap, and we lose a lot of people to drugs—not all those people look like a stereotypical user either."

I eyed the man, frowning again at his attire. "Yeah, but he's not dressed like I'd expect. Working poor would be in a uniform, not looking like they just walked out of casual Friday at the office. I volunteered at one of the cold weather shelters last month, and none of them had nice, clean clothes like that."

My "volunteering" had been court ordered, but I'd signed up for a few additional shifts this month, and three more in December. This was my city. I should do my part.

"You'd be surprised. Steak one day, on the streets the next. Could be he makes enough money to use the laundromat and dress in decent clothes, but not enough to afford rent."

I'd been very close to that just a month ago. This could have been me with my nice clothes living on the streets.

No, it wouldn't have been. I had that checking account. I had a wealthy family who would welcome me back home with open arms, or wire me thousands of dollars in the blink of an eye. And even if I refused their help, I had a car to live in. I had a vampire boyfriend who would have pitched the mother of all fits and hauled me off to his house in Federal Hill, fed me Italian food, and tucked me into bed before going off to wherever it was he sheltered during daylight.

"Head on back home, Ainsworth," Tremelay commented. "We'll take it from here. Nothing for you to concern yourself about on this one."

I watched as they loaded the body into the van to take to the morgue. No. Probably no need for me to worry at all. Just one more death in a city where death seemed to be a brutal reality of daily life.

# CHAPTER 2

It was a busy day at Holy Grounds for a Tuesday. I assumed a lot of people were getting in extra caffeine, trying to cram as much work as possible into the two days before the Thanksgiving holiday, because I was pouring double and triple shots left and right. We were all cheerful—even those of us who would be coming in early Friday after gorging ourselves on turkey the day before.

I was one of those people. It was going to be a scramble driving down to my parents' house Wednesday night, eating and spending time with family Thursday and driving back late to make sure I got in for my early shift. It sucked being the low person on the seniority totem pole, but I was grateful for the extra hours. From what Sean had said, other employees tended to want time off during the holiday season, so I'd have the opportunity to make a whole lot of extra money if I was willing to be flexible about my schedule and work the occasional double shift.

I didn't mind as long as I could hop down to Middleburg for Christmas Day, and as long as I could squeeze in a Wednesday night here and there for my game with Zac and the others. Thankfully there didn't seem to be much LARPing or reenactment activities over the holidays and my presence wouldn't truly be required until early January when I was expected to make a royal appearance at some Twelfth Night celebration.

"What are you doing tonight?" Brandi interrupted my thoughts with the question and a cup that had chai latte with soy and one-shot written on it.

"Date night. Dario and I are going out for dinner." That was the plan anyway.

"Incurable Optimism is playing down at The Ottobar tonight. Anna, Grace and I are going. You guys should join us."

I hesitated because outside of introducing Dario to my family, to Janice that one time, and to Raven, I hadn't included him in any of my other activities. Of course, a lot of those activities took place during the day when he was unavailable, but there was no excuse for why I hadn't included him in evening reenactment events, or role playing games, or when I went out with the girls. It seems when Dario and I were together, we were together alone.

Why was that?

We'd only been romantically involved for a short time, and he was so busy with the *Balaj* that I wanted some one-on-one the few times we managed to get together. Yes, that was it. It wasn't that by including him in activities with my other, human, friends, I'd somehow be making this thing we had together real—making him my official boyfriend. Introducing him to my friends would be like changing my status on Facebook from "single" to "in a relationship". It would be a public proclamation that we were a couple. And for some reason I balked at that.

Frothing the soy milk, I made a decision. "Sounds good.

What time are you all going to be there? We've got dinner reservations at nine, but we can show up afterward."

Brandi grinned. "The band doesn't start until ten. I'm psyched you're coming. We've all been dying to meet your boyfriend."

Boyfriend. I gulped and finished the drink, calling it out as I put it on the pickup counter and grabbed the cup for the next order.

Yes, I guess Dario *was* my boyfriend, although we'd never really sat down and discussed the details of our relationship. We'd communicated that exclusivity was a requirement for both of us. We both clearly had an emotional attachment to each other. We had mind-blowing sex every chance we got. That seemed to check off all the boxes of what would make Dario a boyfriend. But him being a vampire, and now the Master of the Baltimore *Balaj*, made me hesitate to use that label.

*My boyfriend is a vampire.* It sounded like an absolutely delightful campy horror-comedy, but in real life I didn't see a happily ever after to this relationship, no matter how emotionally invested I was in it. Could I go on like this forever, giving up the traditional marriage and kids I'd always assumed were somewhere in my distant future? And more importantly, would the pair of us be able to hold off on the blood thing that would end with me an addicted blood slave?

I never thought there was much appeal in having some dude bite me and drink my blood, but each time I had sex with Dario, it grew more difficult to resist—especially since I'd actually been bitten against my will twice by that asshole Master from the Philadelphia *Balaj* and knew firsthand how it felt.

You'd think having someone blood rape me twice would totally turn me off the idea. Yes, I still had nightmares about it. And the worst part of those nightmares was, along with the fear and helplessness, the anger and hatred, I'd still be turned on, my body rebelling against my mind because of that stupid narcotic in vampire venom. Just thinking about it made everything south of my waistband come alive—which pissed me off to no end.

And sicko that I was, I wanted Dario to erase all that. I wanted to associate the feeling of having a vampire feed from me with *him*, not that asshole in my nightmares. But I was pretty sure if we went down that path, it wouldn't be a one-time occurrence, and I didn't want to end up a blood slave to a vampire, no matter how much I cared about him.

I ended up working until three, overlapping a bit with Chalese to help Sean restock the syrups and pastry case, then with a promise to see Brandi and the girls later, I headed home, bundled Fulk into my car, and drove to my appointment with a necromancer.

# CHAPTER 3

*R*ussell stared at the crystal ball in front of him, then at the dog, then back at the crystal ball. His coffee table was littered with divination items—Ouija board, Tarot cards, the ball, two empty cups with tea leaves wet and slimy in the bottom, a pile of small bones.

The bones kinda weirded me out, but then just about everything to do with necromancy kinda weirded me out.

"He's a dog," Russell pronounced. It hadn't been the first time he'd made that statement.

"Yes, I know he's a dog, but Raven was in there. This dog rose from the dead at the animal shelter. He made her signature checkmark on the cement floor. I looked into his eyes, and I swear I saw Raven."

The necromancer gave me one of those looks, like the kind you give toddlers on the edge of an exhaustion meltdown. "I'm so sorry, Aria. He's a dog. There's no spirit possessing him. At the moment, anyway."

I seized on that last sentence. "But maybe there was? Maybe she's in one of the figurines, the *lelek raktarban*? Or floating around the house?"

"I'm sure if she was in one of the *lelek raktarban* or in your house, she would have made herself known to you by now."

I knew he was right, but I also knew that for a moment there at the animal shelter, I'd been positive that Raven was communicating with me through this dog. The fact that I'd sensed no sign of her since then didn't negate that fact. She'd been there, I was sure of it. And I held on to the faint hope that she might still be somewhere nearby, waiting for the right moment to return to communicate with me again.

Was I wrong to hold on to hope like this? Should I be praying instead that she had found peace in the afterlife? I needed to let go. I really needed to let go. But that moment in the animal shelter had given me questions, and I needed to answer those questions before I could even think about letting go.

Russell sighed once more and scooped the bones into his hand, tossing them on the table as he'd done twice previously. "Let me see if I can divine her spirit's whereabouts."

He stared at the bones intently. Squinting. Leaning closer until his nose practically brushed the surface of the coffee table. "Her spirit is not on this plane of existence."

My heart sank. Was she in purgatory? Hell? In Balsur's clutches?

"But..." Russell hesitated.

"But?" I held my breath. Watching Balsur crush Raven's fox figurine in his demonic hands, hearing her screams as he'd forcibly ripped her spirit from the *lelek raktarban* had devastated me. It had devastated her lover, Reynard, who'd been ready to throw me under the bus and make a deal with the demon to bring her back to the land of the living. She'd given her life for me twice, erasing the demon mark and saving my soul. And now it was my turn to help her.

Fulk hadn't shown *any* signs of Raven's presence since the animal shelter. I'd been so positive, but had I imagined it?

Was it all in my mind? Was it grief that filled my mind with memories of Raven's screams, with dreams of her terrified eyes, full of agony and desperation as she reached out toward me from a lake of fire?

"But… It's like when you jam a foot in a doorway." Russell rubbed his nose and frowned at the bones. "There's an opening. There's something that's not letting the veil shut all the way."

My heart skipped a beat at the thought. "Veil in general? As in it didn't close completely after the Halloween window? Or as in Raven's got one foot still in the land of the living?"

He shook his head. "I don't know."

I hoped it wasn't the first, because then the nasty creatures that inhabited the underworld might be able to squeeze through. During the three days surrounding Halloween, the veil between the worlds thinned, and under certain circumstances, the demons and other unsavory beings could communicate, or even sometimes cross. But I wasn't sure the second of my scenarios was much better. From what I'd read, a spirit that didn't fully cross over risked being torn apart until nothing remained.

"This isn't completely unusual, Aria," he added with a sympathetic smile. "Yes, the veil is thin around Halloween, and it is easier for spirits to cross over, but a skilled medium knows how to find the tiny gaps in the veil and use their talent to communicate through those gaps."

I stared at the bones, realizing what I knew about magic involving the dead wasn't much. As a Templar, I knew how to put restless souls at ease, and about the various types of ghouls and undead that we might need to fight and battle. What I didn't know was more than the vague and somewhat contradictory Christian dogma about what happens to a soul after death.

Maybe that's where I needed to start in order to figure

out if Raven was okay in her afterlife, or if she needed my help.

"When you communicate with spirits on the other side of the veil, do you temporarily bring them through? What's on the other side and what's it like? Is there a way to tell if a spirit is in heaven, or hell, or purgatory?"

Russell sat back. "The veil shrouds many places, and each spirit's afterlife is individual. Some rest in slumber until the call of end-times. Others exist in a calm peace, other spirits appear to be distressed. None of them has ever communicated specifically what their afterlife is in concrete terms. Necromancers and others talented in spirit work only get emotions and abstract expressions of what the spirit experiences. And no, we cannot fully bring a spirit across, at least not without a difficult ritual and either an incredibly powerful necromancer or the combined efforts of a group. Even then, it would be a temporary ritual. We channel the dead. We communicate with them. I can raise the dead for a limited time with only an echo of their former spirit, but that's the extent of my abilities."

I thought back to séances I'd attended, to readings where mages skilled in spirit work communicated with the dead to divine the future. "So when you communicate with those who have died, it's like a telephone call reaching through the veil?" I asked.

Russell collected the bones on the table, moving them to the side. "It's something like that, but a portion of the spirit being *does* reach through to inhabit the medium or communicate through our tools. But it's temporary. We may be able to sense and utilize the small gaps in the veil, but we cannot hold a spirit across two worlds for long."

I frowned in thought. "Can a spirit find the gaps and temporarily send part of itself across without the help of a medium?"

I was pretty sure there had been no medium at the animal shelter calling Raven's spirit across the veil to communicate through Fulk, so either she'd done it on her own, or at the time she'd still been on this side of the veil.

"Normally I would believe that an earthbound spirit temporarily possessed the dog, as it would take an incredibly powerful being to communicate through the veil unassisted, but you said you were sure it was Raven, and my divination says she is no longer in this world…"

"Maybe she was on this side of the veil at that time," I guessed.

Russell scrunched up his face. "It's possible. But if she'd been determined enough to communicate with you that she possessed a dog, then I can't believe she would willingly cross. And from what you've told me about this Balsur demon, I'm sure he would have flung her spirit across the veil."

I agreed. In fact, my greatest fear was that Balsur had cast her down to hell to torment personally. Seeing her for that brief moment in Fulk, watching her make the raven mark on the floor, had given me hope that she'd escaped the demon's clutches, but still I had to know.

"Raven was a skilled mage," I told Russell. "She knew her stuff when it came to Goetic demons. She'd have more knowledge than most people since her expertise lay in bringing demons across the veil. Completely. If any mage would have known the gaps and how to use them, it would have been her."

I wasn't nearly that skilled. Yes, I'd been involved in some mid-level rituals during my short time in Haul-Du, and I'd led a few where I'd brought across a low-level Goetic demon —including the time I mistakenly got Balsur instead. Yes, I understood demons as a Templar, knowing how to send them back across the veil. But I didn't fully understand the veil itself, or everything that lay on the other side.

"If she was able to find the gaps and powerful enough to cross, then she may well have been able to communicate with you briefly through the dog," Russell said. "Besides the small gaps that mages skilled in spirit work use, there are larger, more temporary openings. At the point of death, when the deceased's spirit crosses the veil, there is a brief doorway. A spirit with considerable power and skill can take advantage of that, cross the veil and take the body in that twilight moment, possessing it."

I stared at Russell, open-mouthed. Was he saying a powerful being could come back from the dead? Take over a deceased person's body? How long would that continue, especially if the body itself were badly damaged or failing?

"You mean a spirit could permanently possess the body of a person or animal who had just died?" I looked at my dog, suddenly wondering who the heck was in there if the original dog spirit had crossed over and Raven had only been able to be in the body temporarily.

"Oh no. At least, not without an incredibly complicated ritual and a powerful mage. What you're talking about is basically a resurrection with a soul-swap. There are so many variables involved that the risk of failure is high. If everything isn't just so, if the mage hasn't sufficient power to complete the ritual, then all sorts of disasters could occur."

"Such as…"

Russell shrugged, as if we were talking about the chances of rain tomorrow. "The wrong spirit could come through and take the body. The desired spirit could fail to cross completely and the body would end up a zombie. The original spirit could snap back as a resurrection. Both spirits could end up possessing the body. Lots of things."

"What happens if two spirits possess the same body?" I looked down at Fulk once more.

"In that case the spirit crossing the veil is pulled back along with the desired one, and two spirits inhabit the same body." Russell shook his head. "The two will always battle for control. Either the stronger spirit will prevail, or both will go mad. Unless a necromancer is able to force one of them out of the body and across the veil, that is."

"But a necromancer wasn't involved with what happened at the animal shelter," I told him. "Or a medium, or any sort of mage. Just me, and I wasn't doing anything magical at the time."

Russell smiled sympathetically. "Then I would guess that Raven's spirit was able to temporarily communicate through a gap in the veil. That action blocked the animal's spirit from crossing, and when she left, the dog's spirit returned to the body."

I scratched Fulk behind the ears. "But according to the people at the shelter, he's not the same. They told me he'd been used as an attack dog, used in dog fights. He was aggressive, unpredictable, violent. They were putting him down because he was a danger to whoever would adopt him."

They'd tried repeatedly to dissuade me from rescuing the dog. And the Fulk I'd brought home was nothing like the aggressive monster they'd described. He was happy and slobbery and goofy. I thought he'd probably protect me if needed, but he might be just as likely to run away or lick my attacker to death.

"Our personalities are not only formed by our spirits, Aria," Russell said. "Yes, a spirit will carry the memories of its former body and life, but returning to the body after it has died…well, the longer the body is dead, the longer the spirit is separated from it, the more they both change. Joining them back together doesn't always result in the same personality as the person—or dog—was before."

I thought of Russell's sister, now known as Bella. She'd been dead before being turned as a vampire and although she had some memories of her human life, she was a child in her mind, and disabled to the point that she needed a caretaker. Dario had turned her, and his devotion and love for her had meant she'd survived and was enjoying a happy life when most vampire *Balajs* would have put her down. Had the same sort of thing happened to Fulk? He didn't seem mentally disabled to me, he just seemed like a normal, happy dog, but I guess he hadn't been dead for over an hour like Bella had.

Raven was on the other side of the veil. And she'd tried to communicate with me. What had she been trying to say? To tell me? Was she safe and happy? Did she need help? I glanced at Fulk once more and looked up at Russell.

"Do you think it would be possible to communicate with Raven? If she was strong enough to slip through that one time at the animal shelter, then do you think you could call on her? I just want to make sure she's okay."

Russell met my eyes with a long, hard stare. "And what exactly do you plan to do if she's not? What will you do if her spirit is in distress, or hurt, or possibly in hell?"

I swallowed hard. "I don't know. I just...I just need to know."

It was a lie, because I'd do anything to help Raven out. It might take me years, but I'd do it. I'd try to contact Reynard again. I'd find another mage to mentor me. I'd read every book in my father's library, in the Temple itself. I'd light thousands of candles in thousands of churches and ask every holy person I came across to intervene. I'd help her, because she'd given her life to help me.

Russell nodded, and I got the feeling he'd seen right through my lie.

"Okay. Come see me Saturday morning and I'll do my best."

I thanked him, collected my dog and left, hoping that Saturday would give me some answers—and that those answers would put my worries at ease.

# CHAPTER 4

*I* got home with barely enough time for a quick workout before I showered and prepared to meet Dario, but I managed, even squeezing in time to curl my hair and put on more than the bare amount of makeup. Satisfied that I looked as good as I was going to get, I checked that the leak from my ice maker wasn't any worse and that the towel was in place, then I grabbed my keys and got ready to head out. That's when I got the text.

*Problem with a group of rogues at the north end of town. Need to reschedule dinner. Tomorrow? If I can wrap things up before dawn, maybe I can swing by your place.*

I gritted my teeth, torn between disappointment, frustration, and worry. He had a responsibility to what remained of his family. I couldn't fault him for putting their needs and future before romance. Part of me longed for the days when he was second in charge and had more free time, but if I was honest with myself, even then he'd been at the beck and call of Leonora and been just as busy.

*Heading down to my parents tomorrow night for the holidays.*

*If I don't see you tonight, then let's do Friday night instead. Be safe.* I finished the text with a heart emoji, trying, knowing full well that I'd make the same decision in terms of priorities if I were in his place, and that it would be hypocritical of me to think otherwise.

Still, here I was, hungry, dressed up, with makeup on and my hair done, and nothing to do for another hour until the band started at The Ottobar. I looked down at my phone and texted Brandi.

*Want to meet for a late dinner? Pregame before the band? Dario had to work tonight and I'm starving.*

A few seconds later my phone dinged.

*We're at Maisy's on Charles getting pizza and beer. Come join us!*

I glanced in the mirror, thinking I might be a little over-dressed for pizza and beer. Five minutes later I was in jeans and a fitted t-shirt, my curled hair in a ponytail, and my makeup a little less smoky eye. Dinner and drinks. A cool band. Some time with my friends. And hopefully I'd come home to a sexy vampire waiting for me.

Hopefully.

The Ottobar was a hipster homage to a grunge dive bar. There were bar stools with tall tables, booths, couches, a pool table, and scribbled graffiti on the walls, pillars, and beams in black Sharpie. Opposite the bar was a pinball machine and a row of gumball and candy dispensers that looked straight out of the '70s. The band was setting up on the small stage fronted by an equally tiny dance floor. We were there early, and the place was already crowded.

"Beer or booze?" Anna asked as we wove our way to the bar.

I'd had a few beers with the pizza and was definitely feeling a buzz, but with that buzz came a sense of freedom. Screw it. I hadn't indulged in ages, and I deserved to cut loose a little. If I got drunk I could just Uber home. It's not like anyone would steal my car or lift the worn tires. And if Dario managed to come over before dawn, he could watch my drunk ass sleep it off. I'd worked my butt off today. I'd fallen over a dead homeless man while jogging this morning. My boyfriend was a vampire.

I totally deserved to tie one on.

"Vodka and cranberry," I told Anna, knowing that I'd need the cranberry to cover up the taste of the cheap rail vodka. Back home I would have sipped expensive whisky, but that was out of my budget here. Honestly, vodka and cranberry was out of my budget, so after this one, I'd probably have to go back to the cheapest draft beer they had. Unless some guy was kind enough to buy me a drink, that is.

Hey, I had on makeup. It could happen.

I dug some money out of my wallet and passed it to Anna, standing behind her to help carry the drinks as Brandi and Grace went off to search for any available seating.

Stepping back, I bumped into someone and felt a splash of something wet and sticky on my arm.

"Oh, I'm so sorry!" I turned around and looked up into a pair of blue eyes.

"My fault." The man smiled and wiped the beer from my arm with his sleeve. He was tall and lean with over-long brown hair and a thin angular face. It was his eyes that held me—deep-set between high cheekbones and a heavy brow, they were an odd gray-blue, like shifting storm clouds over the ocean.

"I'm Aria." I held out my hand—the one that didn't have beer on it. "Aria Ainsworth."

"Rick Dimond." He shook my hand, still trying to wipe beer from my other arm. "Let me buy you a drink. It's the least I can do after practically dousing you with mine."

In spite of his concern, it had barely been a splash, and

my arm was hardly injured by a little bit of beer. But I recognized the offer for what it was, and I wasn't averse to having someone buy me a drink, or chatting with a man who clearly was admiring my appearance.

"I'd love a beer," I told him. "Whatever you're drinking."

Yes, I was absolutely okay with trolling for free drinks in a bar, but I wasn't about to take advantage of the situation by making this man buy me some top shelf booze. I had a boyfriend, and although I got the impression this guy wasn't looking for a hookup, I didn't want to give the wrong idea. Besides, there was a vodka and cranberry waiting for me somewhere with my friends and although I intended on cutting loose a bit tonight, I didn't want to get so drunk I ended up facedown on the floor, or waking up on someone's couch—or in their bed.

So beer it was. I waited while Rick flagged down the bartender, then thanked him as he handed me a frosty mug with some kind of local IPA.

"So, are you local or in town visiting for the holidays?" he asked as I sipped my beer.

"I just moved to Baltimore this year from Virginia, where I'll be headed tomorrow night so I can eat turkey and stuffing with my family. What about you?"

"In town for work actually." He tilted his head. "I'm from Massachusetts, if you couldn't tell by the accent."

I laughed. "I was getting a Boston vibe there."

"The only thing I share with the Kennedys," he quipped.

"So what's work?" I asked.

He grimaced. "Funeral services."

I nearly choked on my beer. "You work in a funeral parlor?"

"It's a family business. There's a seminar tomorrow on facial reconstruction for extreme cases when the family wants an open casket."

I stared, open mouthed.

"And there goes any chance I've got of getting a date." He laughed.

"In all honesty I've got a boyfriend, so your date chances were zero before you told me about reconstructing corpses' faces. Actually, if I didn't have a boyfriend, that would have considerably upped your chances of getting a date."

"Good to know." He saluted me with his beer. "So, what do *you* do for work, Aria-with-a-boyfriend?"

"I work at a coffee shop as a barista."

I don't know why I didn't tell him I was a Templar. It would have been a heck of a lot more unique and impressive than making espresso for a living. Maybe I didn't feel like explaining what the Order did and didn't do, or go into convoluted explanations of our actions during the Crusades, or why I hadn't taken my vow of Knighthood. I wasn't going to see this guy ever again. We were just chatting over a beer. No need to impress him or to feel ashamed that I worked in a coffee shop.

"Cool. Hey, I like coffee probably more than I like beer. Are you going to college?"

Everyone assumed that if I worked at a coffee shop part-time, I was in school.

"No, I graduated a few years back. History degree. Which is why I'm working in a coffee shop," I joked.

"What kind of history?"

"European. I specialized in the tenth through the fifteenth century. If you like, I can deliver a riveting lecture on the Baltic campaign to recapture Edessa in 1147."

"Oh, there's probably not enough beer in this bar for that one," he teased. "I can see why there wouldn't be many job opportunities for that kind of specialty unless you ended up getting your doctorate and teaching at some university. Or becoming Indiana Jones."

"I was hoping for Indiana Jones."

"They're showing Indiana Jones? I thought there was a band tonight?" a woman interjected, pulling the mug of beer from Rick's hand and taking a swig before handing it back. "Hi. I'm Liz. The sister. And now I know why I was left all by myself at a table, wondering where my brother was with my beer."

I shook her hand. "Aria. I think I'm probably drinking your beer."

She rolled her eyes and punched her brother in the arm. "Figures. A pretty face and he forgets all about his poor thirsty sister."

"I'm getting you a beer right now." Rick laughed and turned to flag down the bartender again.

"So you work in the family funeral home, too?" I asked Liz.

"He told you that?" She shook her head. "The man has no game. He might be my older brother, but I swear he's thirteen when it comes to picking up women."

"I think he was doing pretty good. If I didn't have a boyfriend meeting me after he gets off work, I might be interested," I told her.

"Ah well. It's not like we're here for more than a few days anyway. We're leaving tomorrow night to head back home, and in my experience long distance romance doesn't last."

"The seminar." I nodded and polished off the rest of my beer. "The day before Thanksgiving is a weird choice for that sort of thing."

"I know, but when we got the invitation we had to come. This is a really specialized skillset and not a lot of people know how to do this sort of reconstruction. If we can offer this, we'd be serving a niche that no one else in the county, or probably even state, can serve."

Rick turned back around and handed Liz a beer just as the manager got on stage to introduce the band.

"I'm heading over there to my friends," I told Rick. "If you want to dance later, or if you two want to hang with us, then come on over."

They both nodded, replying something that was completely drowned out by the band introduction. With a smile and a mouthed "thank you" for the beer, I headed over to our table.

"He's cute." Anna screamed in my ear as the band began their opening number. "It's okay if you ditch us for him."

"I've got a boyfriend," I shouted back. "But I told him and his sister to come over and join us if they want. They're cool. They own a funeral parlor."

"They own a beauty parlor?" Anna yelled. "That *is* cool."

I didn't bother to correct her and gave up on trying to communicate, just enjoying the band and my drink, dancing with my friends when we got tired of sitting. I caught a glimpse of Rick dancing with a blonde woman and assumed he'd moved on to a more available female prospect for the evening. His sister was sitting at a table chatting with two men, and seemed to be having fun, so I turned my attention away from them and just enjoyed the night out with my friends.

Going on past midnight, I'd danced my little feet off and had drank way too much. Switching to water, I headed through the crowd to find the restrooms. They were on the opposite side of the bar, around a corner and down a short hallway. Thankfully there wasn't much of a wait. I stood behind a sweaty woman with blue hair and crossed my legs, hoping the line moved quickly. That's when I saw Rick. He was in a corner over near where the fire door was. The blonde he'd been dancing with was with him. She and the wall were pretty much the only thing keeping him upright because he seemed to be so drunk he could hardly stand.

Huh. I hadn't really expected that of him. He hadn't exactly been pounding his beer earlier, and I just didn't get that "I'm going to get wasted" vibe from him. Whatever. Maybe he'd gotten talked into one shot too many.

The blonde turned and caught me staring, then frowned, turning back to lock lips with Rick in a passionate kiss—one which he seemed to return wholeheartedly. Well, at least as wholeheartedly as a really drunk guy could. Pushing him hard against the wall, the blonde grinded up against him. I felt my cheeks heat and turned away.

Whew. I certainly hoped to be doing something like that with Dario later. In fact, I was wishing I was doing that with him right here, right now but I hadn't expected that of Rick. I mean, yeah, I'd gotten the idea that if I'd been willing he might have been interested in some light smooching over in the corner and maybe exchanging numbers, but I didn't think he was the make-out-in-public type. Of course, I didn't think he was the drunk-in-a-bar type either.

I decided not to be a creepy voyeur and studiously keep my gaze averted, inching forward as the line moved. It took forever, and by the time I finally got into a stall to relieve myself I was practically dancing around. When I came out of the restroom, I couldn't help glancing over in the corner, but Rick and the blonde were gone, no doubt either back on the dance floor or perhaps taking things to a more private location.

Grabbing another glass of water, I caught sight of my friends on the dance floor and made my way to them, noticing that Liz had left the two guys at her table and was on an intersect course with me.

"Hey! Come dance with us!" I told her, figuring that with

her brother otherwise occupied, she could probably use a friend or two to hang with.

"Later. I'm trying to find Rick. Have you seen him?" She scanned the room with a much better vantage point than I had with her height.

Ugh. Here's where I bust her brother. Sorry dude, but the woman asked and girl-code meant I needed to be honest.

"Yeah, he was in the corner by the fire door, drunk as all get-out, with that blonde all over him." I winced. "If they're not here, they might have headed outside and back to his hotel or something."

Or something meaning her place if she lived nearby, or one of their cars if they were the impatient sort—and the blonde definitely looked to be the impatient sort.

"He's not drunk," Liz protested. "He only had the one beer. Rick doesn't really drink much."

Well then, that might be why he was so drunk. If he didn't drink much, a couple tequilas would totally do him in. "Maybe he did a few shots with the blonde?" I asked.

She rolled her eyes. "Gah, he's such an idiot. We've got the seminar tomorrow. He's going to be useless if he's hungover. And I can't believe he left me here. He's got the car keys."

"He'll probably be back soon," I assured her, thinking he'd be indulging in a parking lot quickie and returning. Or he'd be passed out in his hotel room while the blonde caught an Uber back home. If the latter, the poor guy was going to get an earful from his sister. A massive hangover would be the least of his worries.

I saw Liz glance over at the two men at her table, and something about the tension in her face made up my mind.

"Dance with us. Sit at our table. I'm too tipsy to drive, but you can share an Uber with me later."

She smiled gratefully. "Thanks. It's just I don't know

anyone in this city and those guys are a little handsy and pushy with the booze. Not that I really know you, but…"

I totally understood. We'd spent all of two minutes conversing, but I wasn't trying to get her to do body shots or come back to my room. Plus there was safety in numbers. And if those two guys tried anything…well, I might not have my sword on me, but I was perfectly capable of improvising when it came to defensive weaponry, and I did have a spell or two up my sleeve, or in my pocket.

I introduced Liz to my friends and we all danced. I was completely sweaty and starting to sober up a bit when a pair of strong hands grabbed me from behind and pulled me against a muscular chest. I would have elbowed the guy if I hadn't felt the static buzz of vampire the moment he'd come in the door. And this particular static buzz of vampire was as familiar to me as his face.

Dario.

"Hey, babe." He nosed my hair aside and nibbled on my ear, swaying to the beat in time with my hips.

"Hey, you." I turned to face him, wrapping my arms around his neck. "How'd you find me?"

I hadn't texted him about where I was going, thinking I'd be home either the same time he arrived or a bit beforehand. Don't get me wrong, I was thrilled he was here, but how he managed to track me down in a city this large was astounding, even for a vampire.

Someone in his *Balaj* had probably seen me and let him know where I was. And knowing Dario, I doubted that had been a random occurrence. He knew how I felt about his need to protect me, but no matter how much I argued, I'd realized he wouldn't stop, he'd just make those efforts stealthier and less obvious. I was human, mortal, and terrifyingly fragile in his eyes, even though as humans go I was better suited than most to handle whatever baddies might cross my path.

Still he worried. And although I chafed under that worry, a part of me found it a bit charming and somewhat flattering.

"Doesn't matter. I'm glad you're here," I told him before he could reply with some sort of lie. "How did things go up north of the city? With the rogues?"

He grimaced. "Let's not talk about that. Let's dance and drink, then go back to your place and make love."

That sounded good to me, although I did want to know what happened up north. If there was a rogue band of vampires that had snatched part of his territory, then I needed to be aware of what was happening. Protecting pilgrims on the path was part of my self-imposed vow, and although I counted vampires among my pilgrims, protecting humans from violent supernatural elements was a priority.

"How was your day?" His little nibbles trailed from my ear down my neck and I felt the familiar scrape of fangs. Everything south of my waistband tightened and I pressed myself against him, limiting our dance moves further.

"Let's not talk about that either. At least for now."

I ran my fingers along the back of his neck, feeling the cool smoothness of his skin. One of his hands left my rear to slide up my back. I felt him twist my ponytail into a fist and tug playfully.

"Good. From the moment I woke, I've been thinking of what I want to do to you," he murmured against my neck. "I've been thinking of you spread out before me, of tasting you. I want your tight wetness around me. I want to make you come so hard you can't do anything but say my name and beg me for more."

The erotic breathlessness that his mouth and words inspired came crashing down with unwelcome memories of my nightmares.

Beg.

Dario lifted his head and looked down at me. "What's wrong?"

"Nothing." Now wasn't the time to get into a discussion of my horrible dreams, how I couldn't seem to bury the memories of that asshole from Philly, how the pain and fury was all twisted up with a seductive need that all came rushing back unbidden at the most inopportune times, like when I was hot and bothered on the dance floor with my sexy boyfriend and he said the word "beg".

He pulled away and lifted his hands to cradle my face. His eyes searched mine, and I saw the flash of awareness in them, followed by an expression that made me shiver.

Dario knew what had happened to me. He'd seen me the night after the first attack, seen how torn up my neck was. With a vampire's heightened senses, I was sure he'd noticed my runaway heartbeat, the smell of fear and anger twisting with an unwelcome craving.

Reaching down, he smoothed his fingers over the scar on my neck. "Death was too good for him."

"It was a pretty horrific death," I replied with a wry smile. "And knowing I was the one that killed him was probably the most torturous of all."

"I wish I could make all this go away," he told me, that murderous gleam in his eyes softening to something that looked a lot like love. "I hate that he did that to you. I hate that in death he still finds a way to intrude on what we share together. I want to smash his head in, wipe those memories from your mind, take this scar, this reminder, from your beautiful skin. I want you to be safe, protected, to never know fear."

I smiled, because that's not the way life went. And as much as I hated the nightmares, Dario's alternative was a bit too much of a suffocating protective cage for me to ever allow.

Pulling his hand from my neck, I brought his fingers to my mouth and kissed them. "*I'm* the knight in shining armor in this relationship, not you. You'll just have to get used to my hundreds of scars, and the panic attacks you're going to have every time I face down something scary with sword in hand." My smile faded and I put his hand against my cheek. "Time, Dario. It'll take time, but I'll be okay. Just…just please be patient with me as I work all this crap out."

He leaned his forehead against mine and whispered, "Of course." Then he kissed me and I let all the fear and anger wash away with the touch of his lips. And then we just danced, wrapped around each other, my cheek against his chest.

"Do you want a beer? A glass of wine?" he asked me when the song was over and we finally eased apart.

I laughed. "No way. I'm just now starting to sober up. But I do want to introduce you to my friends. They've been hoping to meet you."

I disengaged my arms from around Dario's neck and grabbed his hand, leading him over to the table where my friends eyed our approach with raised brows and expectant expressions.

"Is this the hottie boyfriend?" Brandi asked. "Holy crap. Does he have a brother?"

He had a whole family, all of them vampires. But in my opinion, none of them were nearly as hot as *my* vampire.

"Dario, this is Brandi, Anna, Grace, and Liz."

The vampire shook hands with all four women, smiling with the sort of charm that I was sure had gotten him the body and blood of every woman he'd wanted. My friends were enchanted. Everyone scooted over and Dario and I took a seat. I watched as he chatted easily with my friends, and felt a strange, giddy warmth in my chest.

My boyfriend. Yes, he was a vampire. Yes, he was now responsible for the Baltimore *Balaj*. Yes, we had a whole lot of issues we'd need to overcome in the course of what might be a short and emotionally devastating relationship, but there was no way I was backing out of this now.

I reached out and took his hand, smiling as he turned his dark eyes to me.

"Let's dance," I told him as I tugged him out of his chair and toward the dance floor.

# CHAPTER 5

The last set was over too soon. As the lights came on I was wrapped tight in Dario's arms, my face resting against his chest. It was perfect, and as much as I wanted to go back to my house and get busy, I also wanted to stay here.

"Did you drive?" I looked up at him, starting to ease myself away.

"Of course." He chuckled. "Did you think I jogged here from Federal Hill?"

He could have. Vampires were insanely fast. Plus who knew where those tunnels under his house went to besides Leonora's former residence.

"I kinda promised Liz a lift and I'm not sure I'm sober enough to drive yet. Do you mind? Her brother took off with some blonde and she doesn't have a way back to her hotel. She's in town for a seminar."

"Of course I'll give her a lift." Dario stepped away from me, taking my hand as we walked back to the table where my friends were gathering up their belongings and paying the bill—and where Liz was looking rather forlorn.

"Where are you staying?" I asked her. "Dario and I can drive you back to your hotel."

She shot Dario a wary look, then glanced across the room. I followed her gaze and saw the two men she'd been sitting with earlier. They were back by the fire door where Rick had been making out with the blonde woman. And while they weren't staring creepily at Liz or anything, I could tell she was worried that they might follow her or something.

Or something.

"The Sheraton at the Inner Harbor," she said. "Is that out of your way?"

"Not at all," Dario lied. If I'd still been living in Fells Point, we would have gone right past the hotel, but with my new place, we'd need to double back. It wasn't far, though, and traffic should be light at two in the morning on the Wednesday before Thanksgiving.

"Thanks." She looked around the room again. "I can't believe Rick took off like this. It's so unlike him to not even say something to me."

"He did look pretty drunk when I saw him last," I reminded her.

She shook her head slowly. "That's not like him either."

"He's probably back in his hotel room right now sleeping it off," I said as we headed toward the exit.

She bit her lip and nodded, following us out. Dario unlocked the black SUV and opened the door for me, then let Liz in the back seat before walking around to get in the driver's side. Liz was quiet as we headed through town, but her worry was starting to infect me. Did guys get roofied? If the woman wanted to drug and rob Rick, then wouldn't she have just left him passed out in the bathroom hallway or outside somewhere? He was here for a work seminar. I couldn't see any reason why someone would want to slip him something besides robbery.

I glanced in the back to see Liz looking out the window, a frown on her face. What if Rick *was* passed out in an alley somewhere? Would a club patron notice him? Would the police pick him up? What would Liz do if she got back to her hotel and Rick wasn't there? Clearly he'd not called or texted her, or she would have said so.

Digging in my purse I pulled out a piece of paper and wrote a name and number down on it before turning around and handing it to Liz.

"Look, I'm sure everything is okay, but just in case you can't find Rick, here's the name and number of a friend of mine with the city police. Tell him I gave you his number and he'll make sure you're taken seriously."

She looked down at the number and slipped it into her purse. "Thanks."

Her voice was small, and I felt another lurch of worry in my stomach. What would I do if this was Roman who was missing like this? Of course, Roman was a Templar Knight and could take care of himself, but I would still worry just as much as Liz was doing right now.

Dario pulled up to the Sheraton, and Liz had the door open practically before we came to a stop, thanking us once again for giving her a lift as she ran to the doors.

I watched her as Dario pulled away, that sick feeling still in my stomach.

"You want to tell me what happened?" Dario asked, his deep voice soothing my worry. "I thought the brother hooked up with some woman and just didn't tell her."

I sighed, leaning back in my seat. "I'm sure that's all it is. He seemed pretty sober when I was talking to him earlier. Then he was dancing with this blonde. Then he was drunk and barely able to stand and making out with this blonde. Then the pair of them were gone."

Dario chuckled. "Sounds like a hookup to me."

I frowned. "Maybe she was a vampire. The blonde, I mean. Not Liz."

I hadn't sensed any vampires in the club until Dario had come in, but I'd been pretty tipsy, and not all vampires packed quite as powerful an aura as Dario. That would explain Rick's sudden drunkenness, as well as his forgetting to let his sister know he was leaving. If that was the case, then he'd show up tomorrow morning, hung over, having had the night of his life.

Unless…

"A rogue wouldn't come this far into the city, would she?" I asked, worried again.

"I doubt it, but I can't completely rule it out. There aren't many of us left and it's a big city."

I thought through the remaining members of Dario's *Balaj* that I'd met and couldn't recall any of them who might be the blonde woman. Maybe she wasn't a vampire after all. I was probably fretting over nothing. Besides, a drunken hookup by some guy I'd just met tonight wasn't really my business. If there was a problem, his sister would call the police. And if not, she'd probably chew his ear off tomorrow morning.

I was going to forget about it, and just enjoy the early morning hours with Dario. Reaching across the car, I snaked my fingers through his.

"Your place or mine?" I asked.

He squeezed my hand. "Yours. That way we're less likely to be interrupted."

I laughed. "Have you *met* my dog?"

He shot me a grin. "Yes, and he's a hundred times better than the five vampires, two Renfields, and half a dozen blood partners that are probably at my house right now."

My eyebrows shot up. "Blood *partners?*"

"I took to heart what you said last month, but with

Leonora in charge, there wasn't much I could do either in the terminology we use, or the nature of our relationships with each other or our human romantic partners."

"So no more blood slaves," I mused, a bit shocked. Dario was more modern than Leonora, but he was still hundreds of years old, and I knew tradition meant a lot to him.

"It's not just the term. I want blood partners to be a subset of the *Balaj* family, not the property of their vampire. I want addiction management for them, a system to help pairs avoid what had always been considered to be an inevitable loss of control and death. I want an appeal process for any issues a human might have, as well as paid treatment for anyone who wants out of the relationship. I want them to have as clear a path to turning as Renfields, if that's something they're interested in. I want a fund to give assistance to the blood partner's family if needed—medical, emergency funds…that sort of thing."

I was absolutely gobsmacked.

"There's no *Master*. I'm still the boss, the head of the family, but no one's Master. I'm putting together an advisement council. Right now our numbers are small enough that everyone could come straight to me with any issues, but as we grow that might not be practical. Besides, I want vampires in our family to have options in bringing concerns to light, and I realize it might be intimidating for the newly turned to come to me directly."

He parked the SUV on the road and let me out of the car. I followed him up to the house, thinking about all he'd said. We went inside and he allowed Fulk to greet him with the dog's usual enthusiasm, then he scooped up Gaia and headed to the sofa.

"I wanted to wait until everything was in place before I told you because this might take a while. A good many in the *Balaj* are as old or older than me, and changing the way you've done something for hundreds of years isn't easy. But I wanted you to know a few of the reasons why I've been so busy lately, and why I'm not over as much as I'd like."

I sat down beside him and curled up against his side, my head on his shoulder and my hand on his thigh—right next to the purring cat on his lap.

"I'm glad you told me." I was. And I was thrilled at the changes he was trying to make in their structure and traditions. This was a *Balaj* that humans could work with, that *Templars* could work with. This all eased so many of the worries I'd had about Dario's and my relationship and the potential for us being on opposite sides of an issue.

"I was worried that you were spending every evening fighting off rogue vampires determined to take the city, and that you didn't want to tell me," I continued. "I'm happy to hear it's more administrative stuff that's keeping you away."

He shifted beside me. "Well…about that…."

I tensed. "Yes?"

"There aren't many of us left after what happened last month, and the word is out that we don't have the numbers to hold the entirety of the city, or any significant part. Rumors are that a group of rogues are banding together to reduce our territory with the goal of eventually pushing us out. If we can't keep Baltimore as ours, then I foresee four or five outside factions taking parts of the city, and warring amongst themselves to seize the whole territory."

This was bad. It would be bad for Dario, and it would be bad for all the humans caught in the middle of something that would make a gang war look like a tea party.

"What can I do to help?"

He reached out a hand to stroke my hair. "Be patient with me when I cancel dates or can't see you for a few nights. Be my sanctuary, the one person I can turn to and talk about things and not need to be the boss. Take my mind off this whole mess."

I snuggled against him once more. "I can do all that."

I felt like such a shit for mentally griping about how our relationship had seemed to turn into nothing aside from a quick dinner and a booty call. He was fighting for the survival of his family. I needed to give him the understanding and the space he needed to take care of these vampires who'd been an important part of his life far longer than I had.

"You don't have to do this alone, you know. I can help. The police can help. Maybe I can get a few of my family to come up for a weekend to patrol your borders."

I knew as soon as I said it that I was wrong. My family were all Knights. They wouldn't come to Baltimore to help my vampire boyfriend secure his territory. They'd taken a vow, and unless the Elders sent them here on assignment or unless I was in danger, they wouldn't help. In their minds, it didn't matter which vampires controlled the city, or if Dario's *Balaj* was pushed out of their territory or not.

"I'll let you know if I need you, but I really don't want to involve the police. We have some human alliances that are helping us as paid mercenaries. I have to tell you now that I'm worried, Aria. The one thing going for us is that these rogues mostly operate on their own. If there is a group, it doesn't seem to be very large or have the family loyalty, the blood bond, that we do. If a large *Balaj* were to splinter off and come for us as Simon did, we would never survive, but I'm hoping we can hold out against these individuals and a potential group of ten or twenty rogues."

"I'm so sorry." A vision of more vampire deaths filled my mind, of Dario's small family fighting for their existence and losing, fleeing Baltimore and wandering without a safe territory with whatever few remained of their family just as they'd done in those centuries when they'd left Haiti.

And Dario would never leave his family. Even if only one or two remained, he'd still fight and risk his life to keep them together and provide for them. It wasn't just that he was the Master, or boss, it was who he was inside.

He kissed the side of my head. "We've survived worse. And I mean a hell of a lot worse. I've personally survived worse. We'll make it."

"How can you increase your numbers?" I asked. "I know you guys tend to bond over shared blood lines but there are occasions when a *Balaj* will welcome in outsiders. Is that a possibility? Is there anyone you can bring in to bolster your numbers?"

He shook his head. "We're so small right now that I don't think either I or any of the others would trust bringing in a stranger. There's too much potential for them to do damage. We have quite a few candidates to turn—some loyal Renfields and several blood partners who lost their vampires in the last month. We just can't spare anyone to turn them right now, though."

I nodded, knowing that it took a lot out of a vampire to sire a newly turned human, and that both of them would need the support of their *Balaj* until the sire regained his or her strength. It seemed all they could do right now was focus on holding their territory, and as soon as there was a breather, expand their family.

I had mixed feelings about that. I'd always been taught that in exchange for immortality a vampire gave up not only his or her ability to live in the daylight, but their soul. I didn't want to believe that, but I still worried that the humans who accepted this bargain weren't always completely informed of the tradeoffs.

But I also believed in free will. And I knew that Dario and the other vampires I'd met felt they'd made a good choice. Only God should judge. I certainly shouldn't.

"So tell me about your horrible day." Dario's voice was low, rumbling through his body and into mine.

"Work was crazy. The ice maker in the fridge broke and is leaking on the kitchen floor. Raven's not in Fulk and I'm scared she's in hell being tortured or something. Oh, and I tripped over a dead homeless person on my run this morning."

Dario scowled glancing toward the kitchen with a rather fierce expression before turning back to me. "I'm so sorry. Can Russell contact Raven's spirit? Find out where she is and allow you to communicate with her?"

It was mildly amusing that Dario completely overlooked my falling over a dead homeless person, and fixated on my worries over Raven. He'd been living in Baltimore longer than I had, but it wasn't that he was jaded about the plight of the city's homeless. Dario was hundreds of years old. He'd seen slaves murdered and die of untreated illnesses and wounds as well as malnourishment growing up as an enslaved child in what was now Haiti. He'd seen his followers die while fighting against the slave owners. He'd seen his vampire family die. He'd seen blood slaves and donors die, watching generations of humans grow old as he remained the same immortal age. He'd become numb to death. Or he'd become numb to most death. I knew there were those in his family who he grieved for terribly. And I knew that he'd be wrecked when I eventually died.

Hopefully that was a long way in the future.

"I'm meeting with Russell Saturday morning and I'm hoping he can contact Raven." I sighed. "And I have to let you know that I might not be too lively of a conversationalist Friday night after driving home Thanksgiving and working the early shift Friday."

I wouldn't see Dario Wednesday or Thursday night, and I really wanted to be able to see him Friday, but I knew I was going to be exhausted. Maybe I could squeeze a nap in some-time between work and my visit with Chuck at the prison.

"If you're too tired, then we'll do something special Saturday night instead. I owe you dinner after cancelling on you tonight."

I covered my mouth to hide a yawn. "I think you owe me several dinners, buster."

Dario laughed. "I'll send some cannoli over this weekend to make it up to you." Shifting my cat off his lap, he scooped me up and stood. "I'm taking you up to bed. Sunrise is in a little more than four hours, and you need some sleep."

Ugh. He was right. Even though I really wanted some sexy-times, I had to be up and at the coffee shop early. Maybe I'd skip my morning run and get an extra hour of sleep.

"Stay with me?" I asked as he carried me up the stairs.

"Always."

Always. He *did* always stay with me, only leaving when he needed to be safe from the rising sun. Maybe this *could* work out between us. There were still a million hurdles we'd need to overcome, but maybe, just maybe, a vampire and a Templar could have a happily ever after.

# CHAPTER 6

"Have you seen this?" Janice slapped an eight-by-ten glossy on the counter. The other customers edged away because the photo clearly showed a dead body—a *naked* dead body in a room with bright lights and a stainless steel table. I guess I should have been grateful that the picture was only from the waist up.

"Janice, crime scene photos don't really belong in a coffee shop," I told the reporter.

Sticking the milk under the frother, I leaned over to eye the picture. I'd had my fill of dead bodies for the week, but Janice wouldn't have come to me unless there was something odd about this. I wasn't a cop, but as a Templar the odd fell under my self-imposed job description.

Self-imposed, because the job that paid the bills was the one I was doing right now. And even though I had been born into a Templar family and thus had all the skills and abilities that came with that birthright, I hadn't taken my oath and wasn't a Knight. Although, a Knight wouldn't care about a dead guy in the morgue. Templar Knights removed magical artifacts from the public and safeguarded them in the

Temple, and researched and cataloged information on magic and the supernatural. They were also supposed to protect Pilgrims on the Path, but no one knew what the heck that meant anymore.

I did. And although I wasn't a Knight, I took my "safeguarding Pilgrims on the Path" duties seriously.

"Notice how pale he is?" Janice waved the picture at me.

I shuddered, thinking of the homeless guy from yesterday morning. "Yes, in my sadly extensive experience, dead people are usually pale."

Janice ignored my comment. "My contact at the morgue says he was drained of blood. Zippo. Nada. No blood."

The other customers were still giving Janice a wide berth, but they all had an expression of rapt attention on their face. Everyone loves a good murder mystery, although most people don't want to see the actual photos.

I did. Finishing up the latte with a swirl of caramel on top, I handed it to my customer and grabbed the picture from Janice's hand. The dead guy was as pale as my bedsheets, but I couldn't see anything really notable about him.

"There have been an increase in what the police are calling animal attacks as well as what they're claiming are overdose deaths, but no one shoots up in their neck and these mysterious animal attacks are suspect." Janice looked at the scar on my neck and I lifted a hand to touch the mark.

I knew what she meant. "If those deaths *are* a result of what you're implying, then it's not Dario's *Balaj* doing it," I told her, trying to be vague because of the interested customers listening in to our conversation.

Janice made a huff noise. "Right. So how do you explain this guy then? No blood, Aria. None."

"How the heck are you getting this information? And pictures?" I asked her. "What are you paying this morgue employee, because I'm pretty sure he's not supposed to be snapchatting pics of bodies on the slab to reporters."

Janice looked smug. "It's not a regular thing, but I've got contacts. The only reason he sent me this one was because when he went to take a blood sample for a tox screen, there wasn't any. I mean none."

I handed the photo back to her and took the outstretched cup Brandi was handing me. Templar duties aside, I really didn't want to get fired here and needed to keep up with the orders.

"Anemic junkie? Or the guy bled out and the body was dumped somewhere other than where he was killed?" I hadn't seen any knife wounds, but the guy was face up in the picture and could have been stabbed, or shot, in the back. Or below the waist.

"They're calling it an OD in the preliminary report because the guy has track marks, but no junkie is that anemic," Janice informed me. "The guy had no blood in his body. None. Maybe those track marks aren't really track marks, if you know what I mean. *I'm* thinking you need to have a serious chat with your boyfriend."

I flinched, worried this was the sort of thing that would eventually end whatever I had going on with Dario. *Ugh, don't let this be a vampire killing. Don't let me be forced to deliver justice to one of my boyfriend's* Balaj.

"I can't ask Dario about every anemic junkie overdose and fatal animal attack in Baltimore," I protested. "Go back to your friend at the morgue, and ask if this guy has bite marks on his neck. Maybe send a picture of them over for me to show to Dario. *Then* I'll have a chat with the *Balaj.* Otherwise this is just another upsetting statistic in Baltimore's war on drugs."

"Drained. Of. Blood," Janice insisted. "Not anemic. Drained. Your boyfriend needs to rein his people in."

Janice wasn't a fan of Dario. She felt I should date a nice human man instead, like Zac or Detective Tremelay. She'd had a brief relationship of her own with a guy who wasn't human, and couldn't get around the whole predator/prey dynamic. I wasn't sure I could get around it either, but for now I was in denial.

I finished making the double-shot mocha and handed it over in exchange for another cup from Brandi. "So the preliminary report is overdose? They're not ruling that the cause of death was the blood loss?"

Even if a vampire had been extremely careless with his donor, an overdose was still an overdose.

"Yeah, but it's just preliminary." Janice shrugged. "There's no final report yet. They just got the guy in yesterday. Some jogger tripped over him on South Fulton right before dawn."

Crap, that jogger was *me*. This was *my* guy on that slab, the guy I'd discovered dead on the sidewalk. At least, I was pretty sure it was the same guy. What were the odds that two dead guys would have been tripped over by two joggers on South Fulton within the same hour of each other?

"Surely your friend at the M.E.'s office noticed something on the body, like say a knife wound or two giant puncture marks on the guy's jugular?" I asked, feeling a bit sick at the thought that the very man I'd fallen over yesterday morning might have been killed by vampires. No, it couldn't be. Janice's morgue contact was probably exaggerating with the no-blood thing. The dead man was probably severely anemic from an illness, or giving too much plasma, or getting stabbed early yesterday before shooting up and freezing to death on South Fulton.

Janice squirmed. "The body had some bruises, and had a set of what my contact called track marks on the inside of both elbows, but I don't know what else. They could have been bite marks. He could have bite marks elsewhere. I don't have any closeup pictures yet, and didn't want to be too specific about asking if the dead man had anything that looked like you-know-what bites."

I knew what she meant. We both knew there was a supernatural element in Baltimore. So did Tremelay, and my friend Zac. It was one thing if we slipped and the customers in the coffee shop overheard us talking about vampires, and thought we were a bit off our rockers, but Janice wouldn't want to jeopardize her contact at the morgue with that sort of talk.

I hesitated, not wanting to completely dismiss Janice's concerns even though this dead man probably had some illness or condition that, combined with drug use, led to both his anemic state and eventual death. Inside elbow *did* seem like the usual place for a junkie to shoot up.

And as far as I knew it wasn't a typical place for a vampire bite, unless maybe one of them got off on inside elbows. I'd seen vampires bite from neck and wrists. I knew they bit from the thigh as well. Maybe some liked arms. I flushed, my mind detouring to an image of Dario between my legs and all that might entail. Wow…that…whew.

I took a steadying breath and concentrated on making the vanilla spice latte. I hated to think that a vampire who got carried away and drained someone would set them up on the street to look like death from overdose, but it might have happened. Homeless people wouldn't be missed, and it wouldn't have been unexpected for a vampire "oops" to end up where the body would never be found. Maybe the vampire cared enough that he wanted his dinner to have an appropriate burial. I remembered the guy's clothes under the blanket. Or maybe he wasn't just some homeless guy, and the vampire didn't want it to come to light that one of his donors had met an untimely death. Dario would normally have taken a dim view of an accident like this, but with his *Balaj* so decimated, he might be more forgiving than normal. I knew he needed every vampire in his family, and really couldn't afford to lose even one right now.

A blood donation gone bad. The vampire goes to the Master—or boss—of his family, begging forgiveness and asking for help. Dario covers it up as an overdose, and keeps it all a secret from me.

I wasn't so in love that I didn't realize the dark side of my relationship with a vampire, nor that his family's survival came first in his mind right now. But if Dario had been involved, I would have thought that an "oops" like this would have never seen the light of day. That body would have vanished, never to be found. Dario wouldn't take chances like this on a sloppy disposal, especially so near my home on a route that he *knew* I jogged regularly.

If this death was due to a vampire feeding gone wrong, and it wasn't one of Dario's family, that would mean the rogue elements outside of Baltimore were emboldened enough by the unsettled state and shrunken size of the *Balaj* to do more than chip away at the territory boundaries. If so, this was something Dario needed to know about.

But not before I verified a few things. And not until I finished my shift. A girl had to pay her rent, you know? And a girl also had to hustle down to Middleburg Virginia for Thanksgiving dinner with her family as well.

"Let me see if I can reach Tremelay." I eyed the photo, realizing the chances I had of getting any information on this the afternoon before a major holiday were slim. "Can you text that picture to me? High-res? I'll check into it, but don't expect anything soon with the holiday and all. I'll call you Monday or Tuesday after I do some digging and let you know what's going on."

Janice wrinkled her nose. "I was hoping to get a story out for the weekend."

That so wasn't going to happen. But I really did owe her one—more than one. Janice had been a good friend and a good resource, and having a bulldog of a reporter on my side wasn't something I wanted to take lightly.

"I promise I'll get right on it. I'll text you as soon as I know something definitive, and you can call me back."

If I managed to reach Tremelay and he confirmed it was a stabbing and body dump or an anemic overdose victim, I'd be texting her before the turkey was on the table. If it wasn't…well, I wasn't sure when I'd actually get to see Dario. I wouldn't get back in town until late Thanksgiving night, and Friday would be a hectic shitshow of work and other obligations. I might be able to see him Friday night, although being the new head of his family meant there were a ton of things he needed to take care of upon awakening, the first of which was feeding.

And now my thoughts were back to the idea of bite marks on my inner thigh.

* * *

I'D TEXTED Tremelay on my break, and drove home after work to an enthusiastic greeting. There were several perks of my new digs—one of which was the charged magical circle inscribed and inlaid into the basement floor. The other was that I was allowed to have pets. I'd barely put the dishes in the kitchen cabinets before I'd headed to the local animal shelter for a cat.

I'd come home with a cat and a dog. The dog wasn't planned, but when the bull terrier mix had come running at me in a jailbreak attempt, and had scratched Raven's symbol into the concrete floor, I'd immediately adopted him.

As I petted Fulk, I felt tears well up in my eyes at the memory. My best friend. She'd been killed, murdered and left in a gruesome display for me to find. Then she'd been killed again, her spirit ripped from the *lelek raktarban* that had housed it by the frighteningly powerful sun demon who had marked me. I'd hoped when I saw this dog that she'd somehow survived, that her spirit roamed this plane looking for a safe place to land. But the other *lelek raktarban* on my shelf remained empty, and ever since I'd brought the dog home, he'd shown no signs whatsoever of possession by anything but a sock-chewing, slobbering, pizza-stealing dog.

I knew Russell had his doubts, but I'd been sure that day at the animal shelter that Raven was somehow in there, possessing this dog. Hopefully Friday's séance session would reveal more. The necromancer could open a channel of communication with the dead, and my hope was that somehow he could manage to get in contact with Raven on the other side of the veil and let me talk to her. Had she been briefly possessing my dog, or had I just been imagining it? Was she safe and happy in her afterlife, or had Balsur dragged her down to a fiery hell when he'd broken the *lelek raktarban*?

Would she ever return, even if in spirit form?

The bull terrier danced around my legs, breaking through my grim thoughts. Even if Raven hadn't possessed the dog, I still loved this guy. Even when he ate my socks.

"Fulk, you adorable little blockhead, my goodest boy ever. Aren't you? Who's the best boy? You are. You're the best boy."

I knelt down so he could paint my face with his tongue and wedge his blocky head under my arm, tail going a hundred miles an hour.

"And Gaia." The cat chirruped, then shoved the terrier aside and wound her way around my legs. I'd named her after the primordial goddess because Gaia always insisted on being first—first to be fed, first to be petted, first on top of my bed at night. Once she'd claimed her right, she turned back into the stereotypical aloof cat—until another occasion to be first presented itself.

Fulk wisely moved aside and let the cat receive my affection. From the scars on his head and body, and from what the shelter had said, he'd been used as a fighting dog—and clearly had come out on top of his many fights. Badass he might be in the fighting ring, but one swipe of Gaia's paw had put him right in his place. He stood aside, impatiently waiting his turn. It didn't take long. I stroked Gaia's soft fur, picked her up in my arms to cuddle against my face, then set her back down when she began to squirm. One last pat and she was off to the kitchen to check her food bowl, replaced in my arms by a sixty-pound, muscled mass of slobbery, whining dog.

I couldn't help it. Once more I did my ritual, taking his head in my hands and staring deeply into his eyes. Still no sign of Raven. I'd give anything for her to take up residence in one of the figurines on my shelf, to haunt my dreams with her sass, to stare back at me from Fulk's eyes. Anything.

But she wasn't there, and I'd grown to love Fulk for Fulk. I might have gone into the shelter wanting a cat, but I was glad I'd walked out with both animals. They made my house a home.

Fulk followed me upstairs as I went to change out of my coffee-shop clothing. Once I was in my yoga pants and t-shirt, I headed into the bathroom to unwrap the scarf from around my neck and check the scar.

The scar. I ran my fingers over it, thinking of what Janice had said about the animal attacks. That was what I'd told my coworkers at the coffee shop—that a dog had attacked me. Somehow they believed it, horrified that a dog had mauled my neck and amazed that I'd somehow survived it.

Kyra had stitched up my wound after the second attack. Dario had sent the vampires' physician over to do a salve-

and-bandage routine. Wolfram had even shown up the next day with an IV bag and some weird herbal concoction. I had no idea how he'd found out about my run-in with Simon but whatever was in that IV, or whatever was in that tea, had cut the physical effects of the vampire venom right off. I swear it was like venom Narcan. And just like Narcan, negating the physical effects of the drug didn't do anything for my remembrance of what it felt like when it hit my veins.

But my neck… Kyra had said the scar would fade. It had healed nicely, but I still looked like a dog had tried to bite my throat out.

I not only gave that excuse at the coffee shop but to my gaming friends as well. Zac knew. He'd been there. And ever since that night, things had been rather strained between us. Which was awkward given that we were king and queen of a reenactment group that I still got confused with an animal charity, and that I played in his Wednesday night Anderon game.

Rubbing some of the salve Kyra had given me onto the healing scar, I threw the little pot into a bag with my toiletries. I was going to spend the holiday at my family home. None of them would bat an eye at the gnaw mark on my neck, not with all the scars that Templar Knights tended to have decorating their bodies, but I still wanted it to heal as best as it could. The questions, the eyes of strangers that drifted to the scar all were a constant reminder of something I was trying very hard to put behind me, even if I could never forget.

Fulk was my shadow as I headed downstairs, only abandoning me once I'd poured food in his bowl—after filling Gaia's first, of course. Then I went into my living room, picked up my sword, and began to practice.

There was no sense in leaving for Middleburg until later this evening when the traffic may have thinned out a bit. I figured I might as well get in my fitness routine before throwing a few clothes in a bag and heading out.

Normally I tried to squeeze in some daily study on the magical texts Raven had given me, as well as familiarizing myself with my magical space downstairs by using it to create little charms. If I'd ever wanted to open a charm and hex shop, I had plenty of inventory. And where most of the magical groups I'd encountered would turn up their noses at such basic stuff, I didn't. Yeah, it was impressive as all shit to summon a demon and return it back to hell, but a spelled butter knife had saved my life once. I wasn't going to discount how useful a variety of ready-made spelled items could be.

I'd only swung my sword a few times when I heard a knock at the door. Dario? No, it was still daylight out. And as I put my sword aside and jogged for the door, I realized I wasn't sensing the staticky feel of vampire. It wasn't Dario.

I opened to door to find Detective Justin Tremelay on my doorstep, his unmarked car parked right behind mine at the curb.

"An in person visit?" I grimaced. "So I take it this wasn't just an anemic junkie after all?"

"Can't a guy pay a social call? Maybe I wanted to drop by after work for a beer or something." He came in, patting Fulk on the head. Yes, the dog ate that fast. It was a wonder he hadn't choked to death on his food by now.

"If that's the case I hope you brought the beer," I joked. In spite of the increased hours at work, I was still skirting the poverty line. Beers were a luxury reserved for payday. And sometimes not even payday.

"Coffee then?"

I eyed him and went into the kitchen to put on a pot, more worried by the minute. Yes, Tremelay and I were sort-of friends as well as sort-of professional liaisons, but I got the feeling this request for beverages meant we were about to have a serious discussion about something unpleasant. And it worried me that this "unpleasant" was going to be about the vampires I was trying very hard to see the good in.

Pilgrims on the Path. That's what I kept reminding myself.

Gaia finished her dinner in her typical dainty fashion while the coffee brewed. Tremelay stayed out in my main room, yanking photos from a folder and spreading them across my table while Fulk looked on.

Ugh. I wish I had beer. I wish I had something stronger than beer.

"I just got this case," Tremelay called out to me. "So when I got your message, I pulled a few files and found something."

Yep. I wasn't going to like this at all. Pulling two mugs out of the cabinets, I added the requisite amount of milk and sugar, and carried them both into my living room. Gaia followed, took one look at Tremelay, then stuck her nose in the air and went upstairs. The cat was very particular about who she associated with. She was an absolute lovebug with me, especially late in the evenings when I was sprawled across the couch watching TV. She adored Dario, Brandi, Zac, and all my gaming friends. For some reason she was cool around Tremelay, though. Maybe she sensed he was more of a dog person?

"That's a lot of pictures. Was it a slow day in homicide, detective?" I asked him.

"It's never a slow day in homicide in Baltimore," he drawled. "But I know better than to sit on something that grabs your attention, Ainsworth. And as you know, I don't really sleep."

Or fold his clean clothes. Or iron them. Or make sure his socks matched in the morning when he put them on.

"So whatcha got here?" I handed him one of the mugs.

"Dead people," he replied.

I could clearly see that from the photos spread out on my coffee table. Three dead people to be exact.

My heart sank.

"Your reporter friend was correct. We've had a rash of what we're calling animal attacks. Perring Parkway, Cedmont, and Belvedere."

I thought for a second. "Northeast?"

He nodded. "We're not ruling out some whacked-out dog-fighting gang, but knowing what I know I think you should make your boyfriend aware that he's got a problem in the northeast part of the city."

"Judging from what he told me last night he's already on it, but I'll let him know the specifics just in case."

Tremelay pointed to the photos. "I didn't have time to do a complete search, but I wanted you to take a look at these."

I eyed the pictures, not sure what exactly I was looking for. "You think that these all have to do with the man I tripped over on South Fulton?"

"I'm not sure." He nudged a picture toward me. "These are the potential vampire-bite deaths that I think your friend Janice was talking about. Cause of death was listed as cardiac arrest due to overdose and their cases are considered closed, but I wanted you to see them—again, just in case."

"Only three overdose victims? What, in the last day?"

"Week," Tremelay replied.

Baltimore was a big city, and there was definitely a drug problem here. I'd assumed there would be a few more than three overdose deaths in a week.

The detective scooted one of the pictures over. "Oh, trust me there are more than three, but I focused on people who had been found in the streets—people who seemed to be homeless. If I counted the rich kids we've found overdosed in the cars, or the people in their homes, or the ones the cops got to a little too late to Narcan, then there'd be more. Plus I had limited time to look things up, because if you hadn't realized it, there's a major holiday tomorrow and nobody besides patrol and those on hot cases will be working. I figured it was prudent to start with these few, then expand the search if there seems to be a pattern, or if you think we've got a vampire problem—well, more of a problem than usual, that is."

I took a deep breath and sat down with my coffee, looking closer at the photos. I didn't recognize any of them.

"So, what else can you tell me about these three?" I asked Tremelay.

"They were found in Upton, Druid Hill, and Franklin Square, so a relatively close geographic area in the middle of the city. They had heroin in their systems, which was the main cause of cardiac arrest and death. All had severe anemia, and track marks on their inner arms. All were homeless individuals."

"Did the anemia play a part in their deaths? How severe was the anemia?" I knew that a good number of the regular blood donors on the *Balaj's* payroll were active drug users, enjoying not just the high from the vampire venom, but the cash they received for their "donation". If one of Dario's family had imbibed no more than their usual pint, and the donor had died later from an overdose, then I was hardly going to hold the vampires responsible.

"Several factors could have contributed to the deaths, but the main cause of the cardiac arrest was attributed to drug overdose. All three had signs of long-term drug usage according to the report. The anemia was significant, but as usually the case with indigent overdose victims, the M.E. didn't do extensive testing beyond the cause of death. Nothing stood out as an obvious cause of the anemia, and since it wasn't ruled a homicide, there was no need for a ton of other, frankly costly, lab work."

"But these three weren't drained of blood'?"

"Nope, although the report notes that with that level of anemia, the M.E. would have expected to see some sort of underlying disease like cancer, or sickle cell disease, or an autoimmune disorder. Not to sound callous or anything, but beyond the typical tox screen and routine organ inspection on autopsy, the M.E.'s office doesn't normally do a deep dive into what subtle diseases a homeless junkie found dead on the streets may or may not have, especially when there's no sign of foul play."

As sad as these deaths were, I was relieved that this wouldn't be something I needed to address with Dario.

"Now, the guy you stumbled upon yesterday is a bit different," Tremelay added. "I'm still not saying it's vampires or werewolves or the monster-under-the-bed, but there's a couple of weird things that have me scratching my head."

I motioned for him to go on and he pulled another photo out of the folder—a photo of the man I'd found on South Fulton.

"As the reporter told you, the prelim is potential overdose but unlike the other three, this guy didn't appear to have any prior drug use history or the usual street drugs in his system, although that's going to be hard to test for since this guy is *way* beyond anemic. He basically doesn't have any blood. The M.E. said they managed to pull some from his organs and send out some tissue samples, but that it's the weirdest thing he's ever seen. The man basically bled out, and there's no obvious reason why that would happen."

I caught my breath, knowing a non-obvious reason for that to happen. "But why call the death an overdose in the prelim? Why not say the guy died of blood loss?"

"Because blood loss isn't a cause of death. Gunshot or knife wound resulting in fatal blood loss, yes. Mysterious blood loss, no. The only marks on the guy were the track marks on his arm, and some bruises here and there. Nothing to have caused the blood loss. I think the M.E. is hoping the tox screen comes back and he can rule it a heroin overdose and not have to deal with the why and how of the missing blood."

"But he didn't show any signs of habitual drug use," I argued. "How likely would it be for a new user to overdose?"

Tremelay shot me a grim smile. "More likely than you think. New users don't always know the dosage their bodies can handle, and they're not good at figuring out what dealers have more potent stuff and which ones have the weak stuff. Plus there's a ton of drugs laced with all sorts of crap that can kill someone with one shot. Fentanyl is a real problem in street drugs as well. Could be this guy was moving from prescription drugs to IV, and got really unlucky his first time."

"Still doesn't explain the blood loss," I muttered. This could be bad. This could be really bad. Either Dario had a rogue smack in the middle of his city, or a member of his family drained this man. If the other three deaths were somehow related… I could imagine someone feeding a little bit too heavily with three homeless donors, then taking it waaaay too far with the fourth. Was the situation with the rogues far more serious than Dario had shared, or was someone in his family taking advantage of the change in leadership?

Before I went and pointed fingers, I needed to dismiss other possible suspects. Vampires weren't the only beings that drank human blood. And there certainly was a possibility that some horrible virus or disease slowly emptied a person of their blood supply—a disease the homeless were more susceptible to than others.

I pointed to the photo in Tremelay's hand, the one of the man I'd found. "Any closeup photos of the track marks?"

"They'll be in the M.E.'s final report, so not yet. The notes I got said inner arms."

Fang marks, or needle marks? I wouldn't know until I saw them—heck, I might not even know then. But I certainly couldn't confront Dario until I saw those marks and at least had a reasonable suspicion that they *were* caused by a vampire. The guy had enough on his plate without me having him chase down what could be a non-existent killer.

Tremelay took a sip of his coffee. "I've got this case, but right now it's more about identifying the man and trying to locate his next of kin. Any actual investigation is on the back burner until we know if it's an overdose, some weird natural causes thing, or a murder."

I nodded, knowing that suspicious deaths fell into a gray area. Sadly, Baltimore homicide was so darned busy that they prioritized and devoted manpower to the cases that were clear homicides while these others had to wait.

"So there were track marks on the inner arm of the other three? That's kinda the normal place for drug users to inject isn't it?"

Tremelay nodded. "As well as other areas. Inner arm is pretty common, but some users shoot up in areas that aren't so readily visible. People hiding their addiction from family, or a job, might use toes or upper leg so the track marks wouldn't be openly visible."

"Toe means taking your shoes and socks off," I mused. "Thigh means taking your pants off. Are there really that many guys willing to shoot up with their pants around their ankles? Don't users pass out or something? How many times do you get a call where someone is passed out with his pants down?"

Tremelay chuckled. "Ainsworth, sometimes you're really

naïve. It's cute. Really. Pants down, means someone is probably shooting up with a girlfriend or boyfriend. If things go wrong, that girlfriend or boyfriend usually puts the guy's pants back on before calling 911. They also hide all the drugs and try to sober up before calling 911 as well, which is why sometimes we get there too late to help."

I scooped up the photos. "Can I keep these? And can you let me know when you get any more info on this guy from yesterday morning?"

"Help yourself. They're all copies." He stood and turned to leave. "You working Black Friday? I can swing by, or if not we can meet for lunch. I'll buy."

"My shift is six to noon and I've got a couple of afternoon appointments." Which sucked because lunch on Tremelay's dime wasn't something I wanted to turn down.

"You out of town for the holidays?" Tremelay asked as I walked him to the door. "You're welcome to join Kyra and me. Nothing fancy, but I can manage to roast a turkey and Kyra makes a darned good sweet potato casserole."

"I'm heading to Middleburg in a few hours where I plan to eat like a complete pig all day then drive back Thanksgiving night with a trunk full of leftovers. Maybe we can do something Saturday morning?"

"As long as I'm not slammed at the station." He stood in the open door and looked out across the street to a boarded up row house. "Of course, we're always slammed. I'll call you Friday afternoon and let you know how my weekend looks."

"Cool. Oh, wait!" I stopped him as he started down my porch steps. "I wanted to ask if a woman called you this morning about a missing person report. Her brother. Her name is Liz Dimond, and her brother is Rick Dimond. I gave her your number in case he didn't show up at the hotel."

Tremelay thought for a second then shook his head. "No. She might have filed it with someone else though."

"I gave her your number, so I'm sure she would have called you." I felt the tension drain out of me in relief. That was one thing I guess I didn't need to worry about. "He ditched her last night for a hook up. Dario and I drove her home, and she was worried because it was out of character for her brother. I guess he finally staggered in, though."

The detective chuckled. "Hung over and exhausted, no doubt. Hope he wrapped it or he'll end up at his doctor's office in a few weeks getting antibiotics."

I winced at the implication and waved Tremelay off as he trotted down the remaining stairs and into his car. Then I turned back to eye the photos on my coffee table. Picking them up, I stuck them in my backpack and glanced at the time. I really needed to get going because it would probably take me four hours to get home on the day before a major holiday.

While I was at my parents' house, I planned to do more than eat turkey and pumpkin pie. Dad was a Templar Librarian and had some of the most rare and detailed books on the supernatural right in his own personal library. These deaths might be natural causes, or they might be vampires, but if they were something else, then my father and his books were the best chance I had of figuring out the "who" in this potential whodunit.

# CHAPTER 7

My mother wasn't thrilled that I'd brought a guest home for the holiday. No, Dario was still in Baltimore. My "guest" this Thanksgiving was of the four legged variety.

Gaia was fine alone in my row house for what wouldn't be much more than twenty-four hours. She had a litter box, and I just put out a few extra bowls of food and water. Fulk would have lost his mind solo in the house for that long. I would have returned to shredded furnishings, poop every-where, and a very anxious canine who'd thought I'd left him *forever*.

Boarding was expensive and probably completely booked up for the holiday, and none of my friends were available to stay in my house over Thanksgiving to dog-sit Fulk, so I'd loaded him in the car along with an overnight bag, and headed down the road.

Fulk quickly climbed up to ride shotgun, panting happily as he slobbered all over my seats and made nose-prints on the windows. I pulled into the drive about ten o'clock and he immediately began to bark excitedly at everything—the barn, the trees, the front door.

"Do not pee or poop in the house," I warned him once I could get a word in edgewise. "One wrong move and Mom will have you locked in a horse stall in the barn for the night."

I can't say Fulk was the perfect gentleman, but his excited wiggles didn't escalate to jumping up on my parents. Roman's boys were thrilled that I'd bucked the rules and brought a dog into the house. Jet coo'ed at the "puppy".

And Mom glared. Fulk came to sit before her in solemn attention.

"I don't like pets in the house, Solaria," she told me.

"That's no way to speak to your grand-dog," I teased. "This is the closest thing you're going to get to a baby from me, so you should probably make the best of it."

She ignored me and reached down to pat Fulk's head. "He's a handsome boy, but if he chews anything or relieves himself in the house, he's going out to the barn."

"See?" I told Fulk. "Told you so."

"Well?" She stood and scowled at my dog, who was actually behaving himself for once and not racing around the room, or humping her leg. "Introduce us to our grand-dog."

I stepped to the side, gesturing toward the bull terrier as if I were Vanna White showcasing a brand new luxury car. "Everyone, this is Fulk."

Roman's boys giggled, and were quickly shushed. My mother stiffened.

"Solaria. We did not raise you to use such vulgar language, especially here in our home. And what possessed you to name your dog such a thing?"

"Fulk, Mom. F. U. L. K. Fulk the Fifth? You know, after the Count of Anjou who was King of Jerusalem from 1131 to 1143."

"Isn't he the dude whose first wife ditched him to marry the King of France?" Ajax asked.

"Yeah, and then he married Baldwin the Second's daughter to become King of Jerusalem after Baldwin's death." Bors waved his hand. "But his first wife had died by then, so he wasn't a bigamist like she was."

"Bertrade," Hilda informed her boys. "His first wife was Bertrade. And Melisende was to succeed Baldwin with Fulk as co-ruler, but he basically cut her out until she got fed up with his nonsense and took charge in a coup."

Mom shook her head, ignoring the history lesson going on in the background. "Why Fulk, Aria? If you wanted to honor that particular Templar, you could call this dog Count."

"Count's a good name," Ajax chimed in.

"Like Dracula? Chocula? The guy on Sesame Street?" I rolled my eyes. "I'm dating a vampire. Don't you think it's a little weird to have a vampire boyfriend and a dog named Count?"

Mom's eyebrows shot up at that, and I realized that I'd never told any of my family that my relationship with Dario had taken a turn to the romantic. I hadn't wanted to break it to them this way, but the cat, or vampire boyfriend, was out of the bag now. I guessed this would be one more thing for them to lecture me about over the next twenty-four hours.

"You could call him Anjou," Bors suggested.

His brother swatted him in the arm. "Dummy. She's not going to name her dog after a country."

"It's not a country," Bors shot back. "It's a principality, or a duchy or something, isn't it, Mom?"

"How about King?" Athena asked. "Or name him Baldwin. He was the better ruler and military strategist, in my opinion."

"His name is Fulk," I informed them all. "I'm not changing it."

"Fine." Mom folded her arms across her chest, glaring down at the dog. "We'll call him Fulk. But if he pees on anything—"

"He goes out to the barn," I finished for her. Then I picked up my bag, whistled to my dog, and headed upstairs to my bedroom.

Once inside the Pepto-pink bedroom I'd occupied since my childhood, I examined the contents of my closet while Fulk explored the room with his nose. When I'd moved to Baltimore, I'd left all my formal outfits behind since I couldn't see myself needing them living solo in a ratty apartment while working part time as a barista. Now, I was considering hauling one or two back with me. Christmas and New Year's were coming, and I had some vague hopes of maybe being invited to a formal event somewhere. Plus Dario was the head of his *Balaj*. I assumed that might mean a formal occasion sometime in the future once he sorted everything out and the *Balaj* was on more of a stable footing. Plus I was eyeing anything I might be able to use as a dress for this medieval reenactment thing I'd somehow found myself a queen-elect of. The last event I'd attended, I'd just worn my armor and borrowed a dress from someone for the dinner. I really couldn't keep doing that, but didn't have the funds to be buying or renting costumes. Could I attend dances in armor? Be coronated while wearing my armor? I was going to push for yes on the latter, but I couldn't see myself getting away with plate mail during a fancy Twelfth Night celebration, even if I *was* the regent monarch.

In the end I selected a black and a red dress, and grabbed two bridesmaid things from the very back of my closet to hopefully retrofit into something reasonably medievalesque. Then I unpacked my bag with the clothes for tomorrow.

Thanksgiving in our family wasn't as formal as Christmas or our family weekend dinners, but jeans and a t-shirt would be heavily frowned upon. I'd grabbed my trusty blue dress and figured I'd jazz it up a bit with pearls from the jewelry box I'd also left behind when I'd moved.

Just as there was no need for formal gowns in my Baltimore life, there was no need for pearls and diamonds. Besides, I had been worried someone would have broken into my apartment and stolen them. A few of these pieces were heirlooms, and I would have been gutted to see them lost from the family. But just as I was hauling a few gowns home, I now looked at my jewelry box with renewed interest.

No. This was ridiculous. I felt weird enough bringing formal dresses back to Baltimore with me. I wasn't about to bring expensive jewelry that I'd probably only wear once a year.

That decided, I turned to Fulk. I wasn't sure how the dog would feel about being left alone in what for him was a strange room while I went downstairs. On the other hand, I'd pushed things pretty far by bringing him into the house, I didn't know how my parents would feel about the dog trailing around after me. I weighed the two alternatives and decided that having a howling dog tearing up my bedroom was worse than having him hopefully sitting quietly beside my chair. Maybe I'd get lucky and my nephews would take him outside to play fetch.

I lucked out. Ajax and Bors were downstairs, and clearly bored to death with sitting politely while the adults talked about unexciting stuff and got into the booze. They were more than happy to take Fulk outside to play for the next couple of hours until bedtime. Yes, it was dark, but this was one of the benefits of growing up in a wealthy family with a historic mansion on hundreds of acres of land—the only danger the boys would encounter would be tripping over something in the dark and landing face-first in the soft, manicured grass. There was no poison ivy, no poisonous snakes, no monsters lurking in the dark. Everything that could possibly harm a young child knew better than to be within a mile of a Templar home. And if not, I completely trusted Fulk, as goofy and friendly as he normally was, to take care of any possible menace and protect the children.

With my dog happily in the company of my nephews, I made my way back into the sitting room where all the adults were gathered around in leather chairs, sipping whisky, or port, or sherry. I paused on the threshold, overcome for a moment with nostalgia.

My parents, looking much the same as they did when I was a child, albeit with silver hair and a few lines in their faces. My brother and sister, only now with their spouses. The chairs, the paintings on the wall, the antique rugs, the wallpaper were all the same as when I'd grown up. How many times had I come down before bed to sit beside my parents with a glass of warm milk while they had their more adult nightcaps?

Mom or Dad would read us bedtime stories, or tell tales of their adventures, glossing over the scary parts so we wouldn't have nightmares. The story I'd always wanted to hear, though, was the one about when my parents had met. Mom attending the private college that ensured Templars had all the knowledge and skills they needed before taking their vows. Dad a professor teaching Beasts of Myth and Legend. She'd thought him a pompous ass with all knowledge and no sword. He'd thought her a brash, overconfident woman who was probably going to get herself killed rushing into her first fight without an adequate understanding of what she was up against.

How wrong they'd both been. They'd fallen desperately in love when they realized that their strengths complimented each other, and that together they were an unstoppable team.

Standing there at the entrance of the room, I saw the way Dad looked at Mom, the way she reached out to take his hand. All these years and they were *still* an unstoppable team. I loved them so, and I hoped one day I'd have what they did.

Would that be with Dario? In spite of the obvious hurdles a long-term relationship between a Templar and a vampire would face, I could see a glimmer of this future ahead of us—a possibility, if we could somehow manage to trust each other fully and work together, to be partners. If we could manage that, then maybe one day the pair of us would be sitting like my parents were right now, only in Dario's Federal Hill home, me with silver in my hair and Dario looking exactly the same as he did now—the same as he had for hundreds of years.

But I knew he still kept things from me about the *Balaj*, and I couldn't commit to unconditionally supporting him because I knew his loyalties were first to his family—and the actions he might take to safeguard them and their territory might force him to do what I couldn't support or even accept.

We weren't there yet, and I wasn't sure we would ever be.

Roman turned to me and smiled, holding up a whisky decanter in one hand and a decanter of port in the other, his eyebrows raised in query.

I hated sherry. But was this a whisky night or a port night?

"Port, please," I told Roman. Then I walked over and gave my father a hug. He hadn't been in the foyer when I'd arrived and I'd yet to greet him.

"I hear you brought a dog." His voice held a note of humor, and I knew that he'd gotten an earful of my mother's complaints.

"Your grand-dog, Fulk."

He chuckled. "Interesting choice of names, Solaria. Sit. Tell us about your new house. I hear from Athena that you've moved."

It was then I noticed that one member of our family wasn't in attendance. "Where's Gran?"

I'll admit a brief moment of panic. My great-grandmother was probably close to one hundred and twenty-five years old as far as anyone knew. She was spry, and didn't look a day over eighty, but I still worried about her.

Dad waved his hand toward the doorway. "She went up to change. Claimed her outfit smelled of horses and dogs, so I'm assuming she was out in the barn this afternoon. She'll be down soon."

I didn't like the way Dad had said that and glanced with worry toward the doorway. Gran was...odd. My great-grandfather Tarquin Ainsworth had brought home his Hungarian bride to the consternation of Templars every-where—especially Templar women who'd considered him the catch of the century and longed to combine their genetic pool with his. Essie was a witch, although the exact nature of her magic had never been explained. She was eccentric, vulgar, and I loved her with all my heart. I hoped she was okay. I hoped she outlived me.

Roman handed me a glass of port and I took a seat, sipping and listening to Athena and my mother debating the best way to introduce little Jet to the art of swordsmanship. I'd had foam and flexible plastic weapons since before I could walk, and I agreed with Mom that it was never too early for a young Templar to start.

Just as we were moving on to gossip over who was poten-tially next in line for an Elder opening, Essie entered the room. Much to my relief, she seemed as hardy and strong as ever. Her eyes sharp and clear and her step sure, but when I got up to kiss her on the cheek, she seemed warmer than usual—as if she were running a low-grade fever.

"You feeling okay, Gran?" I asked her.

"Soon as someone gets me a whisky I'll be okay. And don't you dare water it down, Solomon," she shouted to my father who'd gotten up to fetch her the beverage.

"Tell us about your new home, Aria," Essie commanded as soon as she'd gotten herself seated and taken a sip of the whisky to assure herself it hadn't been diluted. "Your father has been worried sick that it's in a bad neighborhood, or that it's got rats or bats or mildew or something. I told him if a Templar can't manage to live with a little mildew, then she's not a real Templar."

I grimaced, thankful that my new place didn't have mildew or rats or bats. And although it *was* in a sketchy neighborhood, I wasn't about to tell my family that fact.

"Well, it's a block west of MLK, so farther from the water than my apartment, which is a bit of a bummer. But it's much larger with two bedrooms and something that might be a bedroom or could be a study or studio. It's a row house with a little yard out back for Fulk to play. And it's got lots of privacy since the house next door is boarded up and vacant."

Neither my parents nor my siblings seemed too thrilled about my description so far, but Essie at least didn't appear to be put off by my little slum rental.

"The best part is that there's a permanent ritual space in the basement next to the furnace," I continued. "A circle, acid etched into the concrete with interlocking rings and pentacles of cemented rock salt, silver, and gold."

That was met with an uneasy silence.

"Solaria," Mom scolded. "Please tell me you're not summoning demons again. I would have thought you would have learned your lesson the last time."

Yes, I'd summoned what was supposed to be a Goetic

demon and gotten something far worse instead and ended up marked, but that hadn't been my fault. And with the help of friends, I'd managed to rid myself of both the demon and the mark.

"I'm not summoning demons," I told my mother, neglecting to add the word "yet". I was sure there might come a time when I'd need to do that, but I was trying to make sure that time was far in the future when I'd developed more skill as a mage and maybe had an entire group to back me up in case things went sideways.

"I'm sure such a space would be useful in creating charms and illusions," Dad chimed in.

"Or sex magic," Essie added. "Get that vampire of yours down there and make shit happen. Although you'd get more done with a virgin, and I doubt that sexy bloodsucker is a virgin. Men who look like that never are."

"I've been using it for things like detection spells and such," I assured them, ignoring my great-grandmother's suggestion. I was always up for sex with Dario, but doing it on a cold basement floor wasn't exactly erotic, no matter what the magical boost might be.

"Your new place sounds lovely," Athena said with a wince. "I can't wait to visit."

That would require me to actually get a bed in the spare bedroom that was now empty except for a few boxes. Maybe I could get a futon or cheap bedroom set off Craigslist with my overtime money. It would be nice to have my parents come up for a weekend, or Roman or Athena. Before I could suggest appealing touristy things to entice them to visit, Bors and Ajax returned with a panting, but still energetic, Fulk beside them.

The dog made the rounds, greeting everyone with a subdued politeness I hadn't thought possible, then came to sit between me and Essie. We said goodnight to the boys and

Jet, and my siblings and their spouses headed upstairs to put their children to bed, leaving me with my parents and Gran, and Fulk.

"Did you know Solaria is now referring to that vampire as her boyfriend," Mom informed Dad in a tone that practically frosted the windows.

Gran snorted. "Like that's any surprise. Let the girl have her fun, Mavia. If he turns out to be a dick, she can just run him through with her sword."

"We just worry about you," Dad told me. "His loyalties aren't your loyalties. And then there's the whole blood thing."

"I'm well aware of the issues, but we're trying to make this work. Let's talk about something else instead."

"When are you going to take your Oath?" Mom asked.

That hadn't been the choice in topic I'd envisioned. "I don't know. Maybe never. What should I get Jet for Christmas? The boys are so easy to shop for, but what would a toddler want?"

"You are one of the most knowledgeable and skilled Templars alive," Dad told me. "The Order needs you. We have a responsibility that was given to us at birth, and it's time you accepted that and served the Lord."

"I do serve the Lord," I snapped back. "I do more to fulfill the Oaths of Knighthood than most of the Elders in their posh estates. I protect humanity. I safeguard Pilgrims on the Path. When I came across an artifact, I brought it to safety. If the Temple is ever attacked, I will rush to its defense. The only thing taking my Oath does is put me under the thumb of a bunch of Knights who have lost their way. I will not be put in a position where I have to choose between my pilgrims' safety and whatever the Elders decide is more lucrative or important. I won't allow myself to be in a position where I have to choose between the Oath I made to God, and the Oath I made to the Order."

My speech was greeted with a shocked silence. Then Essie chuckled.

"Dear, an Oath to God always comes first. And if the Elders fail to realize that, then shame on them. Your great-grandfather always did what he felt was right no matter the opinions of others. And yes, there were many times when he told the Elders to get bent. Facing the hard decisions and making difficult choices is part of being a Knight. It's part of being a Templar." She waved a hand and drained the rest of her whisky. "Bah. But what do I know? I'm not a Templar and never will be. I'm just an old woman who has seen far more than anyone except the divine and the dead. I'm going to bed. Try not to kill each other while I'm gone."

We watched Gran leave, Fulk following her to the doorway, then trotting back to me with a whine. I looked down at his chisel shaped head and scratched between his ears, not wanting to see the expression on my parents' face.

"She's right, you know," my mother said, her voice soft. "An Oath of Knighthood never displaces an Oath to God. And if you ever found yourself having to choose between the two, then know this, Solaria Angelique Ainsworth—every member of this family will stand behind your decision. Every one of us. We are Knights. We serve the Order. But we serve God and all that is right first."

"Agreed," my father chimed in. "Well said, Mavia."

Tears blurred my vision as I blinked. If I were to take my Oath, and the day came where I had to go against a direct order by the Elders, my punishment wouldn't be a slap on the wrist. And it wouldn't be a slap on the wrist for those who supported me.

But knowing that my family would be willing to give up all they had to stand behind me...that made me love them all even more. We were family, and family always protected each other. I wasn't alone. I was never alone. Even if things didn't work out long-term between Dario and me, even if some horrible monster attacked Baltimore, even if I had to stand between what I knew was right and the Order I'd been brought up to respect and obey, I'd survive.

Because I'd always have my family right there to catch me if I fell.

# CHAPTER 8

"So what's happening up in Baltimore? Necromancers, death mages, Boo Hag, warring *Balajs*... Are there dragons now? A gorgon?" Dad leaned his arms on the counter, nudging the bacon toward me. As usual, we were the first two up in the morning, and Dad had made the pair of us breakfast. He'd clearly been up at the crack of dawn getting the massive turkey in the oven. Normally we had staff that prepared family dinners, but they'd been given Thanksgiving off, so my father was handling the turkey, and we'd warm up all the dishes the staff had prepared earlier this week when it was closer to dinner time.

I grabbed a piece of bacon and took a bite, relishing the thick crisp texture and the smoky, applewood flavor. "I don't want to say things are quiet. I tripped over a dead homeless man Tuesday morning on my jog."

Dad shook his head. "That's such a tragedy. Perhaps we should donate to Baltimore area homeless shelters or addiction treatment programs in the city. Now that you've made Baltimore your home, we have a responsibility to help the less fortunate there."

I winced, knowing Dad meant well, and donations were better than "thoughts and prayers" or just shrugging over the whole thing, dismissing it as a sad state of affairs.

"That would be nice, but this man wasn't just the usual homeless drug addict. He was severely anemic. He was so anemic that the M.E. had to draw blood from an organ. There were three other homeless deaths this month where the decedents were unusually anemic, but not to this extent."

Dad smirked. "Decedent. I can tell you've been hanging out with cops."

I smiled, knowing Detective Tremelay's lingo had seeped into my vocabulary. "The first three died from cardiac arrest due to a heroin overdose. They were clearly long-term drug users, and their anemia might be due to some undiagnosed underlying disease or genetic condition. But this last one… it's like he was drained of blood."

"Vampires." Dad shot me a sympathetic glance. "I know you're dating one, Aria, but they're the likely culprit when it comes to these things. There's a *Balaj* in Baltimore. There are rogues outside the city. They usually cover these things up, but sometimes one gets sloppy."

I got the impression Dario never got sloppy. And I didn't want to jump to the assumption that these deaths were due to vampires—especially not Dario's family.

"The only puncture wounds were the victim's inner arms, which is consistent with drug use. Yes, it could be vampires trying to cover up their feeding by taking blood from a site where a junkie might shoot up, but I'm trying to explore other potential causes."

Dad slapped some French toast and bacon on a plate and sat down beside me. "Perhaps the anemia *is* from a disease. Some of those needle marks might be transfusions for medical care and these homeless people died from the disease."

I took a bite of French toast and thought about that. "But what disease could cause the lack of blood in the last victim? How could he have been still walking around the night before if he was that bad off? I'm just trying to think outside the box here, to figure out if something other than a vampire could possibly be responsible."

Dad frowned as he chewed. "Plague demon? If you've got a plague demon in your city, then the guy could have been fine the night before, and dead from advanced leukemia by morning."

"Maybe. But I'm sure the M.E. would have noted in the preliminary if the guy had been riddled with cancer. And leukemia doesn't drain the body of blood."

Dad thought a moment. "More of those death mages?"

Ugh, I hoped not. Most of them were dead or in jail, but I knew of at least one that had gotten away. I doubted he would have returned to Baltimore, but who's to say there weren't more lurking around? I'd certainly bring it up tomorrow when I went to the prison to talk to Chuck, but there were a few things about the body that made me doubt a death mage was responsible.

"There's nothing about the body that indicates a ritual killing. Maybe blood magic, although I don't know any blood magic rituals that require more than a few drops. And usually it's the mage who needs to supply the blood. I can't imagine any magic that would need six or more pints of a homeless drug-user's blood."

"Black market blood banks?" Dad shrugged. "Like those waking-up-in-a-bathtub-without-a-kidney stories only it's blood and not kidneys?"

Wow, I hadn't even thought of that. Homeless people would be a quick supply of blood, and they'd be willing to donate for a quick buck. But would homeless blood be usable? Especially those who were drug users? I knew they screened those people out at community blood drives, so I couldn't imagine that paying for multiple blood donations from the same at-risk individuals would yield…well, anything. And it wasn't like blood was something that could be sold at a premium, unlike black market kidneys.

Dad waved a piece of bacon at me and continued. "Maybe it's a rare blood that's actually in demand, either for humans with autoimmune problems, or those who live on human blood and are willing to pay big for preferences."

I suddenly remembered Dario commenting to me that certain human illnesses lent blood a very pleasing flavor, and caught my breath. Rich people with exotic illnesses. Rich vampires with kinky blood preferences.

"But how would the killers know the homeless people's blood type?" I mused. "It doesn't make sense to go around taking blood from a whole bunch of people in hopes that one of them might be the right type. There has to be some prescreening."

"Doesn't take much to test blood. A quick finger stick, and you've got it." Dad frowned. "But I'm assuming this would be more than just blood type, otherwise I doubt there would be enough money in it to be worth the bother. Maybe a specific genetic abnormality creates the value? Something that only one in tens of thousands of people have?"

"Then it wouldn't be worth it to go around finger sticking a gazillion homeless people," I replied. "That's far too much work for what might potentially be no reward."

Dad swirled a piece of French toast in syrup and popped it in his mouth. "If it's humans killing for blood to sell, I'd think the best plan would be to steal the records from an actual blood donation site. I'm thinking if this is the case, then one of them works there. Prescreened. Already knows the blood type and all the information about someone. And who cares if they donated last week if you're going to kill them anyway."

Dad scared me sometimes. "It *is* the most logical scenario if we're talking about blood-for-sale," I agreed.

"But..."

"But..." I grinned. "I am down here for the day and I want to go through all possibilities. So, who drinks blood that isn't a vampire?"

Dad gave me that one-eyebrow look. "Or what sort of magic requires blood—lots of blood—but doesn't involve a death."

That was the question of the year, and I wasn't sure who to go to on that one. I had been in touch with Reynard after the ritual on Halloween, and his knowledge was strictly Goetica. I also doubted this was a specialty area that Russell could help me with.

I knew who to go to and he was in Jessup prison. I had a visit scheduled with him on Black Friday of all days, and was bringing his tub of Fisher's caramel popcorn up with me as well.

"Think we can do a little research after we eat and before I need to head home?" I asked.

"You know I'm always willing to research something with you, Aria." Dad saluted me with a piece of bacon. "Right after dinner, when everyone is having their turkey coma, we'll head into the library."

I grinned and saluted him back with my own piece of bacon. "Then it's a date."

* * *

IN TYPICAL THANKSGIVING TRADITION, we ate our turkey around two in the afternoon, which gave everyone plenty of time to lay around in a food stupor for the rest of the day. We'd hit the kitchen again around eight o'clock for a second round. I planned on leaving sometime before ten since I'd drawn the short straw at work and needed to be at the coffee shop at six in the morning. I was pretty sure traffic would be light getting back to Baltimore, but I wasn't too worried. It wouldn't be the first time I'd worked a shift on a few hours' sleep. And after my shift, I could catch a quick nap before having to be at the prison for my scheduled visit with Chuck.

But all this meant I couldn't do a late night research session with Dad. Instead we waddled into the library after gorging ourselves with food and sat down with a stack of books to look for supernatural beings who had needle-like fangs or mouth parts, and fed on human blood.

"Manananggal?" I asked, pointing to the entry in Schumer's Creatures of the Night.

"I've never heard of one leaving the Philippines," Dad confessed.

"They've been sighted in Indonesia and a few other areas, but they get lumped in with Aswang, so there's an issue with reporting accurate numbers." I turned in surprise to see my mother sitting down across from me at the table. "What?" She grinned. "I'm not about to let your father have all the fun. Besides, I've never been much for napping after a big meal. You're thinking there's a Manananggal in Baltimore?"

Dad smiled at her. "Aria possibly has a non-vampire bloodsucking supernatural being in her city, but I doubt it's a Manananggal. They separate themselves into two parts, then sprout wings and fly to hunt their victims. They'd be biting humans on the neck and actually chewing on their faces, not draining them of blood via punctures on their prey's inner arm."

Mom's eyebrows shot up. "Inner arm? Drained of blood? Sweetie, it sounds like vampires to me."

"It might be, but I'm trying to cover all bases here. Vampires. Some blood-for-pay scheme where the guy had a rare form of blood. Magic that needs a huge quantity of blood. Or possibly some creature other than a vampire. I'm just trying to be thorough."

"Always a wise idea, Solaria." Mom nodded in approval, pulling one of the books over to her and leafing through it.

Dad read down an entry from Predators of the Orient. "Ekek, Chonchon. Krasue. Nukekubi. Penangglan. Tiyanak. Wak Wak. Most of these have a similar attack method as the Manananggal, so I doubt it's one of them. Besides, their populations are pretty much limited to Asia."

"Isn't Chonchon a shapeshifting sorcerer?" I leaned over to look at the illustration.

"It's more a permanent transformation spell where a sorcerer becomes a Manananggal," Dad said. "So again, the method of blood feeding isn't consistent with that sort of creature."

"And the Krasue looks like a floating female head with entrails below the neck, so I'm guessing no on that one," Mom chimed in.

I grimaced. "Yeah, I'm pretty sure there would have been reports of floating female heads if it was a Krasue."

"Outside of the Tiyanak they all detach their heads and fly around," Dad commented. "I'm thinking if this man was killed by something supernatural, it would be a creature that was comfortable or adapted to urban living and would be fairly unnoticed in a high-population area. Possibly the Tiyanak, but I doubt any of these others."

"So I should consider a Tiyanak?" I asked

Dad shook his head. "Probably not. Tiyanak aren't very mobile. They lure their prey in by sounding like a baby in distress. That might be a successful hunting strategy in the city, but they're not the sort of creature who would go unnoticed. Plus having to crawl around everywhere would be a huge disadvantage. Besides, they chew their prey with claws and fangs, and you said the only noticeable injury to the victim was puncture wounds on their inner arms?"

I nodded. "And some bruises, but I'm pretty sure the M.E. would have noted if the bruises were the kind that might have led to internal injuries, so I'm thinking we can discount those."

Mom waved her hand to halt the pair of us. "Look, there are thousands of supernatural beings who feast on human blood. Let's start with the ones common to this continent first, rule them out, *then* consider the more exotic ones."

She had a point. Dad and I tended to go down the rabbit hole and get lost in the fascinating details of various creatures, all while losing sight of our original question.

"Chupacabra?" Dad turned a questioning glance to mom.

That's right. She'd battled a nest of Chupacabra down in Puerto Rico a few years back. I turned to my mother. "Would the injuries from a Chupacabra attack be limited to puncture wounds on the inner arm and some random bruises?"

"If the victim didn't fight, which might be the case with someone who was passed out from drug use. Although as far as my experience goes, they only drain the blood from goats and animals. They'll attack humans who they see as trespassers and rivals for territory and food," Mom commented. "But I doubt they'd drain the blood from a human. From what I've seen, a Chupacabra killing on a human would look more like a wild dog attack."

Dog attack. Crap. I made a mental note to mention that one to Tremelay as well as Dario. Those murders in the north part of the city might be rogue vampires, or some nutjob with an attack dog, but it could also be Chupacabra.

Was it wrong that I was hoping it was a nutjob with an attack dog?

I pulled up the picture that Janice had sent me and showed it to Dad. "I don't have any close-ups of the actual puncture wounds. This is the guy I tripped over, the one who was basically drained of blood."

He looked at the photo and turned my phone to show it to my mom.

"How about a Soucouyant? Or as they call them in Haiti, a Loogaroo?" My dad asked.

"Hold on, Solomon." Mom took my phone and zoomed in on the picture. "Let's look at the limiting factors here. Male victim. The only injuries appear to be on the inner arms where there are puncture wounds. Blood was drained from the body."

"That's all I know at this time," I told them. "The earlier victims, which may or may not be related to this, didn't have any other marks or diseases, although they had heroin in their tox screen. They had severe anemia, but this last guy basically didn't have any blood left in his body at all."

Mom and Dad were both silent—Dad flipping through Schumer's Creatures of the Night, Mom frowning down at the picture.

"Outside of a vampire attack, which is the most likely scenario in my opinion, I'm leaning toward a Dearg-Due, or possibly a Mandurugo," Dad announced.

"Femme fatale," Mom mused. "With one victim we can't really be positive, but I agree. The puncture wounds could be the barbed tongue of a Mandurugo, or the needle-like one of a Dearg-Due."

"And both would easily lure a man back to their lair," Dad said.

"How *do* they choose their prey?" I asked. "Is there something special about their blood, or do they just select randomly?"

Dad shrugged. "They tend to choose cheaters, enticing

men in with promises of sex only to drain them and kill them, but the homeless would be an easy mark. You could definitely have a Mandurugo in your city."

Mom rolled her eyes. "What is it with you and the Philippine supernaturals? I'm leaning toward it being a Dearg-Due."

Dad grinned. "Okay you're right. Mandurugo fly. But they tend to take the most convenient prey, and the homeless are certainly convenient."

"How would I kill it if it were a Mandurugo?" I asked.

Mom shrugged. "Stab it. They're pretty fragile as supernatural creatures go. Stab it in the chest, or cut off its head."

I winced at the thought of cutting off a young beautiful woman's head, even if she *was* killing someone.

"But if it's a Dearg-Due..." Dad frowned.

"If it's a Dearg-Due, we're in trouble," Mom added.

I turned the book around and read the summary. A Dearg-Due was a combination of vengeful spirit and ghoul. Abused and tortured during her life, she came back from the grave each night and took her revenge—first upon those who had witnessed her abuse and never stepped forward to help. After she'd killed them, the Dearg-Due went on to kill others, sucking the air from their lungs to incapacitate them, then draining them of all their blood. There was no mention of which body part she preferred to do her blood-sucking from, but the article did say the Dearg-Due had very sharp, needle-like teeth she used to puncture flesh and drain her victim's blood, so I was assuming their site of attack could appear to a human as if the victim had been a recent drug user.

"It's in keeping with the neat appearance of the body," Dad noted. "Dearg-Due don't chew or maul. They just drain blood."

"How do I kill it?" I asked, flipping the page.

"Schumer says to stack rocks on the grave, but a guy in Dungarvan told me that was a waste of time," Mom said. "Sometimes they still get out of the grave, and even if the stones hold them, all it takes is one tourist or teenager dare, and you've got a Dearg-Due on the loose again."

"Best to enlist a necromancer then," I murmured, eyeing the photos that accompanied the article. From what Schumer said, it was a sort of ghost, so I was thinking Russell would be better suited to handle the situation than me slapping rocks on a grave.

"Maybe, but I don't trust necromancers," Mom commented. "Dig her up, burn the body and replace it in a lead-lined casket, then salt the grave with an End Times blessing. That's what I'd do."

Mom was the expert. Dad did the research. Mom did the killing. Or in this case, the containment.

So I had three theories running around in my brain right now. One, a Dearg-Due was loose. If that were the case, then this body would only be the first in a whole lot of dead men. Two, a group of mages were doing spellwork that required a whole lot of blood. To check the plausibility of that theory, I'd talk to Chuck and possibly see if Reynard would return my call. Three, some humans had a blood-for-money scheme and were trying to get rich draining homeless people who had a rare blood type. If that theory were the case, then this whole thing got dumped in Tremelay's lap.

It didn't escape me that the most implausible of the three theories was the human one. The logistics of identifying who had the appropriately valuable blood type, then finding them among the homeless seemed a whole lot more farfetched than a vengeful blood-drinking ghoul or some sort of overkill blood magic.

Either way, I already had plans to meet with Russell for

the séance and could ask him what he knew about Dearg-Due.

But in the meantime, there was a turkey sandwich in the kitchen calling my name, then a long drive home, and an early morning tomorrow.

## CHAPTER 9

The coffee shop was insanely busy. I got there at five thirty and there were people standing outside the door, right in front of the "we open at six" sign, demanding to be let in for coffee. Seemed we weren't the only ones opening at six, and half of Baltimore wanted to be fully caffeinated before hitting up their Black Friday deals. There were no breaks for us, and I was pretty sure as I eyed the clock, that I wasn't going to be getting off work at noon as originally planned.

Turning to take an order, I saw a familiar face across from me.

"We need to talk," Tremelay announced, placing something on the counter.

It was the second time this week someone had slapped crime scene photos on the counter in front a bunch of customers. I shot a quick glance over at my manager, thinking that I was probably on the edge of getting fired here.

At least these weren't of a corpse on a morgue slab. These

were closeup shots of someone's arm—an arm with two big-ass holes in it.

There was also a ruler helpfully placed next to the holes. Picking up the photos, I looked closer at the marks, my mind cycling through everything I knew about vampire feedings. Their fangs were sharp and needlelike, leaving much smaller holes than this. The goal was to quickly pierce the skin and vein, allowing their euphoric venom to cover up any of the donor's pain as the vampire drank. There was an anticoagulant in their saliva that allowed them to quickly consume a pint of blood before clotting began—a fast feeding reducing the chance of detection at a rather vulnerable time for the vampire.

If they wanted more than a pint, they could bite a second time either from a different or the same location, or they could bite deeper, widening the puncture marks and allowing for a more rapid blood flow—although with that technique, there was a significant risk that the pain to their victim would overcome the euphoria of the venom, and that the fang marks would be very noticeable afterward.

Unfortunately I knew that personally. Simon had bitten me deep, not caring about my pain or leaving a scar. In fact, that had been part of the thrill for him. He'd not just widened the puncture marks on my neck, but chewed the flesh, ripping and tearing it so my scar looked less like a vampire bite and more like the savage attack that it was.

The marks in the photo were not what I would have expected for a stealthy vampire feeding. From the diameter of the holes, a vampire would have sunk his fangs in practically to the gums. Beyond these, there were no signs of other teeth marks or damage in the area of the photos. Interestingly, the measuring device showed the marks at two inches apart. If this were a vampire, he had a really wide jaw and some tusk-like fangs. I was pretty sure a dude like that would stand out.

It all made me believe this wasn't a vampire attack, but something else. I wondered briefly how big Dearg-Due fangs were. Hmmm. I might need to call Dad on that one later.

I looked up to see Tremelay scowling at me. "What? Why are you looking at me that way? I didn't do this."

"I know you didn't do this. I'm just tired and grumpy because I spent most of Thanksgiving on this case. And I'd like to know who our leak at the morgue is, because waking up to 'Homeless Man Found Dead and Drained of Blood' as the headline in the paper this morning along with these very same pictures didn't do much to help my mood."

I winced. Poor guy. "Go yell at Janice, because I don't know who her contacts are."

"Well, she wasn't wrong, but now I've got my lieutenant breathing down my neck because people are flooding the hotlines with calls about satanic neighbors, vampire co-workers, and mutant giant ticks from South Africa—none of which I'd rule out given the weird shit-show of cases I've had in the last few months."

I blinked. Mutant giant ticks? Was that a thing? Should I call Dad and ask him about South African tick-monsters, or perhaps these were a genetic experiment gone bad? Glancing over at Sean, I held up the pictures. "Do you think I can grab a quick break?"

He looked at the line behind the detective, then at the pictures. "Fifteen minutes max, Aria. Try to make it quicker. We're swamped."

I nodded, smiling in appreciation as I led Tremelay away from the curious eyes and ears of our customers and to the back room where we tended to take our breaks. We'd barely gotten seated in the hard wooden chairs before Tremelay began.

"Here's what I've got so far. The first three people I showed you two nights ago were long-term addicts who had been on the streets for several years. As I said, anemia was a contributing factor to their deaths, but not the main cause. They appeared to have been down a couple pints of blood in volume, which the M.E. says could have been due to an unknown underlying illness as no blood donation site would collect from an active drug user."

I nodded, thinking that was in line with what he'd mentioned Wednesday night at my place.

"This man here. He doesn't show any signs of habitual drug use, and he basically was drained of blood, as the rather sensationalist headline in today's paper announced."

"This is the guy I found, right?" I asked, just to make sure.

"Yep. We've got an ID on him, and he's not homeless like the other three. He's not even from Baltimore. His name's Melbourne Cassidy. He's a financial analyst at some company I've never heard of in Chicago. He's not even supposed to *be* in Baltimore. His wife said he'd flown out Monday for a consulting gig at some firm in Philadelphia and was due to return home next week. She didn't even know he was missing until a uniformed officer showed up at her home to give her the news."

I caught my breath, wondering how the heck a man on a business trip ended up on the sidewalk of a sketchy neighborhood in Baltimore.

"Didn't she worry when he didn't text or call her or anything?" I asked, knowing *I'd* be worried. But then again, sometimes a few days went by without my seeing Dario depending on what was happening. I hadn't heard from him beyond a quick text Wednesday and Thursday night, but I'd still be concerned if he didn't check in at least every few days.

"She says when he's doing these consulting gigs, he's

buried in spreadsheets and focused. He let her know he'd landed and checked into his hotel, and texted her that he'd see her this coming Monday."

I nodded, acknowledging that she'd hardly expect her husband to lose his life looking over accounting files for some corporation. Not like that job was particularly high on the list of risky careers.

"She's on her way out here now," Tremelay added. "From what I can tell, this Cassidy guy landed in Philly, checked into his hotel room, then never showed up the next morning at the company he was supposed to be working with. They called his firm, but with the holiday and everything, they figured maybe they got the dates wrong and he'd show up next week."

"So he went missing sometime between Monday and Tuesday morning," I mused.

Tremelay nodded. "Given that you stumbled across him Tuesday morning and the suspected time of death, we're thinking Monday, probably soon after he checked into his hotel."

I looked at the pictures again.

"There's more," Tremelay continued. "They found faint traces of a sedative in the blood sample they took from his organs but, as I said, there was no sign of habitual drug use at all. His wife says he's clean as a whistle, and it wouldn't be like him to suddenly decide to shoot up out of the blue."

"Something really bad was going on in his life and he turned to drugs?" I asked. Sometimes people lived a life that their spouses knew nothing about. Although why the man would need to come all the way to Baltimore to get high was beyond me. There were plenty of dealers in Philly for that sort of thing.

"According to the wife and his company, he gets regularly

tested at work because of the financial nature of the projects he's working on, so it seems unlikely."

I frowned. "Either way drug use doesn't explain the blood loss."

Tremelay sat back in the chair. "But here's where it gets weird. The wife insists he's not a drug user. She said the only needles that have ever been close to her husband's arm were for blood donation, which he did regularly according to her. Evidently he's got some rare blood type and a strong sense of moral duty around giving blood. Twice a year, like clockwork. I'm verifying it with the American Red Cross, but she texted me one of those little booklets they give out and he's got more stamps than frequent flyer miles. The guy gives a lot of blood."

I frowned, thinking that Dad's implausible blood-for-money scheme was looking more and more plausible. "Any idea what's so special about his blood?"

The detective took his notebook out of his pocket and flipped through a few pages before finding what he wanted. "Rh-null. He's one of forty known people in the world that are Rh-null. It makes him slightly anemic, which is why he's only allowed to donate twice a year. Plus, if he's ever in an accident and needs an emergency transfusion, he's pretty much screwed since he'd need Rh-null blood. His wife says because of that he always was a careful driver, and not much of a risk taker as far as hobbies and activities. She gave that as one more reason why he'd never have turned to drugs—especially IV drugs."

I shook my head, perplexed by the whole thing. "I get the rare blood thing, but with only forty known people in the world with this blood type, I can't imagine it would be in so much demand that a blood-for-money scheme would be profitable. I mean, they'd need to figure out Cassidy had the blood type they needed, plan to grab or entice him and transport him from Philly to Baltimore, then basically take every bit of blood in his body. Seems like a lot of work for blood."

"I hear ya." Tremelay flipped a page in his notebook. "Unless there was an Rh-null rich guy who needs ten to twelve pints for open heart surgery."

I nodded. "I guess. With forty people in the world with that blood type, it shouldn't be too hard to track that sort of thing down."

Tremelay rubbed a hand over his eyes. "That's what I'm hoping. I'm trying to see if there's been any blood flown out of the country in the last few days, and trying to get a list of any surgeries that happened Wednesday or today, or are scheduled for the next few weeks that might require this much blood and which Rh-null was a requirement in the transfusions. Fresh blood only keeps for four weeks, so whatever someone was doing with this blood, they'd need to use it pretty soon after collecting it."

"So this isn't supernatural after all, but the equivalent of a black market kidney operation? Only with rare blood?" I looked down at the picture again. "Those punctures look way bigger than the ones I get when I've donated blood. Are you sure about this?"

"They're needle marks," Tremelay assured me. "I was scratching my head over this Thanksgiving, so I asked Kyra to take a look at them."

"Lovely Thanksgiving dinner conversation," I teased. "Hey Kyra, take a look at these morgue photos and tell me what you think. Oh, and pass me the sweet potatoes."

He laughed. "She's a doctor. I'm a cop. That's pretty much been our dinner conversation since the day she went to college."

I nodded, thinking it was pretty close to the dinner conversation I'd grown up with at my house, only we were usually debating whether the wounds we were looking at in photos were caused by a wraith or a ghoul.

"So what's her take on it? If they're really needle marks, then why are they so huge?"

"First, my theory is that he was either lured down to Baltimore with some sort of emergency that needed his specific blood type, or he was nabbed and hauled down here. I'm putting my money on the first, because kidnapping someone and driving them down from Philly has a whole lot of risk. Plus I get the idea based on what the wife says, that if Doctor So-and-So called his hotel with a medical emergency, he'd want to do the right thing. It's a short drive from Philly and I'm willing to bet his rental car shows up in the city in the next few days. I've got patrol officers looking around the hospitals, thinking that would have been the best place to lure and grab this guy."

"That makes sense. But why are the needle marks so big?" I pressed.

"I'm getting to that. Be patient, Ainsworth."

I was so not patient, especially with my allotted break time slipping away, but I knew that arguing with Tremelay would only waste more precious minutes so I waved him to go on.

"The human body holds five to six liters of blood, and it wouldn't have been easy to get that all out of his body. There's no way for the blood to exit aside from these puncture wounds on his arm."

I frowned down at the picture. "Would they have used a pump or something? I've given blood before and they're having me squeeze rubber balls like crazy just to get a pint out of me before it clots and stops flowing."

"I checked with Kyra, and she said if someone wanted to take a large quantity of blood from the body, they'd need to do it fast before clotting set in. If they didn't care whether the person lived or died, then they'd go for an artery and use a large bore hollow hypodermic needle and possibly an anti-coagulant to keep clotting to a minimum."

I stared in shock, thinking how painful that would have been. Although from what little experience I had with sudden blood loss, the guy wouldn't have been conscious for long.

"Twelve gauge," Tremelay continued. "She said from the photos showing bruising, she thinks they restrained the guy, but he clearly didn't fight hard or for long. It would have taken a while, even with the large bore needle and an antico-agulant. The multiple marks mean as the blood clotted and slowed they moved to a different spot. She also said they'd need to use negative pressure, and as the heart slowed, possibly gravity by elevating and tipping the body to get as much blood out as possible."

This was horrific, with such a careless disregard for this man's life. It was almost on par with the brutality shown by the death mages. Their victims had died fast with a knife wound to the heart, but they'd still been terrified, knowing that their death was coming. I'm sure it was the same with this man. He'd been restrained, painfully stuck with a thick needle in an artery. He'd probably lost consciousness fairly quickly, but he had to have known these men meant to kill him.

Tremelay picked the photo back up. "The M.E. report isn't finalized yet since they're waiting on lab tests, but I trust Kyra's expertise on this. She's taken enough blood samples to know her way around an IV."

"This means whoever did this knew what they were doing," I commented. "They had access to databanks of rare blood types. They knew to use a large bore needle and had access to them. They knew how to hit an artery. They had access to anticoagulants. They knew to apply negative pressure. And they had the means to collect, store, and transport the blood in a safe and sterile manner."

"Four degrees centigrade," Tremelay added. "The blood has to be at that temperature consistently or it starts to break down and would be useless. Kyra said our killer is probably a doctor or possibly a nurse with emergency room experience. Evidently it's hard enough to hit the vein right, for this they'd need to support the artery so it didn't slip aside when the needle was inserted. They'd also need to know how to speed the blood flow so they could remove a significant volume as quickly as possible before clotting began to occur."

"Even with an artery?" I shook my head, envisioning a firehose of blood. Arterial spray was a real thing and not just something in the movies.

"Twelve gauge is big, but not all that large, Ainsworth. Speed is limited by the size of the needle, and the longer it takes, the more likely the blood is going to clot."

I shuddered. "How long?"

"A few hours at the quickest. Less if they used some sort of anticoagulant drug. A whole day if they had problems hitting the artery right or didn't know how to speed blood flow. Given that the guy went missing Monday and showed up dead early Tuesday morning, I'm agreeing with Kyra that at least one of these guys is a doctor or an ER nurse. They knew what they were doing."

"So you're really thinking this is a blood-for-pay scheme?" I asked.

Which meant it wasn't my responsibility any longer. No supernatural baddie. Just a human killer. I was grateful that Tremelay had shown me all this, explained it all to me, so I wouldn't spend any more time obsessing or worrying over it. And I wouldn't embarrass myself by going to Dario and asking if one of his family might have caused this man's death.

But something about this still worried me. There was something in the back of my mind that wondered if Tremelay wasn't quite right about the murderer or the motives.

Janice had immediately suspected vampires. They would definitely have a reason to take five to six liters of blood from a guy. There were other supernatural creatures that liked blood and quite possibly had fangs that were similar to twelve gauge hypodermic needles.

"I'm putting my money on a rich guy needing heart surgery who is Rh-null blood type, but I could be wrong about that. Could be someone…or something…else that is willing to pay big for ten pints of rare blood." Tremelay fixed me with a hard stare. "Vampires with exotic tastes, maybe? Vampires who would pay big and store blood in bags in a freezer for later."

"They don't like stored blood. It doesn't satisfy their hunger. If it's vampires, then they would have gorged on it all right away. And they wouldn't have wanted to drink from bags no matter how fresh. Part of the nutrient transfer is by drinking right from the vein. If Kyra's right and this was from needles, then it's not vampires."

One of Tremelay's eyebrows went up. "And this is information you got from your vampire boyfriend? You're sure he wouldn't lie to you…oh let's say because he doesn't want you to get mad that one of his buddies has kinky tastes and killed a guy, and have you cut him off from the bedroom nookie?"

Nookie. I smirked knowing full well that Tremelay could curse like a sailor when he wasn't in the storage room of a coffee shop. He'd throw around photos of dead people, but didn't want to drop the f-bomb in public. Silly guy.

"It doesn't make sense as a vampire killing. Plus I've have up close and personal experience with vampire bites. They don't look like this."

They didn't. And now that I had decent photos, that fact was glaringly clear.

"There was another of those 'animal attacks' in the north part of the city Wednesday night, and Snyder told me this morning he had a call about a dead man found in Pigtown that had bite marks on his neck."

I sucked in a breath, worried that Dario was losing control of his city. "It's not Dario's *Balaj*. There are vampires coming in from outside the city and his group is trying to keep them out, but it's a struggle since they don't have the numbers they used to. I want to tell you things will get better, but they might not."

Tremelay shook his head. "This is going to blow up, Ainsworth. That story in the paper...what can you do to clamp down on this before these vampires send our homicide rates through the roof and cause a city-wide panic?"

"I'm meeting with Dario tonight," I assured the detective. "Let me get an update from him and see what I can do to help."

If I wasn't chasing down Dearg-Due and Mandurugo, I'd have time to help Dario. I'd just need to convince him to let me help. And somehow manage to squeeze in enough sleep that I wasn't dozing off during my shifts.

Speaking of which...

"Okay then, let me know. You take care of this vampire situation, and I'll work on the blood-for-money murder."

Blood for money. It *was* like the bathtub-kidney urban legend, where someone went to Mexico, got drunk, and woke up in a bloody bathtub with one kidney, a bunch of stitches, and a note telling them to go to the hospital, only with blood and this man never woke up.

It was a bit of an urban legend, but black market organs weren't. They truly happened. People bought and sold kidneys, portions of livers, a lung, or even body parts resulting in someone's death depending on the profit.

Tremelay was right, it *did* sound like a human on human crime. A doctor would have access to all the information, tools, and knowledge. And a doctor might be aware of a patient desperately in need of a rare blood type for a serious surgery—a patient willing to pay big for that blood so he could have that surgery sooner rather than later.

Finding that killer would be his job, and helping Dario would be mine. I followed Tremelay out of the storeroom, wincing at the crowd in the coffee shop. We'd wrapped up just in time, because my break was over, and I could tell from the noise outside the storeroom that once again, the line of customers was nearly out the door.

# CHAPTER 10

The coffee shop was in utter chaos all morning. Chalese and I worked the machines while Brandi and Sean handled the registers and called the orders. By noon we were nearly out of pastries and Sean had been to the back room twice for more espresso and extra bottles of gingerbread syrup. Things had thankfully slowed down a bit, so Sean told me to head home at three—which was a whole lot later than my scheduled quitting time of noon. I wasn't going to complain about the overtime, even though my feet were killing me and I was beat.

My scheduled visit with Chuck at the prison was at five, so I headed home wondering if I'd have time for a decent nap before driving over. Probably not. An hour nap would just leave me groggy, and I really didn't want to meet with the mage while not fully awake and alert. Plus who knows what the traffic would be like to Jessup on a Black Friday afternoon.

Instead of a nap, I ended up taking Fulk for a quick walk, then calling Janice.

"Thought you were going to wait for me to call before you went with that article?" I asked when she picked up.

"I had to get it out there, so I went with what I had. Why? Do you have something else for me?"

I pursed my lips, trying to figure out exactly what I could tell Janice without getting in trouble with Tremelay.

"Well, there does appear to be an issue with some rogue vampires up north of the city, but I'm not absolutely sure they're responsible for the deaths that are being attributed to animal attacks. I'm seeing Dario tonight and we'll discuss it."

"And what about the guy in the morgue that didn't have any blood left in his body?"

"I'm getting to that," I told her. "But first, there are some homeless people who have died of overdoses but are anemic. I'm talking to Dario about them as well."

"The guy at the morgue—"

"The guy at the morgue." I waved a hand to slow her down, even though Janice couldn't see it. "The police are looking for a human murderer on that one."

The reporter made a *pfft* noise. "Because they don't know about vampires."

"Tremelay knows about vampires," I countered. "And he's convinced it's not them or anything else supernatural. I can't go into any details, but the situation is such that this is probably a one-off murder, and not part of a spree or anything."

"You've got to be kidding me," Janice groaned. "How the heck is that *not* a vampire murder? Needle-like fang marks on the guy's inner arms. Drained of blood. Classic vampire."

I winced. "Except it's not. I promise you, Janice. Tremelay is no dummy and he's looking for a human murderer."

Janice was silent for a few seconds. "Wait. Is this like a bathtub kidney thing? Black market blood? How the heck is that profitable? Is there something about this guy's blood that makes it worth enough to kill him for it?"

Janice was no dummy either.

"I can't say. But it's not vampires." I headed into the kitchen, needing a drink. Something with caffeine since it wasn't looking like I'd be getting a nap today. Soda. Or iced tea.

She snorted. "Not that guy, but the others…"

I rolled my eyes, even though she couldn't see that either. "It's not Dario or his *Balaj*. If vampires contributed to or caused those deaths, then it's rogues from outside the city, emboldened since the *Balaj* is all of twenty-five vampires right now."

I yanked a lone can of Diet Coke out of my fridge and pulled a glass from the cabinet while I listened to Janice go on and on about the threat to humanity, and how vampires shouldn't be allowed in the city at all. Popping open the can, I opened the freezer door and scooped a handful of ice cubes into my glass before I realized something.

There were ice cubes. And no puddle of water on my kitchen floor. I frowned at the floor, then looked at the ice maker. Had I called the property management company? I didn't remember calling them. And even so, the thing was broken on Wednesday when I'd left to go to my parents' house. They'd either come out on Thanksgiving to replace it, or this morning when I was at work.

Huh. That was a pretty quick response for an ice maker. These people were a million times better than the management at the apartment in Fells Point. Maybe I should get them a little something for Christmas to show my appreciation.

"Aria? Did you hear a word I said?"

I started guiltily, shutting the freezer door and putting my glass of ice on the counter. "I know you've got your objections about vampires and how they feed on humans, but I don't have any problem with consensual, symbiotic relations between vampires and their blood donors."

Well, I did have problems with it, but not to the level of Janice's issues. My concerns were the addictive nature of vampire venom and how that interfered in the free choice of the donors in their continued service. It veered too closely to drug addiction in my mind, and I questioned whether an addicted person really could be seen as giving consent or not.

It was a conundrum. Vampires needed human blood to live, and they couldn't help the addictive nature of their venom. Still…just thinking about it made my heart race.

"I'll help Dario and the *Balaj* keep these other vampires out," I told her. "And if I find the ones who killed those people, I'll deliver justice."

There were no vampire prisons, well besides the cages in Dario's and Leonora's houses that were meant for temporary restraint. Justice was death. Dario and his family wouldn't hesitate to deliver that punishment, and neither would I. A vampire that killed couldn't be trusted to live among humans.

"Call me this weekend?" Janice asked. "I'd like an update before I run anything on the alleged animal attacks."

"I'll call you as soon as I know anything," I promised before hanging up and pouring my soda.

The caffeine didn't help, but thankfully the quick nap I was able to squeeze in did. Splashing some cold water on my face, I headed downstairs, let Fulk out for a quick potty break, grabbed the huge plastic tub of Fisher's popcorn that was my monthly tithe in return for Chuck's cooperation in going to and remaining in prison, then headed out.

Traffic was reasonably light, and although there were quite a few people visiting friends and family at the prison this afternoon, I got through security with a quick efficiency. They'd taken the tub of popcorn as they always did when I visited, but Chuck had told me that they delivered it to him back in his cell. It seemed the mage had some sort of arrangement that I probably didn't want to know about with the prison staff where he got all sorts of items from the outside that prisoners would normally have been denied. It wasn't just popcorn either. I was pretty sure the guy had his spell book and magical supplies with him. Everyone seemed to treat him with a respectful caution, so I had no doubt he'd been putting that spell book to good use.

The guy could have easily gotten out of there—either bribed the guards, or spelled the guards, or spelled the doors open, or levitated over the fence. I was pretty darned sure at least one of those would have been possible if not all of them. Why he remained here was a mystery to me. I was sure it didn't have to do with the continued supply of popcorn from me, nor from our monthly conversation. No, I got the impression Chuck felt safer in prison than on the outside. And that worried me.

I sat down in the plastic chair and waited. Chuck was escorted in, not cuffed or restrained in any way. He looked good, as if he'd been eating well and getting lots of sunshine.

"Thanks for the popcorn," he told me as he sat. "I love that stuff. It's the highlight of my month. Well, that and your interesting company, of course. Who, or what, chewed your neck up?"

That's right. I'd last met with Chuck prior to everything going down between the two vampire groups.

"It was a crazy Halloween," I told him. "I got evicted. Some asshole vampires came down from Philly and tried to oust the Baltimore *Balaj* and take over. I killed the Philly Master, but not before he mauled me. I got rid of my demon mark."

I didn't mention Dario's and my relationship, nor the

sweet ritual space in my new digs. That stuff was none of Chuck's business. Actually none of this was Chuck's business but our deal was that I told him of my magical and Templar doings, and he gave me hints about whatever horrifying thing Fiore Noir had been sacrificing souls to keep at bay.

"Did you lop his head off?" Chuck asked cheerfully. "That Philly Master, I mean."

It would be best to keep this one vague. "No. Let's just say my body is a temple."

He laughed. "You're clever. You're the sort who thinks outside the box, which I can't say about any other Templar I've had the misfortune of knowing in my life."

I made a mental note to ask my mother and father if they'd ever heard of Chuck. I couldn't imagine that he would have met with more than one Templar and had them not take note. Although the guy didn't exactly look like a stereotypical mage. He looked more like a retired stevedore.

"It's warm this winter," he commented out of the blue. "Warmer than it should be."

It wasn't technically winter yet, and I wasn't sure what he meant because it had been freaking cold ever since before Halloween. But I knew what he was referring to. One of the hints he'd given me about the Big Bad he and Fiore Noir had been spelling against was that it would come in the spring, or earlier if we had a warm winter.

I was so not ready for this…whatever it was, and I immediately sent up a quick prayer for a sub-arctic blast to come our way.

"How cold is cold?" I asked him.

His smile was downright jolly. "Colder than this."

"So if it stays this temperature, when can I expect this thing to appear?"

Chuck shrugged. "Probably after the new year. Sooner if it warms up."

Maryland weather was weird. We'd have subzero days, followed by weeks in the mid-forties, then a few days in the sixties, then back to low twenties. It was absolutely possible that we'd have spring-like weather in December.

I leaned forward in my seat. "What is it, Chuck? I need to know. I need to be prepared."

"Won't matter. There's nothing you can do to prepare for this. Well, except get the heck out of the city, that is."

This was starting to piss me off. "All I know about this thing so far is that without the magic you guys were doing, it's going to come, and that it prefers warm weather. Come on, Chuck. You've got to give me more than this."

He leaned back in his chair and folded his arms across his chest. "It's not just the weather. That development in the north part of the city is hurrying things along. The vibrations have disturbed its slumber. We were keeping it asleep, but now it stirs."

"So it dwells in the ground." I eyed him for confirmation and got none. "It prefers warmer temps, and lives in the ground, and some excavation near the city is waking it up and pissing it off."

Chuck just sat there, looking bored.

"Has it always lived in the ground? Baltimore was founded in 1729. Why now? Why is this thing waking up now and not a hundred years ago, or a decade ago?"

"Before Fiore Noir, others were charged with singing it to sleep. They all died out a long time ago, and we only discovered its presence and the danger a few years back. We lack the magic of the original guardians, but we had to do something." He shrugged. "So we did what we do best. Our own specialized magic."

It still didn't excuse killing human beings, destroying their souls. I don't care how noble Fiore Noir felt their cause, the temporary safety of many did not justify the sacrifice of a few.

But still, his words chilled me. A creature of the earth that had slumbered for ages. Guardians who had died out. I'd need to research this, to find out exactly what it was and how to either keep it asleep or kill it. The worst part of this whole thing was not knowing what the heck I might be up against in the near future.

Chuck shifted forward. "So I've kept my end of the bargain. I've more than kept my end of the bargain. Tell me about what's going on in the outside world."

I told him all about the ritual to rid myself of my demon mark, choking a little when I got to the part where Balsur destroyed the resin fox that had housed Raven's spirit.

"Demons." Chuck shook his head. "Good thing he was busy dealing with you and the other mage or he might have grabbed her spirit and taken it to hell."

I blinked in surprise. "How are you so sure he didn't? Wouldn't the demon have done that when he broke the fox figurine?"

I didn't mention that I wasn't sure about Raven's destination in the afterlife. I'd always considered her to be my best friend, a kind and ethical person, but Raven did what she needed to do and I honestly didn't know how that would stack up when it came to who went up and who went down after death.

"Spirits are slippery. I'd be willing to bet he was more worried about what you were doing in that ritual than snatching up some wayward spirit."

"Then where would she have gone if Balsur didn't get her?" Russell had said Raven was no longer here, but I had no idea what lay beyond the veil other than my Sunday School classes had told me as a child.

"Probably purgatory, although that's really a question for a mage that specializes in spirit work."

Purgatory. But I'd been certain I'd seen her in Fulk's eyes at the animal shelter. Could a spirit still slip through the openings in the veil if they were in purgatory?

Maybe Russell had been wrong and Raven *was* still this side of the veil.

"Do you think it's possible she might have remained here? Like…I don't know, floating around somewhere and looking for a host? She hasn't inhabited any of my other *lelek raktarban*, but I could have sworn she was possessing my dog at one point."

"There are ways through the veil." He shrugged again. "Again, that's something you should ask a medium or a necromancer. People with strong wills can come through for brief moments before they are pulled back. And there *are* ways of bringing spirits across the veil on a long-term or even permanent basis, just as there are ways of bringing demons and angels across the veil."

I was seeing Russell tomorrow for our séance, hoping he could contact Raven. As much as I would love to have her back again, I wasn't sure it was fair to have her stuck in a resin animal or a dog just because I missed my friend. She'd done what she'd promised she'd do before she'd died—she'd gotten me the ritual to release my demon mark. She'd helped with the ritual. I was free, and I owed all that to her. As much as I wanted her back in my life, I would be happy just to know she was okay, and in some sort of wonderful afterlife.

But what if she wasn't? What if Chuck was wrong and Balsur had her? What if she was in hell? Or purgatory?

"So what else is going on in Baltimore?" Chuck asked, eyeing the clock as if the guards were actually going to enforce some sort of time limit.

"Nothing as far as paranormal or magical stuff goes. I

tripped over a deceased man while jogging Tuesday morning."

Chuck made a "tsk" noise. "Drug addiction is a serious problem, and not just in Baltimore either."

"I agree, but it looks like this might actually be murder," I told him. "The guy's got some rare blood, and the police think he might have been killed for it."

Oops. That was probably supposed to be confidential. I was so used to telling Chuck about the supernatural stuff in the city, that this just sort of came out. I couldn't imagine that he'd be in a position to impede the case, though. I doubted he knew a rich guy needing heart surgery that happened to have Rh-null blood and was willing to pay big for it.

"That's almost as weird as the Boo Hag," Chuck commented. "Why kill the man when you can just pay him for a vial? Blood magic is so much easier than death magic. Doesn't pack quite the energy punch, but it's got subtleties that death magic doesn't have. In some ways I prefer it."

I didn't correct him, instead letting him think the motive was magic and not medical.

"Should be easy enough to find the killer," Chuck continued. "There was a reason that individual was targeted. He was either a mage himself, or from a line of mages. Or perhaps a convicted criminal on death row. Or a virgin. The life experiences and lineage of the human are far more important than basic factors about his blood."

All magic I'd done had only ever used my own blood, so this little lecture on Chuck's part was somewhat interesting.

"Would there be a reason to need more than a few drops of blood for this kind of magic?" I frowned in thought. "If someone needed a specific mage's blood for a ritual, would it be better to take a pint or two and save some for later?"

Chuck laughed. "Uh, no. A fresh drop right from the

person during the ritual is ideal. Blood degrades quickly, and unlike for medical use, you can't freeze it if you are using it in a ritual. You've got two weeks max to use it, and each day that goes by after collection lessens the effectiveness. And a drop or three is all you need. There's absolutely no reason to go taking a pint of blood, unless you're stealing it from a blood bank. And that's far from optimal. Unless you can steal it right after collection, that is."

Huh. Well, this just confirmed that Tremelay was most likely on the right track with his blood-for-money theory. Nothing supernatural about this one. No mage would risk kidnapping and murder charges when he could just offer someone a couple hundred for a fingerstick collection.

"Anything else happening?" Chuck asked. "Have you done any magic besides ridding yourself of the demon mark lately?"

I shrugged. "Just some charms. I haven't had much time, what with moving into my new place and my increased hours at the coffee shop."

I didn't want to let him know that a major part of that was my lack of a mentor and my fear that I was going to screw something up. I'd been overconfident, and gotten myself marked by a demon while trying to do a basic Goetic summoning. Without Raven to guide me, I was reluctant to do more than basic charms and illusions. I would have been willing to learn under Reynard, even though I didn't completely trust the guy, but he'd left after the ritual where Balsur had destroyed Raven's vessel, and hadn't returned my calls.

It sucked. No one in Haul Du would have anything to do with me. And I wasn't about to have a death mage as my mentor. Or a necromancer, no matter how friendly I was with Russell. It left me with few options. Should I stay where I was magically speaking, and not progress in those skills?

Take a chance and try to learn on my own? Or accept a mentor who kinda made my skin crawl?

I eyed Chuck. He knew about demons and Goetic magic. He knew blood magic. He knew death magic. I got the feeling he was far more advanced than the others in Fiore Noir, more advanced than Reynard, more advanced than Raven. I got the feeling he was far more knowledgeable than he'd ever let on.

The mage shook his head. "That's a darned shame. You've got talent and you're a decent, if a bit sloppy, mage. You should be doing more than simple charms."

Temptation, just as beguiling as what Satan offered on the mountain.

"I'm a Templar. Magic is an accessory to my sword, not the sword itself. When I need more than charms, I'll do more than charms." It was a bold statement, hiding my fear and insecurity behind the armor of my heritage.

"Just in case you change your mind." Chuck fanned his fingers, then made a fist and slid a spoon across the table to me.

I looked around, expecting guards to descend on us any moment with guns drawn, but no one paid one bit of attention to us or the fact that a prisoner had just passed me a piece of cutlery.

"Taken to petty theft now, have you?" The spoon was a cheap hunk of stainless steel with a nondescript pattern on the handle. From the odd twist to the business end, I assumed the puddings or cereal here required significant force to scoop up.

"I've paid a lot in taxes over the years. Let's just say a spoon is the least I feel the state owes me."

I reached out to touch the dulled surface, still expecting a guard to come racing over. None did, but I did feel the thrum of magic along what looked to be a plain old spoon.

"It gets a little boring here," Chuck told me. "Yes, I can do some limited magic if I can manage to accumulate the correct spell materials. What would really bring me joy would be to spread my wings a bit outside of these walls."

Picking up the spoon, I looked into the curved surface and saw Chuck looking back at me.

"When you're ready to do more than just simple charms," the spoon-Chuck said to me, "just pull this from your drawer and we'll get started."

I should have pushed the spoon back across the table to him. I should have left it on the table, or thrown it in the trash, or heaved it at the wall. Instead I stood and put it in my pocket as I said goodbye to the mage and made my way out of the prison.

# CHAPTER 11

It was around seven o'clock when I got back from Jessup with a whole lot whirling around in my brain. What was this thing whose shadow loomed over Baltimore, waiting to strike? Should I accept Chuck's offer to mentor me or not? Would Dario cancel on dinner again tonight?

As for the latter, I hoped not. The sun had gone down an hour ago, and the joy of early winter nights was supposed to mean that we were no longer eating dinner at nine or ten o'clock at night, but that hadn't been the case. Dario always had a lot to deal with upon his awakening, and the first two to three hours after sunset were usually taken up with *Balaj* business. I wasn't about to be that girlfriend who texted him every evening demanding to know if we were on or not for tonight. I'd just assume we were on, and wait for his text or call.

So I stuck Chuck's spoon in the kitchen drawer, pulled a handful of books off my shelf, and got to work. Curled up on the couch with Fulk snuggled next to me on one side and

Gaia purring against my thigh on the other, I paged through the huge, heavy book on my lap.

I skimmed past the water-based creatures, figuring they'd hardly be living underground even if they'd been magically confined. Suspecting the Big Bad might possibly be an undead or spirit-type monster, I focused on those. I also honed in on those creatures native to the east coast of the continent, thinking that the group who had previously kept the creature at bay had possibly been Native Americans.

I was just starting to get into my research when I heard a knock on the door. Dario? He hadn't called or texted me yet, but I'd be thrilled to have him just swing by like this. Putting the book aside, I scooted my two animals over and made my way around the couch. I swung open the door to find not the vampire, but Kyra Tremelay on the stoop.

The detective's daughter was roughly my age, a third year medical student doing her residency at Hopkins. Kyra was gorgeous, strongly resembling her mother from the pictures I'd seen of her at the detective's house. Her black hair was in a shiny straight bob. Her dark eyes with their thick lashes were wide-set and slightly tilted upward. Her cheekbones and jawline were feminine but chiseled, and her mouth soft and full. Even with the scrubs visible under her thick winter coat, she was beautifully elegant.

And there I stood in jeans and a worn t-shirt, with snarled hair and no makeup.

"Come on in," I told her, standing aside. "Can I get you a soda? Glass of wine? Coffee?"

We weren't exactly what I'd call best friends, although because of the plague demon issue last month, I'd gotten to know Kyra on a friendly professional basis. She'd helped me out with the bite wound on my neck, but after that I hadn't seen or spoken to her. Maybe this was a social visit? I would have thought a phone call inviting me to coffee or lunch would be the way to initiate a friendship, not an impromptu visit, but I wasn't going to say no to a new friend.

"Actually, I can't stay." She gave me a quick smile. "I've got a case over at the hospital I wanted to talk to you about. Totally off the record because of patient confidentiality, you know."

Ah. Business then. I nodded and motioned her over to the couch. I knew Kyra didn't like to bend the rules about patient confidentiality, but after last month, she'd discovered I could be a significant help when her medical cases had a possible supernatural component to them.

I sat across from her, a bit worried. Was this about the "animal attacks" in the north part of the city? The dead addicts who'd been mysteriously anemic? Or had the Big Bad that Chuck was hinting about arrived earlier than expected?

Kyra fidgeted on the couch a few seconds before speaking. "I had a man come into the emergency room today saying that he'd been kidnapped and had some sort of medical experiments done on him."

That was not at all what I'd expected. "Like alien probes, medical experiments?"

"He says they were human, and the medical experiments are why he has track marks, not because he's been shooting up." She shook her head. "We put him under psych observation, but the guy claims he has no history of mental illness. He's from out of town. Says he's here for business."

I grimaced, waiting for her to go on. Clearly there was more to this. Kyra wouldn't be coming to a Templar for help with someone who'd had a bad trip and needed a referral to either a mental health facility or a drug treatment program.

"He did have needle marks in both arms, but he claims he's never used drugs."

I rolled my eyes. "I don't know a lot of drug users, but I'm betting they all deny using drugs."

"Exactly. And many people with serious mental health issues deny that as well. The guy did have some bruising around his wrists and ankles and chest consistent with being strapped down."

I stared at her in surprise. "You know what bruising from being strapped down looks like?"

"I work in the emergency room. We get people who are combative, either coming down off of street drugs or having a mental health crisis, and sometimes they need to be temporarily restrained for their own as well as our safety. This guy might have been into kinky stuff, or the marks could have been from a hospital or an inpatient psychiatric facility."

I had a whole new respect for what Kyra did. "So he's a drug user and has a mental health problem, and he's a John Doe in a hospital?"

"He's not a John Doe. He knows his name, where he lives. Honestly, he seems perfectly normal outside of his claims that he was subjected to medical experiments. Oh, and he also claims that he's possessed."

"So you're thinking he escaped some psychiatric facility? Maybe the track marks are from sedation, or an IV line for a medical condition?"

"I wondered about that too. I checked all the local hospitals and in patient centers and no one had him or a man of his description there in the last week days."

"You really think he was possessed? That he was subjected to medical experimentation?"

I didn't think I could do much about the medical experimentation thing. Honestly it sounded like the guy had a mental condition and needed help that was outside my abilities as a Templar. Heck, even if it was demonic possession, there wasn't too much I could do about it. The guy needed a priest. Luckily I had one I could recommend.

"Heck if I know." Kyra lifted her hands. "We ran some blood tests thinking we might find a trace of a hallucinogenic or sedative, or something that would explain this."

"And?"

"Nothing drug wise, although there was a trace of a drug used to help people with organ transplants avoid rejection. He says he's had no organ transplants or even major surgery in his life, but when we asked, he kind of freaked out on us, panicking that the guys who experimented on him might have done something beyond poking and prodding. He had no signs of recent surgery. The guy is healthy. There's nothing wrong with him beyond his really odd claims. And he checks out as far as where he lives, what business he's in, where he was staying in town."

"So you're thinking demon possession? And maybe the demon put these ideas of medical experimentation in his head?"

"I really don't know. It's just a whole bundle of weirdness, Aria." Kyra ran a hand through her hair. "The restraint marks, the track marks, the trace drug. And his story is really odd. He said the last few days are a blur, but he remembers being hooked up to a whole bunch of IV lines. He said he was there for a long time, maybe days but he couldn't really tell. At one point he said a group of guys who looked like they were wearing surgical robes and masks came in and chanted over him, and that's when he was possessed."

I frowned. "I've been at a lot of demon summonings and no one has ever summoned a demon into a human body. Of course, Goetic demons are never let out of the circle and the times I attended, they didn't summon any of the higher demons. I guess if someone was really crazy, they would invite a demon to possess *themselves*, but not somebody else."

"Not even if they hated someone? Like revenge?" Kyra

asked. "Your wife cheats on you, and you summon a demon to possess her lover?"

"There are far better ways of getting back at someone than bringing a powerful demon across the veil, letting him outside of a circle, and giving him a human body to possess." I thought for a second. "Did he say he was possessed by a demon, or just possessed? Lots of spirit workers channel the dead, and there are many non-practitioners that have the innate talent. Maybe he's gifted and was channeling a spirit?"

She shrugged. "I just assumed he meant demon. He said he was possessed, and that was my first thought. I didn't think to get into any detail about who or what had possessed him. I was more concerned with checking his physical health, thinking I'd need to refer him to psych for the possession thing."

"But something made you think he might be telling the truth?" I asked.

Kyra sighed. "I don't know, Aria. After what happened with the plague demon and the vampires, and then there were those killer mages…I just figured I should run it by you and see if it was something I needed to worry about—beyond mental health, I mean. Sorry, I'm probably wasting your time."

"No, it's okay. I'm always glad to see you, and I really don't mind you calling or stopping by to ask about this stuff. If he really is possessed by a demon, I know a priest who can help. And if it's a spirit…well, I know some people who can talk to him about how to set boundaries and control his talent so he's not at the mercy of every ghost he comes across."

Kyra stood. "I guess I need to ask him some more questions about the possession. We'll probably discharge him tomorrow morning. I doubt they'll keep him on an EP since he's not a danger to himself or others, and as far as I can tell he would have no trouble attending to his basic needs."

I got up as well, thinking it was a good thing that involuntary psychiatric holds were not put on everyone who had a mental illness. Hopefully the guy would get whatever help he needed, though.

Kyra turned to me as she got to the door. "Just in case, I wondered if I could give him your phone number? Have him contact you once we release him if he still feels he's possessed. Maybe you can refer him to those people you talked about?"

I squirmed, uncomfortable with the idea that Kyra was going to be sending me every mental health case in the city, "just in case" their tales of occult groups doing medical experiments on them and demonic possession were true. Did I really want some crazed drug user showing up at my house? Although I was a Templar with some knowledge of magic, living with a rather solid ex-fighting dog, and I had a vampire boyfriend. If I couldn't defend myself against a mentally ill drug user, then I was pretty lame.

"Sure. Go ahead," I told Kyra. If I needed to, I could always drag the guy over to Father Bernard to sprinkle some holy water on him, although I think I might be skilled enough to do some initial assessment myself. And if he was possessed by a spirit, then Russell could either help or refer me to a colleague.

"I appreciate it, Aria." She opened the door. "Are you free for lunch sometime next week? I'd love to get together and talk about non-medical and non-supernatural stuff."

I wasn't sure what that left, but I was willing to give it a shot. It was so nice having friends in the city, and I liked Kyra. I wondered if she enjoyed role playing games?

"Sure. I'm working mornings, but could do a lunch around one or two."

"Perfect. I'll check my schedule and text you next week."

I waved her off and checked my phone. Still nothing from Dario and it was now eight o'clock. Sighing, I picked up my sword and practiced for half an hour. Then I did push-ups and crunches. I glanced over at my phone mid sit-up. Still no messages. Dario had cancelled Tuesday night's Sesarios' dinner to handle some *Balaj* business, and I was really hoping we could go out tonight. I wished he'd call. Or text. Or something. Now I knew why he hadn't wanted to take over when his and Leonora's former Master had been ousted. The leader of a group of vampires had little time for anything except business. True, he'd been busy as the second in command, but now with Leonora gone, and the group's numbers alarmingly small, I felt as if our relationship was constantly coming in second to the *Balaj*.

And that was horribly unfair of me. Dario had responsibilities. His family needed him, depended on him to keep them safe and provide for their future. He didn't want some needy human woman whining over how she never saw him.

Just in the middle of my pity party, my phone dinged.

*Trying to get everything wrapped up in the next hour or two so I can come over and we can hopefully have an uninterrupted evening. Pray for me.*

I laughed.

*You'd probably combust if I prayed for you. Meet you here or at Sesarios' or somewhere else?*

It was a few minutes before he texted me back.

*I hate for you to be waiting around when I don't know how long I'll be. I'll text you.*

My heart sank. This was pretty much the way it was every night. Maybe he'd make it over around midnight. And even if he did, there was a good chance he'd be getting a call that dragged him out of my bed and out the door.

Should I grab something for dinner? Change and go out?

Sit around the house for hours and wait for him to call like some lame needy girlfriend?

Screw that. If he wanted this relationship to work, I needed to be a part of his life, and that included his *Balaj*. I might not be his blood partner, but I was still his girlfriend. Girlfriend. Not late-night booty call. Not some side piece that he squeezed in time for here and there. Girlfriend.

So I headed upstairs to change my clothes, determined to take the initiative for once.

# CHAPTER 12

*I'm coming over,* I texted Dario after I'd changed.

I'd only been to his house a handful of times. It had become vampire command central since Leonora died and he'd become head of the *Balaj.* Normally I would have been thrilled to go over and hang at his house for the evening, but I suspected there would be a whole lot more vampires besides Dario in attendance, and me either the only human, or me in the company of blood donors and blood partners.

*You'd be bored just sitting around here,* he replied.

I immediately typed a response. *I'm bored sitting around my house waiting for you to show up sometime in the next ten hours.*

That was a bit catty, but I wasn't sure how many details of the *Balaj's* business Dario wanted to share with me now that he was in charge. Once again I worried that the day would come when we'd be on the opposite sides of an issue, and we'd both need to choose between what our responsibilities demanded and our relationship with each other.

*Then come over. Maybe with you here things will speed up a bit. And there's something I need to talk to you about anyway.*

Worry spread through my chest. Was he dumping me? Was he going to say this wasn't working out? Give me an ultimatum about the blood?

I took a deep breath and gave myself a mental slap. There'd been no indication of that. If anything, Dario had been making it quite clear he wasn't about to share my blood until he was positive I truly wanted that. He'd always been warm and affectionate, and very passionate in our love making. I'd just been bruised so many times before that every hint of trouble and I was thinking things were over.

*On my way,* I texted back.

*See you then.* He signed off with a little heart emoji that made me laugh. What a dork. The guy was about three hundred and fifty years old. He was a vampire. He was a total badass. And he was texting me heart emojis.

Dork.

I drove to Dario's house feeling a bit like a teenager going on her first date. The whole time I was driving, I kept thinking of Dario saying there was something he wanted to discuss with me. The vampire always had this flat, non-expressive way about him when he was telling me something unpleasant—or when he was about to tell me something unpleasant. Or avoiding telling me something unpleasant. Whatever this discussion was going to be about, I worried that I wasn't going to like it. Maybe that was the reason for my mascara and eyeliner. Or maybe it was the fact that I'd probably be encountering several of his *Balaj* at his house, and I didn't want to look like I'd just come from a session at the gym.

I parked in front of Dario's beautiful historic brownstone house in Federal Hill and took a moment to admire it from my car. I loved his house. The interior was minimalist with modern elements that made it pretty much the opposite of Leonora's big old Victorian. I would have enjoyed coming here more often, maybe even living here eventually, but not so early in our relationship. Plus, ever since Dario had become the head of his family, the house was no longer a private residence, but instead a home-base for the *Balaj*.

It made me wonder who had ended up with Leonora's place. I doubt they'd sold it since the two homes were linked via some underground tunnels—tunnels that probably linked other homes and businesses in Baltimore that I really didn't want to know about.

I grabbed my sword, noting that there were people milling about not just on Dario's front stoop, but the porches of several other nearby houses. The neighbors must love that. I wonder if the *Balaj* bought out these other houses to create a bit of a security perimeter in a neighborhood where the homes were a good bit closer together than in Leonora's.

Strapping my sword across my back I headed across the street and up the stoop, nodding at the two vampires who stood by the front door. One of the benefits of my relationship with Dario was that few vampires gave me shit about my sword anymore. Few vampires gave me shit about anything anymore, but I think that had just as much to do with my killing Simon as being Dario's main squeeze.

I knew they'd considered me just another weak human—one who had some skill with a sword and magic, but still weak. A bag of blood. A food source, whose only protection was my Templar name and the fact that a high-level vampire had dibs on me. It had been humiliating.

But when I'd shown up with my neck chewed up, announcing that I'd killed Simon, *that* got me wary respect.

I wasn't sure how long that respect would last, though. I knew there were those who wanted to put me into the blood slave category, who thought I was lying about Simon, or maybe had just gotten lucky. I had supporters among Dario's family. Opel, who was young and hip and had been my assistant in some magic a few months back. Balen who I suspected admired my sword play more than he did me. And Dario's second, Madeline, who afforded me grudging respect because she felt Dario practically walked on water, and if he said I was more than just a potential food source, then she was going to believe it. Others in his family either gave me a wide berth, or faced me with poorly concealed hostility.

The two vampires at the door, Kayson and Andre, were in the latter category. They eyed my sword and sneered, sharp pointy teeth clearly visible.

"Boss know you're coming?" Andre asked.

"Yes, he knows." I didn't elaborate further because it wasn't any of this goon's business.

"He's already fed. Go home, little girl, and maybe when he's done dealing with family business he'll come over for a late-night snack."

I winced. Of course Dario had fed. He had donors brought in for him so he could feed right upon wakening. Since his feedings no longer included sex, it was quicker to make the whole thing as transaction-like as possible.

But what we had didn't involve blood, and it was more than just sex.

I could insist that I'd been invited over. I could pull out my phone and show these two the texts. I didn't. The idea that I couldn't stop by my boyfriend's house, invited or not, without having to prove I was supposed to be here pissed me off.

I knew I couldn't push past them to get inside. That would be like trying to shove a thousand pound statue aside. I'd only embarrass myself. So I took the least embarrassing option, hoping they wouldn't call my bluff.

"Can I come in, or do I need to put my sword through your guts?"

Kayson shifted uneasily. "Let her in. I'd rather have the

boss yell at us than hope I can regrow my insides from being stabbed by a blessed sword."

Andre chuckled and stepped aside. "Go on then, Templar. Have a good time."

I was barely over the threshold when Opal came running up to grab me in a rather painful hug and drag me into one of the side rooms. It was Dario's study, with a couch, two chairs, a desk and tons of books.

"It's been ages since I've seen you," Opal squealed, holding my hands. "How have you been? Your neck looks great. I can barely even tell that butthead practically ripped your throat out. Can I help you with your magic again sometime? Well, once things are settled down, that is. Right now Dario needs all of us patrolling and securing the territory. I'm about to head out for Upton. Hey, do you think I could hang out with you and your friends one night? Do any of them like girls? Vampire girls? I'm so done with men, I tell you."

My head whirled with the onslaught of topics. "Um, I don't know if my girlfriends like girls that way or not, but you can come out with us sometime. As far as the other… well, I haven't done that much magic lately but I'll let you know."

Opal grinned and bounced. "Keep your eyes open for me, okay? I really want to find a blood sl—partner. A blood partner. Playing around is fun and all that, but I want what you and the boss have, well except I want to be able to drink from my partner. No offense, but that's a deal breaker for me. If you know of anyone… I'd prefer a woman, but if you know a nice guy, then I won't rule it out."

I eyed the vampire and couldn't help but smile at her happy enthusiasm, her unworldliness. Opal's poof of dark hair was pulled back and up high, like an inky medieval halo. With her natural hair, her blue eyeshadow, her bell bottom jeans and psychedelic stretchy t-shirt, she was stylishly retro.

I had no doubt that any number of humans would be happy to fall at her feet—and bare their necks to her fangs. But I wanted more for Opal. If I was going to set her up on the vampire equivalent of a blind date, then I wanted it to be with someone who would love her and not tarnish her innocence.

Opal tilted her head. "Boss is coming. I smelled you coming up the walk and told Richelle to let him know before I ran up to greet you. Don't let him know that Andre and Kayson were jerks. We can't afford to lose any of our family right now and he's a little psycho when it comes to anyone disrespecting you."

I blinked in surprise.

The vampire sighed and patted her chest. "I hope I find a blood partner who loves me like the boss loves you."

With a quick squeeze of my hands and a peck on my cheek, she vanished out the study door in a blur of vampire speed. I was barely able to take a breath before Dario entered the room.

"Opal is trying to get me to play matchmaker for her," I told him, still bemused over the conversation.

He laughed and gathered me in his arms, kissing my forehead and holding me close. "Yes, she's been asking the other blood partners if they have brothers or sisters they could introduce her to. The woman is on the hunt."

I reached up to kiss Dario, then stepped back to remove my sword and set it on the desk.

"She's lonely. No different than women who decide they suddenly want to get married and settle down."

"Except she was all about the casual, one-night-only until that day I sent her over to your house." Dario scowled teasingly and waved a finger at me. "I think she's secretly in love with you."

Really? I didn't get that at all from Opal, but I had often

been accused of being clueless when it came to others' romantic interest in me.

"Well, she's a friend and I'm not setting her up with anyone unless I'm sure they're on board with a vampire partner and I know they'll treat her right." I thought of Janice and her failed romance with a Boo Hag. I didn't want poor Opal to go through something like that, to get attached to someone only to find out they couldn't accept that she was a vampire.

"I'm glad you came by." Dario smoothed a hand over his short, curly hair. "The past few days have been crazy."

I walked over and hugged him. "So I take it you didn't have a good Thanksgiving?"

He snorted. "Was there a holiday this week? I had no idea. I hope you had a good time with your family, though. I'm sorry I couldn't join you."

An ache settled deep in my chest. Would he ever be able to join me? Would Baltimore ever be stable enough that the head of the *Balaj* could leave town and spend a night or two with his girlfriend?

"I'm sorry you couldn't come. Dad makes an amazing turkey. And there was oyster dressing, bourbon sweet potatoes, Athena's mashed potatoes with the Manchego cheese, and the classic pumpkin pie."

He held me tight and we shared a moment of sorrow that he hadn't been there to share a traditional family event with my family and me.

Then I pulled away, because as much as I wanted to wallow in sadness over what we didn't, and might not ever, have, I needed us to move forward with the things we did share—the things we could partner with.

"So, how was your week? Tell me about all the crap that went down when I was gone."

Dario stiffened, then pulled me close against him once

more. "I need you to be my sanctuary, Aria. I want the time I spend with you to be that holy place where I don't have to worry about my family or our territory, or my responsibilities, where I can pretend for just a few hours that I'm a human with a woman I love, holding her in my arms."

My heart twisted. I knew what he wanted. Part of me wanted the same.

But most of me wanted so much more.

"I'm more than your sanctuary, Dario. I stand beside you. I help you protect your family, to help protect my pilgrims on the path here in Baltimore. I need to be your partner, not just your escape."

He looked down at me, running his fingers over my cheeks. "I have this deep need to keep you safe. I know you're a Templar; that you're capable of defending yourself. You're one of the toughest, smartest, most caring humans I've ever met. And still I'm terrified that one day you'll die. I'm terrified that you won't die old, that I'll wake one night to find you gone, or not be able to be there in time to help you. I can't stand the thought of you gone, of never seeing you again."

I reached up to take his hands. "We are born and we die. Even the ageless immortality of vampires is not guaranteed. I know you've suffered more loss than any human in your long life, and I wish I could ease your fears. All I can do is tell you that I have no intention of dying young, but I have a calling, a duty. Just as you do."

"I know. But I just want you to know why I'm reluctant to embroil you in our fight."

"It's my fight too," I shot back. "I…I trust you to ensure your family's actions don't harm the humans, but other vampires won't have the same values and ethics. I don't want someone like Simon and his family here in my city. So let me help you." I took a step away from him. "Or do you think like others in your family do? Do you believe my defeat of Simon was luck? That he somehow tripped and died by accident?"

Dario stared at me, astonished, then he started to laugh. "Hardly. I've seen you in action. I've cleaned up the bodies you've left behind, remember? And as much as I wanted to kill Simon myself, I couldn't deny you that privilege. Aria, your strength is one of the reasons I fell for you."

"Then don't shut me out, Dario. Let me be more than your sanctuary."

He stared at me for a moment, then pulled me into his arms for a long hug. "Okay. I'll try. You'll need to call me out if I get smotheringly overprotective, though."

It was my turn to laugh. "Deal."

He led me over to the sofa and we both sat. "We've been spending a good bit of time and resources in the north part of the city. After your text Wednesday night, Madeline and I went up to Perring Parkway and I sent Zoe, Balen, Geraldo, and Kayson to Cedmont and Belvedere to check out the alleged animal attacks. We spent Wednesday and Thursday night tracking down those vampires. That situation is resolved."

"Tremelay said the last animal attack was Wednesday night," I warned him. "I think we need to make sure there weren't any additional rogues that snuck in or one or two that might have been missed."

Dario nodded. "I sent five up to Taylor Heights and North Harford Road this evening to search for and clear out any others, but I'm confident that area is secure. At least for now. Thursday I sent ten down to Arbutus in a show of force because there was information that three or four rogues were joining together down there to enter the city. Let's just say they've decided to head further west and try their luck elsewhere."

That was one good bit of news I could tell Janice—and Tremelay.

"Sadly, there's more," I warned again. "Remember when I told you there were people in the central part of Baltimore, homeless drug addicts, who had died from overdose but were seriously anemic?"

He sighed and rubbed a hand over his face. "You've got to be kidding me."

I shook my head. "One found last night does appear to have been either a willing or unwilling donor, and Tremelay thinks the others may be related."

He frowned. "How anemic were they? We do have several paid donors who are drug addicts, but I haven't been made aware of any deaths. We keep track of those things."

"Tremelay says they were down maybe two pints. There were at least three found dead the last week and the one guy from Thursday night or early this morning who was down way more than a few pints."

Dario rubbed his forehead and sighed. "And they had fang marks?"

"The recent death had clear fang marks on his neck, but the others… Theirs could have been track marks from drug use," I admitted. "On both arms. Inside the elbow. Do vampires bite there? I'm honestly asking, because I really don't know your preferences."

A faint smile flickered across his face. "It *is* a preference where we choose to feed from, and it can also depend on the relationship between the vampire and the donor. Neck is always the first choice. It's easy to access. Good strong blood flow for drinking deeply, and it gives us the opportunity to leave a visible mark when humans and vampires want that. It's…it's sensual even when you're not going to actually have intercourse with the human. Holding someone in your arms, feeling their breath against you, their hands clutching you as you feed…it really adds to the experience."

Yeah, I was getting breathless just thinking about it.

"Wrist is also very common. It's almost courtly, and not as sensual although for the human our venom always triggers an orgasmic response. Wrist and inner arm have thick veins, but less pressure, so it's a slow leisurely experience. If a vampire is concerned about losing control, wrist and arm are the best choice since those areas clot fairly quickly and it would take a quite a lot of effort to take too much blood when feeding from those spots."

"Could a vampire manage to imbibe two pints if they bit one arm, then the other?"

He nodded. "It would take time, so in that case the vampire probably wasn't worried about being caught in the act."

My mind slipped back to the man I'd tripped over Tuesday morning. "Remember when I said I'd fallen over the body of a homeless man when I was jogging this week? Turns out he wasn't homeless. He was some businessman that the police suspect had been lured to Baltimore where he was drained of all his blood. The only marks were on his inner arms, and from what I saw they didn't look to be the right size and distance apart to be fang marks. The police are looking for a human murderer in some blood-for-money scheme, but I wondered…"

Dario thought for a moment then shook his head. "I'm not sure if a vampire *could* actually drain a human from those veins. There's an artery there, but it's not easy to access unless you're going to bite a chunk out of the human's arm. You'd probably sever the vein getting to it with your fangs. It would be messy, and the human would have more damage than puncture wounds. If the vampire kept it neat and only to the vein, feeding would be too slow to take more than a pint or two, especially with clotting. If a vampire wants to feed deeply and doesn't care about killing the donor, they'll always choose the neck."

"I was just curious." It sounded like Tremelay was definitely on the right path. I was relieved it *wasn't* vampires because Dario had enough to deal with handling the issues up north and now the possible rogue feedings in the central part of the city.

"Where was the recent death? The one with the fang marks on his neck?" Dario asked.

"Upton, Druid Hill, and Franklin Square are where the anemic junkies were found," I told him. "The one with the fang marks on his neck was in Pigtown."

A muscle twitched in Dario's jaw. "Pigtown is near here. It makes me wonder if this isn't a message meant for me."

"Two miles isn't exactly on your doorstep," I commented. "If it was a message, then wouldn't they leave the body on your lawn?"

He shrugged. "Maybe you're right. We got some information on Wednesday that someone had organized a band of fifteen to twenty rogues. We don't know if they're in the city or not, or even where and when they plan to make a move, but it's got me worried."

I stuffed my phone in my pocket curled up next to him. "I really don't understand this whole rogue thing. I know you guys are suspicious of each other, and that family blood means a lot in terms of who gets accepted and how quickly, but why don't more of these rogues band together? You've told me how difficult it is for a solitary vampire to remain safe."

He put his arm around me and pulled me close. "We don't trust easily. We're territorial, so when a vampire is on their own, they'll claim a small bit of territory that they feel they can hold—maybe a few blocks around where they're bedding down for the day. It's difficult because having a safe hiding place while we're vulnerable in daylight hours is as important as finding a safe and available source of donors. Normally you don't want to hunt where you sleep, because that sort of activity risks discovery of your resting place, but waking and traveling elsewhere to find a food source means you risk encroaching on another rogue's territory.

"The death rate is huge. Either you die in a fight over territory, or you starve. Ideally you want to find willing donors, but if you can't and end up feeding from someone you grab off the street, you risk being caught. A lone vampire can be overcome by humans. We heal, but unload a magazine full of bullets into us, and we might not heal fast enough to get away, or get underground before the sun comes up. And if someone finds your resting place..." Dario grimaced. "We're dead during daylight hours. Imagine a human coming across what appears to be a dead body in a basement room or hidden away somewhere? The police are called, and we're brought out into the sunlight and truly die as we sleep."

"Don't they take bodies out of places in black bags?" I asked. "Wouldn't that shield you enough from the sun to keep you from truly dying?"

"If they bag the vampire in the dark, yes. Usually they open up the area for light as they investigate. There have been a few cases where a vampire managed to survive the ordeal only to wake up in the morgue refrigeration unit."

I was horrified at the image running through my mind. Worse, what if they did an immediate autopsy? Removing the vampire's heart would kill him just as sunlight would. Clearly modern times had changed the dynamic between predator and prey quite a bit.

"We're handling the threats from outside the city. My main worry right now is this group—if they even exist. I'm confident that once we take care of them, things will settle down. We've shown that although we're small in numbers, we're strong and organized. The initial rush to test us and try to chip away at our territory is dying down, and I truly believe in the next few weeks, things will somewhat be back to normal."

That was a huge relief, and very different from the stressed and worried Dario I'd spoken to Tuesday night.

I snaked an arm around his waist and scooted even closer. "I'm glad. Does that mean in the near future we'll actually be able to have dinner together? Maybe go see a play or a concert? There's one of those reenactment things coming up in January and I'd love for you to go to that with me. Or maybe even come with me down to my parents' house for Christmas."

"Dinner and possibly a concert or a play on a regular basis, yes. The others..." He pulled me onto his lap. "I haven't been exactly forthcoming about some of my new responsibilities. Remember when I said after we had control of the territory that we'd need to think about turning Renfields and blood partners who were eager to become vampires?"

I took a steadying breath, knowing where this conversation was going. "I'm assuming you're about to tell me that you're going to be one of the vampires who is going to be doing this turning, and that you'll be unable to see me for weeks? Or months?"

"Yes, but there's more. Those of us who remain have a duty to blood partners who have lost their vampires. Some don't want to be turned, but want to remain part of the family. Others want to be turned, but we need to be responsible for their needs while they wait."

I stiffened, realizing where this was going. "How can you feed from another's blood partner? Doesn't there need to be an emotional bond?"

"It's not like that. Blood partners can leave the *Balaj*, or stay and have their needs met by a vampire of their choosing. If they leave, then we provide them with funds for addiction support and enough to get them settled back into a human life. For those that stay, it's their decision who provides for them and how that is done."

They were in mourning. And where I couldn't imagine having an intimate blood exchange with another vampire if Dario died, some might feel comfort in being around those who were their beloved's family. As long as it was their choice, their decision, then I guess I needed to accept it.

"If they choose, we will turn them when we are able. If not, they can continue to be a part of our family as long as they wish. We will make sure their needs are met, and that they are safe and taken care of for as long as they live—or until they decide they no longer want to remain with the *Balaj*."

I suddenly realized there was a deeper layer to his revelation. He'd said he would personally need to help turn new vampires, possibly in the next month. I'm sure with only twenty-five vampires left in the *Balaj*, he was also needed to take responsibility for his deceased family's blood partners. It bothered me. It was one thing to accept that Dario needed to feed each day, and that those exchanges involved an intimate euphoria on the part of the donor even if they didn't involve sexual activity. It was another thing to think he would be providing for and taking blood from someone who was a part of his family.

I tried to put the thoughts out of my mind and imagine it all as if he were simply providing food, shelter, and emotional support to a grieving, newly widowed brother-in-law, or sister-in-law.

"So who are you taking care of? Which blood partner, or partners, are you personally...helping?" I asked.

His arms tightened around me. "Erica, Leonora's blood partner."

Erica. Gorgeous, annoying, bitchy Erica who had blonde hair and the slight feminine form I lacked, who'd been Leonora's beloved blood slave. I know it was uncharitable of me, but as soon as he mentioned her name, I felt a stab of jealousy and wished the woman at the bottom of the Patapsco River.

"I realize our situation is…odd between a vampire and a human," Dario continued, "and I know you have concerns about who I take blood from. Every evening it's a different donor. It's always a man, which is not my preference. My only contact with them is when I feed. That's the first and last time I see them. I'm going out of my way to do this so you don't feel threatened by those who I take blood from. But this is different. Erica was Leonora's blood partner. She had status in the *Balaj*—still has status in the *Balaj*. She has asked me to provide for her and to turn her when I can. It would be dishonorable of me to refuse."

The guy had to feed, and I knew he was going out of his way to make sure the sexual component wasn't there for him, even if those feelings did happen for the donor. But Erica was a part of the *Balaj*. She'd been privy to all their secrets. Leonora had told her things, given her knowledge that I didn't have. She was a member of the family, she was in.

And I wasn't.

And the beautiful woman was now giving Dario something that I'd refused. The thought of her orgasming in his arms as he fed was too much for me to handle. Dario might not feel anything for her now, but eventually he might. How could he not, when she was perfectly suited to be the blood partner to the head of his family, where I'd always be that

Templar outsider, cautiously respected and never fully trusted?

I didn't want that life. I didn't want to be a blood partner, a lesser part of the *Balaj*. But I couldn't help but envy her even more now that I knew Dario was tasting her blood.

I had no doubt she'd be the first to be offered immortality given her status, as a way to honor Leonora. And of course Dario would perform that honor.

And there was nothing I could do about it.

"Okay." It was all I could say at the moment.

Dario eyed me. "Okay? You're fine with this? No argument? No insistence that someone else needs to take care of Erica?"

I took a deep breath and let it out slowly. "I'll be honest here, it bothers me, but I see your side of this. I just wish it was anyone but you."

"I know." His voice was soft, with a note of relief. "There's a hierarchy among blood partners that mirrors ours, and it hinges on which vampire they belong to. This isn't just me being respectful of Erica's former position, it's me honoring Leonora. She loved that woman, and Leonora wouldn't have wanted Erica to lose her position or status after her death."

"But she's not your blood partner?" I needed to clarify this. "She's in some kind of limbo right now?"

"She's still considered *a* blood partner, only one without a vampire of her own. She'll retain her status through me. I'll refresh her mark every night, and take a bit of her blood."

I clenched my teeth. "What other privileges is she afforded? Does she stay here with you? Act as your hostess? Stand by your side as you conduct *Balaj* business? Will you feed deeply from her every eight weeks? She's pretty much your blood partner, only without the emotional attachment or the sex." I hesitated, my stomach twisting. "Or is there sex?"

A muscle twitched in Dario's jaw. "There is no sex—I promised you that. She's not by my side while I conduct vampire business. She *is* staying here though—that's part of her retaining her status. And she does help my new Renfield with various duties concerning the running of my household and daytime operations."

I took another deep breath. "Okay."

What else was I supposed to say? It's not like I could punch Dario in the face and scream at him that he had to throw her out. He was a vampire. This was their culture, their life.

"I don't have any feelings for her beyond respect as Leonora's blood partner. None."

I turned on his lap a bit to face him. "None?"

"None."

I kissed him. "Good. Now, are we going out to dinner or what?"

He sighed and I realized that I probably wasn't getting dinner tonight.

"I need to go out to check on this man who was found dead in Pigtown. Do you have an address? Hopefully there is enough scent left for us to track, or to at least get an idea of how many rogues we may be up against."

"Good thing I brought my sword." Because there was no way he was leaving me out of this one.

Dario glanced over at the weapon.

"I go or you don't get the address." I was still going to give him the address, but hopefully the threat would help convince him to let me go along.

He shook his head with a rueful laugh. "Okay. You win. Just let me text Richelle to meet us there, and we'll head out."

# CHAPTER 13

*I*'d formed a mental picture of Richelle that was completely wrong. The name conjured up a tall, elegant, dark-haired woman with a French accent. Instead Richelle looked like the sort of woman who would sit you down at her kitchen table and serve you a big slice of buttery pound cake with fresh berries and a cup of strong chicory coffee by its side. She had a round, dark-skinned face with huge dimples in her cheeks and eyes that squinted into happy lines when she smiled. Her body was equally round with soft curves on a short frame. When she spoke, her soft accent conjured images of warm rain on a tin roof and lush green ferns swaying lazily in a hot summer breeze.

She was a vampire, and I knew she was as fast and deadly as any of them, but I still half expected her to launch into a story about last week's church bake sale and potluck.

"I took the liberty of askin' Fidel to join us later as he's taken to socializin' in this part of town," she told Dario with a cheerful smile. "I'm hopin' that's okay with you, Sir?"

"Thank you, Richelle." Dario grimaced. "I'm thinking it might be a good idea to keep track of who tends to hunt where so we know what sections of the city are being monitored."

The unspoken part of that was if a vampire went missing, the *Balaj* would know where to target their search.

"It's been a fair bit," Richelle commented as she looked around the street corner where Tremelay had told me the man's body had been found. "Might not be able to pick up much of a scent."

"I'm not getting even a trace of blood," Dario said. "Even with the other odors and twenty-four hours, there should have been a few drops at least."

My eyebrows went up. I knew vampires had a great sense of smell, probably equal to that of a bloodhound, but I hadn't stopped to think what exactly that meant.

"Maybe he was killed elsewhere and dumped here," I said. "This is a mixed use area, with commercial buildings a block away from the residential ones. Warehousing, manufacturing, distribution, a deli, a parking lot—there are all sorts of businesses as well as the park nearby. If they were quick about it, they could have left the body on this corner to be found and gone before the residents across the street even noticed they were here."

Richelle glanced over at me. It was the first time she'd done so since we'd arrived, and I got the impression that she would have rather I remained silent and let the adults, or vampires, take care of this.

"Your detective friend said he was found here?" Dario pointed to the sidewalk.

I nodded. "This side of the power pole, head facing toward Bush Street."

There wasn't any crime scene tape, no chalk outline, nothing to indicate a dead man lay here less than twenty-four hours ago. But it wasn't like the area could be secured, and I was sure the police would have worked fast to get everything they needed from the scene. Plus both the residents and companies wouldn't want a glaring reminder that a crime occurred right on their block as they slept.

"Maybe the warehouse across the street, or one of the residents pressure washed the spot?" I suggested. "Would you be able to smell blood if someone blasted the concrete with water, or bleached it?"

Dario scrunched up his face. "Not bleach, or I'd definitely smell it. I'd smell that from four blocks away. I hate bleach. It takes me hours to get the scent out of my nose and sinuses."

I bit back a smile, making a mental note to check my cleaning supplies.

"Do humans pressure wash in late November?" Richelle asked. "It's cold. Wouldn't there be ice on the sidewalk if they did that?"

It was cold. I was bundled up in my parka with gloves on. The vampires were dressed as if they were out for a summer stroll.

"I don't know." Dario crouched down and looked around the pole. "Was it sunny yesterday, Aria? Would there be ice, or could it have melted?"

I squatted down, then swept my finger along a fine dusting of white. "Salt. Maybe someone washed the spot, then put down salt?"

Dario scowled. "Salt. That's enough to mess with any blood scent I could pick up. Are you getting anything, Richelle?"

The woman shook her head, then pulled her phone out as it dinged. "Fidel is just parking the next street over. Let's see what he has to say."

Seconds later an elderly Italian man walked around the corner. Judging from Dario's and Richelle's expressions, this was Fidel. Sheesh, why did none of these vampires look like they were supposed to? Where was the slicked back black hair with a prominent widow's peak? Where was the silk-lined black cape with its sharply pointed collar? Where was the Transylvanian accent? If it hadn't been for the faint static buzz across my skin that happened when a vampire was near, I wouldn't have suspected any of these three were more than normal, human, Baltimore citizens.

"Boss." Fidel executed a courtly bow toward Dario, then turned to the other vampire. "Richelle."

I waited a second, then decided I was done with this bullshit. "Hey." I stuck my hand out and grabbed the vampire's. "I'm Aria. The Templar. Nice to meet you. As I'm sure you were told, a deceased human was found here at three o'clock this morning by one of the residents heading off to work. From the puncture wounds on his neck and the amount of blood loss, we suspect he was killed by a vampire."

Fidel glanced down at my hand in horror, but didn't withdraw his own. Instead he looked over to Dario, his expression pleading.

Taking sympathy on the guy, I withdrew my hand.

"Aria and I are working on this together as it impacts our relationship with the humans and police in the city. I'd appreciate it if the pair of you treated her as an ally of our family as well as my romantic partner."

There was an awkward moment, then both the other vampires gave me a curt nod of recognition. It wasn't much, but I'd take it.

"What can you tell us about this area, Fidel?" Dario asked.

The man shifted his posture, glancing over at me before facing the head of his family. "It's quiet after dark. Not much of a rich environment, if you get my drift, but I like the vibe. There's an auction house off Ostend, a couple local bars and a pizzeria. The art gallery sometimes has functions after sunset. Oh, and the ballroom. I love the ballroom. Like I said, not a lot to choose from, but nice folk and there's all sorts of private places to go with the park and all the warehousing and distribution companies that are closed at night and don't have much in the way of security."

"Anything unusual in the last few nights?" I asked. "Or even in the last few weeks?"

Tremelay had said the overdose deaths had taken place elsewhere, but I couldn't believe whatever vampire killed this man bothered to stuff him in a car and drive him halfway through the city. If a rogue was giving Dario the finger by leaving a vampire kill out in the open for the police to find, then he wouldn't bother dumping the body ten miles from where he'd fed.

Fidel thought for a moment. "The little market over on Ward. With sunset happening early now that it's almost winter, they're open when I'm awake. I like to go in there and pick up some smokes and the occasional can of herring roe. Billy Joe told me a few customers had warned him about some attacks lately. Some nutjob coming out of nowhere, dragging people into alleyways and sexually assaulting them. I didn't think twice about it until Billy Joe said the attacker was 'bitey.'"

The soft fondness as Fidel said Billy Joe's name told me all I needed to know about his friendship with the store clerk.

"Did he say if the police were aware of this?" I made a mental note to ask Tremelay to check on sexual assaults in the Pigtown area and if the police had linked any of them to this murder.

Fidel shook his head. "Billy Joe isn't fond of law enforcement individuals. Probably because he makes a little money on the side, if you know what I mean." The vampire lifted two pinched fingers to his mouth and inhaled. "He would have told me if the police were hanging around the neighborhood. I got the impression most of these attacks were in the Franklin Square and Mount Clare area, but he did mention a young man was attacked in Carroll Park, which is just a few blocks away. All male victims, which is why Billy Joe was a bit worried, and why he was telling me."

"It's a lovely park," Richelle chimed in with a benevolent smile. "There's a golf course, and many fields for baseball and other activities. There's even an ice rink. And Charles Carroll's house." She sighed. "Such a nice man. He was a supporter of abolition, but he did own slaves. I can't overlook or excuse that fact, kind and learned as he might have been."

I did a double take because Charles Carroll had died in 1783. Richelle's accent was definitely deep south, and I wondered how she'd met the famous Marylander. I also wondered how she'd come to be a part of Dario's *Balaj* when I'd assumed they hadn't made Baltimore their territory until the late eighteenth century. Had Richelle been turned once Aubin and his vampire family had arrived? Or had she met Charles Carroll early in her life and been turned by a member of Aubin's family as they came north following their immigration from Haiti?

And it didn't escape my notice that Fidel had mentioned Franklin Square where one of the deceased addicts had been found.

It hadn't escaped Dario's notice either. He glanced over at me. "Do you have the address for that deceased addict over in Franklin Square?"

"Yes, but that was two weeks ago. If you can't pick up a scent here, then you won't get one there," I told him.

"If I may make a suggestion," Richelle interjected. "Why don't we search the park, dividin' up so we each cover a different area. Mayhap we can pick up the trail of a vampire that clearly isn't part of our family."

"Good idea." Dario pointed to Fidel. "You take the south end working north. Richelle, you take this end heading south. Aria and I will check out a few of these businesses and alleyways and see if we can pick anything up there. If this is the work of that group of rogues we've been hearing about, then they're most likely holing up somewhere around the area during daylight hours."

With a "yes, boss" and a blur of speed, Fidel vanished. Richelle took a more leisurely pace, disappearing once she reached the shadows of a cluster of trees. Dario kept his speed to my quick walk and we headed down the street. The first block had clearly occupied residential homes on either side, so we kept moving. Next was a parking lot with cracked asphalt and a handful of cars. We were close to the north end of the park where Richelle was searching, so we turned left and walked up the next street. The occasional car went past, but the neighborhood was mostly silent except for some muted television noise from a few of the houses, and the faint sound of music coming from a corner deli.

Heading east, we looped down another street, this one a mix of residential and commercial.

"How about that?" I pointed across the street to a multi-story building whose painted exterior proclaimed it to be a sign shop.

"Looks like they're still in business," Dario said. "Vampires wouldn't risk staying in an occupied building. We need something abandoned."

Down from the building was a block of six garages. I wasn't sure if they were for the owners of the neat row houses across the street, the sign company, or leased independently.

"What about a garage?" I asked.

Dario nodded. "That's a good place for a vampire to bed down for the day,"

We headed that way, picking up the pace as we neared the garages.

"Would you be able to smell if one's been here?" I was jogging to keep up at this point.

"It depends on when they were in the area last and how long they stayed." He stopped at the first unit, running his hand along the edge of the garage door and leaning close. "If one or more vampires is using one of these garages for daytime shelter, then I should be able to tell."

He moved on to the next one, and I followed, feeling a bit useless. My nose was registering nothing except the usual city-at-night smells, and in the dim glow of the streetlights, everything was a muted shade of gray. I wasn't picking up the sensation of any vampire except Dario, but there was never any residual or lingering impression once a vampire had left my general area, so that wasn't surprising.

Not happy being the tag-along girlfriend or potential damsel-in-distress, I pulled my sword from its scabbard and decided the least I could do was watch Dario's back. He might sense a threat and react faster than me, but I had a blessed sword and a spelled butter knife on my side.

Dario eyed my sword. "Is something coming?"

"I don't know. *Is* something coming?"

He grinned and turned to the next garage door. "Hopefully not. If something is coming it's going to be a headless something in short order."

I immediately thought back on my conversation with my parents over Thanksgiving. "It might already be headless. Did you know that the Krasue looks like a floating female head with entrails below the neck?"

Dario shot me a horrified glance. "A what?"

"A beautiful female head with a bunch of guts hanging from her neck. Some references claim she is a normal woman during the day, but at night she's consumed by hunger and that's when her head detaches and goes hunting without her body. Other references say she's nocturnal sleeping underground during the day and never has a body but is always a floating head and guts."

"That…that's… Is that a real thing?" Dario eyed me skeptically.

"Oh yes, although there aren't many of them. They're mostly in Thailand, Laos, and Cambodia, although there have been sightings elsewhere in Southeast Asia. The Krasue doesn't have wings, but floats and flies around, probably because she doesn't have legs and rolling on the ground isn't an optimal mode of transportation when you've got entrails dangling from your neck. Oh, and she's got super sharp fangs and drinks blood, just like vampires."

"I'm so glad I've got legs and arms," Dario muttered turning back to the garage door.

Me too. I stood guard as he continued his examination, edging our way along the row. At the last door, I saw him tense and look down at the padlock.

"Let me," I told him, knowing he was planning on just yanking the lock from the door. My way was quieter, and if we found nothing, we could replace the undamaged lock and leave the belongings secure.

Putting my sword back in the scabbard, I pulled a keyring from my pocket.

"You pick locks?" Dario eyed the keys which were clearly not lock picks.

"Yes, but magic is faster." With a whispered word, one of my keys glowed blue. I inserted it into the lock, twisted and smiled as it sprang open. "See? Easy-peasy lemon-squeezy."

The vampire rolled his eyes. "I still don't know what that means."

Not bothering to explain it for the tenth time, I removed the lock and stood aside as Dario eased the garage door open. Given we were having a casual conversation, I assumed there wasn't any threat of attack from inside, but I still held out a hand to caution Dario and pulled my butter knife from my pocket.

As my eyes adjusted to the dim light inside the garage I saw a shelving unit toward the back holding what looked like car parts and paint cans. Leaning against the wall in a corner were a stack of folding chairs. Some dilapidated boxes sagged next to them and on the other side were a few sturdy large plastic bins with lids. It was what was staining the concrete in the empty center of the small garage that caught my eye.

It could be spots of oil from a leaky engine. Or it could be blood. Judging from the way Dario's nostrils flared, I was guessing blood.

I couldn't smell anything beyond mildew and dust, but it wasn't a whole lot of blood, and it clearly wasn't fresh. Holding up my butter knife, I whispered a few words and the garage lit with a faint, warm light. A few sections glowed red, and I reached out to grab Dario's arm.

"Hang on. There's magic."

I felt his arm muscles bunch beneath my hand. "I smell human blood, about a day old. Not much of it either, so if this was where that man was killed, they did a clean and efficient job of feeding."

"They?" My heart sank. "You smell more than one vampire?"

He nodded. "Six. Two humans—one male and one female."

One female? "Two different types of blood?" I asked, wondering where the body of the woman could possibly be.

He shook his head. "No, just the man's blood."

"Then the woman is the mage, unless vampires would be carrying and using spelled items."

"I doubt it," he replied. "We're not averse to using a magical item, but it's just not normally necessary unless we know we're needing to go up against something big. I can't see why a group of rogues who've joined together to hunt and carve out a portion of our territory would bother. And I doubt they'd have the resources to obtain a magical item anyway."

"They're not just some ragtag bunch of rogues if they're with a mage," I told him. "Either they've got money enough to hire one, or they're working for her."

He grimaced. "I don't like either one of those scenarios."

Me either.

"Let's see what kind of magic we're dealing with before we start to worry." I let go of his arm and took a step into the room, setting the butter knife on a plastic tub to free up my hands for my sword. The red on each of the four walls turned out to be a spell I knew and had been trying to master myself the last month. I carefully scrutinized each of the symbols and decided to leave them in place.

"Silence spell," I mouthed to Dario, because if I'd spoken the words he wouldn't have heard them. Everything that took place inside the garage was inaudible to anyone outside. It was a very useful spell if you were a vampire with a screaming captive, or a mage who didn't want the neighbors to know what was going on in your basement.

Dario's phone buzzed and I waited to go to the other magical item until he'd checked his messages.

"Fidel hasn't come across anything so far, but is widening his search. Richelle scented an unknown vampire near one of the ballfields. I'm asking her to hold in place until I can get Madeline to join her." Dario looked up at me. "I don't want to risk her running into a gang of six rogues unless she's got backup."

I nodded then turned my attention to the other red glowing thing in the corner of the room, almost hidden by the stack of folding chairs. It was a splintered rod of hemlock, half of what had once been a wand. The magic was a weird mishmash of what looked like it could have been a safeguard spell and one that I'd never seen before.

I pulled a little velvet bag out of my pocket and turned it inside out, sticking my hand into it before picking up the broken wand. Then I pulled the bag from my hand, sealing the magical item inside. The red vanished instantly and I motioned for Dario to enter.

"Silence spell," I told him pointing at the walls. "I don't know what the heck this is in the null-bag, but I'll take it back to my place and see if I can figure it out."

Dario nodded, looking around the room and taking everything in before bending down to pick something up. "Six vampires, one male human victim, one female human mage, and this."

I edged nearer to see him holding a broken glass vial.

"Heroin." The vampire set the vial on top of an old paint can. "I can smell it on the glass, but not in the blood on the floor."

I frowned, having a hard time putting this all together. "So they lured a man here, or brought one here. They fed from him, and possibly drained him if this was the same man that was found dead early this morning. Then what? They accidently broke the heroin they were going to give him?" I fingered the bag. "And the wand? There's no sign of a struggle that I can see."

"Six vampires and a mage for one man?" Dario's smile was grim. "He wasn't just a meal. They brought him here to interrogate him, or torture him to send a message to someone. I'm guessing the heroin was to cover up the method of death."

"Then it wouldn't exactly be a message, would it?" I asked.

"It would to the right people. They'd know it wasn't an overdose. I think this was *supposed* to look like those overdose victims you were telling me about, but something happened, maybe a brief struggle, and the vial of heroin was broken. The vampires lost their tempers or said 'screw it', and instead of feeding discreetly through the inner arm to make it look like he was a junkie, they just went for the neck."

"And dumped the body a block away," I mused. "That's a bold, risky move on their part."

Dario's eyebrows rose. "Six vampires and a mage? They have every right to be cocky and bold. There are twenty-five of us trying to hold this entire city, and they've got a mage that they're either working for or have working for them. Either way, it's protection, and I'd also be willing to bet that there are more than the six of them in this gang."

I sucked in a breath. "That group of fifteen or twenty organized rogues that you've had rumors of?"

He nodded.

I looked around the room. "Well, they might have a mage, but you've got a Templar. Do you think you can track any of this six? Or the mage? Or even the human whose blood is here?"

"I'm going to try."

I picked up my butter knife and stuck it in a pants pocket, tying the null bag to my belt. We locked the garage back up. I followed, sword out, as Dario did a crisscross search pattern down the road, reminding me of a two-legged bloodhound, and I jogged behind him.

Admittedly he was moving slowly, no doubt so I could keep up, but we still wandered up and down streets for nearly an hour until I had no stinking idea where the heck I was. I was thinking it would be perfectly acceptable for me to skip my morning run when I felt the static buzz of vampires on my skin.

My grip tightened on the sword and I tensed, nearly running into Dario's back as he halted abruptly.

"They're ours." He put a hand on my shoulder, then waited. A few seconds later, three vampires came around the corner, slowing as they approached. It was Richelle, Madeline, and Fidel.

"Hi boss," Madeline stepped forward. "Fidel caught a scent and tracked it until it joined up with the one Richelle and I were following. A few others joined in and we traced it north to Franklin Square before it split off."

Dario told them what we'd found and about the scent he'd been tracking.

"Should we move on to where it split off?" Madeline asked. "We can call in a few more and track further."

Dario shook his head. "No. If this is what I think it is, then I want us to have more information before we potentially wind up facing them down. Text me your routes and exactly where everything split off, and I'll forward it to some trusted allies to look into it during daylight hours. Depending on what they find, we'll discuss and possibly proceed tomorrow night."

"Can I get that information as well?" I asked. I wasn't asleep during daylight hours, and I was off work tomorrow. Outside of my séance with Russell, and research on the broken wand, I should have a bit of free time to head to Franklin Square and see what I could see.

Madeline hesitated for a fraction of a second before replying. "Yes. Of course."

"Fidel, I'd prefer if you continue hunting in the Pigtown area over the next day or two. Keep your eyes open, but do not put yourself at risk. If you see or hear anything, let me or Madeline know and do not follow-up without specific instructions." Dario turned to Richelle. "If you can, please move your hunting grounds to the Franklin Square area. Stealth mode. If you need more donors upon waking, I'll authorize that. I want you to concentrate more on intel gathering than on finding food for the night. You too, Fidel."

They both nodded and left. Dario turned to Madeline.

"Are we shifting focus from the north to this area?" she asked.

"Don't pull completely out of the north," he told her. "I don't want to hear any more of those 'animal attacks' up there, and I'm afraid if we're suddenly nowhere to be seen, other rogues might see that as a sign that we're spread too thin. Leave five up there and tell them to be openly visible in as many places as possible. I want everyone tripled up on donors upon waking so they can focus on this. We've got the resources; might as well use them. Pull enough from the outskirts so that I've got at least ten focused on this area—but I want them discreet."

Madeline nodded. "No sense in warning these people we're coming and finding ourselves with a magic wand up our noses."

"Agreed." He reached out and put a hand on her shoulder. "You've been running all over the city tonight. Go home. Relax."

I loved seeing this side of Dario. His leadership style as the second in command had been fair but firm. He'd commanded loyalty and respect as well as fear. But watching him now I realized how much of his previous demeanor had been not necessarily him, but a reflection of who Leonora needed him to be.

Don't get me wrong, I was positive he could still be fair and firm and absolutely terrifying if needed, but now that he was the one setting the rules as well as the tone of the *Balaj*, he'd become more collaborative. He delivered his instructions with clear authority, but also with a warm kindness that made it clear he valued every member of his family and that everything he did was for their collective well-being and survival.

It made me love him even more.

"Thanks, boss." She turned and gave him a quick hug. "We've got this. There might only be twenty-five of us left, but we're strong and we're determined, and with you leading us, we're going to keep our hold on Baltimore."

It was the first time I'd been able to witness that closeness between Dario and his second. She'd been a young vampire when he was still a human in Haiti, and I knew the two of them had been friends for centuries.

Madeline left and Dario and I walked back to his SUV. In spite of what we'd seen tonight, everything seemed…right somehow. I took his hand in mine and stepped closer, my shoulder brushing against his as we walked.

"This was a good idea." His voice was light and teasing. "I like working with you. And when you're next to me, I'm not twisting myself into knots wondering whether you're getting yourself shot at, or chewed up by a vampire, or knocked unconscious and almost skinned."

Yes, those things had all happened.

"See? And I'm here to make sure you're not blown to bits, or that you don't die from a magic wand up the nose," I teased back. "The two of us can easily take six vampires and a mage."

He shuddered. "You take the mage and I'll take the six vampires."

I laughed. "Deal."

He pulled his keychain out of his pocket, still holding onto me with his other hand, and beeped the door lock. Walking around to the passenger side, he pushed me up against the door, and kissed me so thoroughly that I thought I might melt through the asphalt.

This was what our relationship had been missing the last

few weeks. Not the sex—we'd had plenty of that. No, it was the camaraderie of working together toward a common goal. It was partnership. It was this.

"Spend the night at my house," he whispered into my ear. "In my bed. With me."

I hesitated, not sure how that would work. "Do you…at dawn, are you…"

"I shelter elsewhere. I'll wake you before I go, though."

I felt a surge of relief at his words. Yes, I needed to accept that Dario was a vampire, but that didn't mean I wanted to get used to waking up next to a cold, non-responsive body.

"But Fulk. I can't leave him alone all night long. I know it's only four more hours, but he's used to me coming home eventually at night." I didn't want my dog to worry. And I really didn't want my dog to eat my house because he was anxious.

He kissed me again. "We'll swing by your place and pick him up. And you can grab whatever you need—clothes, a toothbrush, whatever. Just leave them, so you'll have stuff at my place."

It didn't take me long to make up my mind. "Yes. I'd like that."

He drove to my house. I gathered together supplies for an overnight while he fed Gaia and Fulk. Then we bundled the dog into the backseat of the SUV and drove to his house.

I had no idea where Dario's new Renfield or Erica were but his house seemed to be empty except for the two of us— and Fulk. Dario made the two of us omelets, and we headed up to Dario's room. Thankfully Fulk seemed happy to remain downstairs on the couch, while the pair of us made love. I fell asleep on Dario's gloriously cushy bed, him in my arms, a fluffy down comforter over me. Best of all? I woke up at six in the morning to him kissing his way down my body. We made love again, then went downstairs where his

Renfield, David, made us breakfast. Just before sunrise, Dario kissed me and headed off to sleep for the day, while I fed Fulk scraps of bacon.

Erica was nowhere to be seen, and I wondered if that was on purpose. But it didn't matter, because it had been an amazing evening and morning, and I found myself daydreaming about what my life would be if I lived here with Dario.

But we had a long way to go before I'd consider that any more than a fantasy. Right now I'd be happy with what we had—with my spare toothbrush in his bathroom, a handful of clothing in a dresser drawer, and the hope that what we had might beat all the odds and actually have a happily ever after.

"Mom!" Of all the people I expected to find on my porch at eight o'clock on a Saturday morning, it didn't include my mother.

Fulk bounded out of my car and up the steps, his tail wagging furiously as he greeted her. I headed up at a more leisurely pace, a little embarrassed. How long had she been here? Even though I was wearing jeans and a sweater, I still felt as if I were doing a walk of shame the night after a pickup.

"Good morning, Solaria." Mom patted Fulk, then kissed me on the cheek before shifting to the side so I could unlock the door. Nothing in her voice indicated she was peeved at waiting all night for me, or judging me for my sleepover, and my mother was the queen of saying a million unsaid things in a simple tone of voice.

I opened the door and ushered her in, realizing that this couldn't be a social visit. The last time my mother had shown up unannounced she had discovered my demon mark and was pledging her and the family's help in ridding me of it. My demon mark was gone, and I doubted she'd driven this whole way to take me to task about my choice of a boyfriend, so I immediately thought the worst.

"Is Gram okay? Dad?"

"They're fine," she hastened to assure me. "I'm in town on business."

The relief I felt was short lived. Business for Mom meant Templar business. She was an enforcer, and while most times enforcers were tasked with what amounted to a deployment to guard the Temple, Mom was usually limited to special assignments. She took down the baddies that the Order decided needed to go. It didn't happen very often, but when Mom got the call, she flew out and returned with a bloodied sword and some additional scars. She was good, very good. And was only called in when the threat was significant or the case was high-profile for the Order.

"Just passing through?" I asked hopefully. If Mom was in town because her assignment was in Baltimore, I knew it wouldn't be good.

"No, my business is here. In your city."

My stomach felt like a lead weight in my midsection. This wasn't just a visit to see her daughter while she was in town. No, Mom was here for what I'd call professional courtesy. She was giving me a head's up, and I was sure I wouldn't like what she was about to tell me.

I headed into the kitchen to feed Gaia and Fulk, both animals as well as my mother following me. "Is this about the homeless people found dead?"

It wasn't. The Order wouldn't care about homeless victims. They wouldn't care about any victims unless someone paid them to care, or unless the Order were being implicated in some fashion, or the Temple was threatened, or there was a mass casualty event. None of that seemed to apply here.

Mom set her purse on my kitchen table and waited for

me to feed my dog and cat before pulling a picture out of her purse and handing it to me. It was eerily reminiscent of Janice's morgue photos. This guy I didn't recognize, but what I did see is that in addition to the obvious marks on his arms and inner thigh, this guy had a big ole bite mark on his neck. I winced, assuming this was the man Tremelay had told me about yesterday, the one whose crime scene Dario, Richelle, Fidel, and I had been to last night.

But why would the Elders be concerned about a vampire killing? It happened, but it didn't happen with enough overall frequency for the Order to get involved. Unless this guy was the Pope's brother and His Excellency had made a phone call, then the Order wouldn't bother even noticing this dead man in Baltimore.

Mom slid me another picture and I sucked in a breath. There was a tattoo on the dead man's right inner wrist—a cross.

A Templar cross.

"Shit."

It was all I could say at the moment. A Templar, besides me, in Baltimore. Found dead of a vampire attack in my city. Well, now I knew why the Order was suddenly interested in Baltimore, but I still didn't know why this man had been in town, nor why the Elders had sent *my mother* to investigate. Mom didn't investigate, she killed. She took out the trash. She got the job done. Usually on her assignments there was no investigation required, just hunt down the target and send it to an eternal rest.

Which meant things were about to get really uncomfortable between my mother and me.

"Bernard D'Angelo," she said, her voice soft.

I shook my head, vaguely recognizing the name but not knowing the man personally. He looked to be in his forties, although it was hard to tell from a morgue photo. I was assuming he'd been an enforcer judging by the muscular nature of the naked body, but all Templars were required to keep up a minimal level of fitness and fighting skill. But whatever his specialty was, I was perplexed about why he was in Baltimore.

Clearly my mother was paying a professional courtesy call to let me know she was here in my city on business, but no other Knight would do the same. I hadn't taken my vows. I was off the radar as far as the Elders were concerned. They wouldn't consider Baltimore to be my town at all, or even that they should give me a heads-up about the presence of a Knight. In their eyes, I was still a child assigned to my family home in Middleburg. My non-Knight status wouldn't have qualified me for any sort of notification of the arrival of another Templar, and I certainly wouldn't have been made privy to any sort of investigation as a non-Knight.

"I think we both need a drink," Mom said, her voice still soft.

I turned, not even arguing that it was eight in the morning, and went over to my fridge. That's when my brain engaged enough to remember I didn't have much in the way of quality alcoholic beverages to offer my mother. No wine. No decanters of port, or brandy, or high-end whisky. I doubted my mom would be interested in sharing the Emergency Beer in my fridge, so that left the one thing I did have. Anna had given it to me as a housewarming gift and it was in my cabinet, unopened.

"Fireball?" I held the bottle in the air.

"What...what is that?" Mom's tone didn't give me much hope that this qualified as something under her definition of "drink".

"It says whisky, but in my experience it's more of a cinnamon liquor."

Mom scrunched her eyebrows. "Maybe a coffee?"

I hid a smirk and set the bottle on the table, just in case. Then I fired up the coffee maker while my mother searched my cabinets for mugs, milk, and sugar.

"So, Bernard D'Angelo was investigating something, and now you've been sent to take his place since he's dead?" I asked, knowing the answer was "no".

Mom sat the mugs on the counter and turned. "He *was* investigating something, but the Elders have not made me privy as to what he was investigating. I've been sent to avenge his death." My mother's voice was gentle—unnervingly gentle. "Aria, you know that no one murders a Templar Knight and lives. No one."

We might lose a lot of Knights in the process, but eventually we'd kill whatever. Generally our vengeance was by sword, but there had been times in history where we'd needed to employ far more subtle methods—ones that might look "natural". But any way it occurred, no matter how long it took, we always avenged our fallen.

At least that was the story we were told.

"So we'll be working together? Dario and his *Balaj* have been trying to keep rogues out of the city, but they're a bit short on manpower—or vampire power—right now. We actually spent a good bit of last night trying to track down the vampires who killed this guy, although I had no idea he was a Templar." I told her about everything we'd found as the coffee brewed, letting her know that Dario had some of his human associates digging for information and that we were to regroup tonight.

"A mage?" Mom frowned. "Are you sure? Perhaps they purchased some magical devices and the other human there besides Knight D'Angelo served another purpose—a lure to get him into the garage, perhaps."

"It's possible, but rogues generally don't have the sort of

cash to be buying magical artifacts, or hiring a mage. I'm thinking that the mage hired them."

Mom pursed her lips. "Which would mean that Knight D'Angelo most likely had something to do with this mage."

"It's probably best if we both sit down with Dario tonight and get up to speed. Then the three of us can head out and work this together."

"I'm not sure we *can* work together, Aria, but I will need any information you have gathered to date." Mom took the cream and sugar over to the table and I pulled out two shot glasses, thinking that the Fireball was sounding better and better right now.

"Mom, it's not Dario," I insisted. "It's not his *Balaj*. They're too busy fighting for their territory. There are rogues from outside the city who are taking advantage of Leonora's death. If they keep harrying the *Balaj*, then none of Dario's family can be spared to turn their candidates and increase their numbers, and if the rogues band together with enough numbers, they could actually take the city and drive Dario's *Balaj* out. They want these vampires out of Baltimore, and you want them dead. We can work together here. They need help, not accusation, not the Order coming down on their heads."

She opened up the drawer and took out a pair of spoons. "I hear you, Aria. Trust me, I hear you. But time is not on our side here."

"Mom, the local *Balaj* wouldn't draw attention to themselves by killing a Templar Knight in a way that screams the murderer was a vampire, then dumping him on the street to be found. If it was Dario's family, Knight D'Angelo's body would never have been found."

"True, but—ah!" Mom shrieked and threw a spoon across the room. It bounced off the wall and clattered on the floor.

I looked over at the spoon with the battered handle and slapped a hand over my mouth to smother my laugh.

"Solaria Angelique Ainsworth, why is there a man in one of your spoons?"

Now, I laughed. "Never mind, Mom. He's a mage who's interested in mentoring me."

"And why wouldn't he come to your house like a normal person? Why use a spoon as some kind of weird mage FaceTime?"

"Because he's in jail. Now, as I was saying, it's not Dario's *Balaj*. They'd never risk themselves like that. They know the repercussions of killing a Templar."

Mom picked up the spoon and shoved it in an upper cabinet before getting out another, non-magical, one. "Your Dario is a new Master, trying to gain control over a deci-mated family group," Mom said. "Maybe he wouldn't know if a subset of his family were doing things that might have put them at direct odds with what Knight D'Angelo was doing."

I pulled the half-filled pot from the coffee maker and filled our mugs before putting it back. "There aren't that many left in the *Balaj*, and they're all loyal to Dario. No one would do this."

Mom waited for me to sit, then did the same. "I know you don't believe this, but vampires kill and they're loyal only to themselves. Their hunger drives them and few have enough control to restrain themselves when feeding. This would be the perfect opportunity for a group of your boyfriend's family to do whatever they wanted knowing there would be little chance of repercussions."

"That's not true. Vampires are very loyal to their family, and they *can* restrain themselves," I argued as I sipped my coffee. "I've met a lot of vampires in the last few months. The ones that can't manage to control themselves are put down. I've seen it."

"But if a new Master has his hands full securing his territory and managing the transition he may not be able to enforce that. Especially if they're down on numbers. Killing those who drain their victims, might not be optimal if he's trying to fend off incursions on his territory and he needs the numbers to help him fight any attempts to take their territory."

I clenched my jaw. "You're saying Dario knows about this, that he knows about it and has not only lied to me, but he led me on an orchestrated fake-investigation last night?"

She shrugged. "Maybe. Or maybe he doesn't know. Either way, I've been sent to deliver justice."

I swallowed hard, realizing I was going to have to work fast and hard to make sure Mom and I found the real killers, and that any red herrings pointing toward Dario's *Balaj* weren't taken seriously.

But in spite of my outward confidence that Dario and his family weren't involved in these deaths, there was a tiny thread of doubt worrying away inside me. I knew he'd kept things from me in the past. I knew he tried to keep the unseemly side of vampire life hidden from my eyes. Had he lied? He'd do anything to keep his family safe, and that might mean he'd need to shield the killers—and that he'd need to make sure I didn't find out any of his family were responsible.

If it were a member of Dario's family, then that vampire would need to be brought to justice. And then I'd need to deal with how that impacted my relationship with Dario later. In the meantime, I'd work to find the killers no matter if they were human, vampire, or something else.

"I'll help," I told Mom. "Let's sit down and go over what I've got so far, then we can talk to Dario tonight. If it's any of his family…well, we'll deal with that when we find out who's behind the killings."

"Solaria." Mom reached out and took my arm. "I'll definitely listen and take all the evidence into account, but I need you to know that I've been sent here by the Elders with a very specific mandate. I'm supposed to wipe out all the vampires in Baltimore."

I stared at her. "You mean the ones responsible for Bernard D'Angelo's death?"

"With vampires, it's never just a few, it's a culture of predation. I'm supposed to kill all involved, even if they are only affiliated with the one responsible for Knight D'Angelo's death."

I yanked my arm out of her grasp. "That's not justice, it's murder."

"They're not human, these creatures. They prey upon humans. It's no different than putting down a pack of rabid animals."

I glared at her. "And you really think that?"

I knew my mother wasn't the sort of person who just went around killing without a reason, but she'd had a lifetime of taking out all sorts of supernatural creatures that were a threat to humanity. Vampires occupied a gray area as far as she was concerned. She wouldn't lose sleep over a world where vampires had been eradicated, but she didn't make it her mission to do the eradicating.

Basically if the order told her to murder a bunch of puppies, she'd refuse, but vampires? It was no different than killing wraiths or Chupacabra in her mind.

She sighed. "I came here to let you know. Maybe your boyfriend should leave the city for a while."

It took me a few seconds to get my anger under control. This was a professional courtesy call—so I could get Dario out of town while she wiped out his family.

"He's not going to leave his territory, nor his family. He's in charge of the *Balaj* now. And territory is everything to vampires."

Mom sighed. "I expected you to say that. I'll work with you, Solaria. We'll try to find the actual killer and hope it's not someone in your boyfriend's family. Then I'll take out the killer and his colleagues, but we don't have much time here."

Unless Mom knew where the vampires were or where to find them, she could be here a long time—a very long time. They could sense us just as we could sense them, and vampires, Dario as the exception, tended to stay out of our way.

"I've got a few other things going on in town that I need you to know about," I told her. "There's a murder that my detective friend thinks is a blood-for-money killing. I don't think I'll be called on to help with that, but I might. I've got a meeting later this morning with Russell about…some information. Then Dario's fighting to keep his territory and his family safe, and I'm helping him with that."

Mom shook her head and smirked. "Solaria, I never thought that you'd be dealing with all of this when you refused to take your Oath and went off in a snit to make coffee drinks and live in poverty in downtown Baltimore."

I sighed. "Me either."

We both looked at the bottle of Fireball. Mom reached out and picked up the bottle, unscrewing the cap and taking a sniff. I pushed the two shot glasses over to her. Ignoring them she took a sip out of the bottle and passed it to me.

I did the same. "I'm going to text Dario so when he awakens for the night he knows I've got company and that we need to talk. I'll have him meet us here to go over everything."

Mom nodded and reached for the bottle. "Do you mind if I stay here? I'd rather shack up on your couch or put a bed roll on the floor in a spare room than deal with life on the streets."

I nearly choked on my sip of coffee. "Streets? Doesn't the Order shell out for hotel costs?"

She took another brief sip of the Fireball and passed the bottle back to me, picking up her mug of coffee. "Yes, but this isn't a vacation, it's an assignment. I'll be tracking when I'm not sleeping. I need to be somewhere more central than where the ritzy hotels are, and I need to be able to adjust my overnight space depending on where my hunt leads me."

I eyed the booze, then set the bottle down on the table, knowing I needed the caffeine more this morning. "You're seriously going to go on a vampire hunting spree in the city like a Van Helsing or something? Lurk in dark alleys with a handful of stakes and your sword? Lure them in with the promise of blood and sex only to stake them? How will you know when you get them all? Do the Elders have stats on how many are in the city? You do know that if you wipe out Dario's *Balaj,* another group will swoop in to take the territory."

"I don't want to wipe out your boyfriend and his family, I just want to find who killed Bernard D'Angelo and deliver justice. The Elders aren't asking me to take on every vampire in the Northeast, just the group who murdered Bernard," she assured me. "If that's someone in Dario's *Balaj,* then I think you need to advise him to get out of the way. If that's another vampire family, then we need to find them."

I looked down at my mug of coffee. This was insane. It was like the Crusades all over again—kill them all and let God sort them out. Our order had been formed to deliver divine justice, to protect pilgrims on the path, to guard and protect the Temple and the holy objects therein. Things had gone horribly wrong during the Crusades and a lot of innocent people had died for what had amounted to greed. When we'd fallen from grace, some had felt it was politics and greed at play, while others believed we were being served a helping of our own divine justice. Either way, I didn't want to see history repeat itself. The Elders might not be motivated by greed, but either way, the actions were the same. We Templars shouldn't be exterminating an entire group, just because one may or may not be a murderer.

"What if it's someone trying to pin D'Angelo's death, on the *Balaj*? This is insane, Mom. If a human in Glen Burnie killed a Templar, would you be killing the entire human population there? No. You'd be investigating, finding the person or persons responsible and bringing them to justice."

"Aria, this isn't a random killing." Mom leaned forward. "Knight D'Angelo wasn't a drunk wandering the streets who got drained by a hungry vampire. He was a skilled Templar, and he was murdered on purpose."

"It would be a lot easier to find his killer if we knew motive, which is most likely tied to whatever he was doing in the city. If we knew what his mission was, then we might have a clue who killed him and why," I muttered.

"I know." Mom eyed the Fireball bottle. "But the Elders haven't seen fit to give me that information. I figured that you knew this city better than any of the other Templars, and you'd most likely have an idea why he would have been here. He arrived two weeks ago."

I held up my hands. "I know there's something that the death mages were trying to hold back, something that required serious magic, but I've yet to figure out what that is. It could be that the Elders got a hint and sent someone here to check it out. Other than that, I don't know. Maybe there's an artifact here I don't know about that he was sent to retrieve. Seriously that's the only other thing I can think of."

Mom pursed her lips in thought. "If it were a patron who was paying us to remove a supernatural threat, then I think you'd be aware of that threat. You're right. It most likely was an artifact that the Elders caught wind of."

An artifact that put a Knight at odds either with vampires or someone who was eager to blame the Knight's death on vampires.

"In addition to meeting with Dario, I think we should probably meet with the police as well and get as much information from them on D'Angelo's autopsy as possible," I told her.

"That's a good idea. I know you said you had some other commitments. When do you think we can get started?"

I looked at my phone. "I need to shower and change and be over at Russell's at ten. I should be back around noon or one. I've got that broken portion of the wand we found in the garage, but I wanted to examine it later this afternoon while in the circle downstairs, just in case it's rigged to explode or something."

Mom grimaced. "I'm going to go over to where the body was found, look around, and check out that garage. I'll meet you back here later in the afternoon. Please wait for me before you go examining that wand."

Honestly I'd be grateful for her help in that one. Mom had handled a lot of artifacts over the decades. She might not perform magic beyond the Templar blessings and prayers, but she knew enough to identify a lot of spells.

I held up a hand. "I promise that I'll wait for you to get home before doing anything with the wand. Also, Dario wakes at sunset. He'll probably need an hour or two to feed, take care of any *Balaj* business and get over here. I can order pizza or Chinese delivery for dinner and we can meet here as soon as he's available. I'll text Tremelay and see if he has any additional information about the case he can give us, too."

Mom's eyes widened. "Tremelay?"

I nodded. "I know. But his family hasn't been Templars for ten generations at least."

She shook her head. "Just because someone didn't take their vow, or even train, doesn't mean they're not a Templar. Their family pledged their lives and the lives of their future generations to the Lord. That makes him a Templar in my eyes and in the eyes of the Order."

Just as I was still a Templar even though I'd not taken my vows. Although I couldn't imagine Tremelay would be all that thrilled about being pledged to serve the Lord as a Templar by some ancestor hundreds of years ago, and I didn't see how that might help our case.

"Well Templar or not, I'm glad he's on our side," I told her. "He's a heck of a detective, and he's saved my butt several times."

Mom smiled for the first time since she'd arrived. "Good. I'll be happy to have another Templar working with us, whether he's a Knight or not. Go ahead and text him as well as your vampire boyfriend. Maybe the detective can also meet with us tonight if he's available. And I think Chinese food for tonight. I'm in the mood for some Hunan Chicken and spicy tofu."

I went to write it down and hesitated, mentally calculating what four adults could eat as well as the balance in my checking account.

"I'll buy," Mom added. "Actually, the Order is buying. I have an expense account, so don't skimp on the egg rolls."

I grinned. If the Order was buying, then I was going all out tonight. And I most definitely was *not* going to skimp on the egg rolls.

$I$ sat across from Russell, overly sweet tea on the table in front of me. This time I'd left Fulk at home, assuming Russell wouldn't need the dog to communicate with Raven. He definitely wouldn't need the dog to communicate with the other spirit I needed to speak with.

"Do you have any personal items from this Bernard D'Angelo?" Russell asked. "Often a close friend of a loved one has enough of a connection with a deceased person that I can establish a link, but since you didn't know him, a personal item would be helpful."

"I don't have anything," I confessed. "I don't even know what he looked like. We're both Templars, so maybe that is enough of a connection? The only other thing I've got is a morgue photo of his body and a close up picture of the Templar tattoo on his wrist—also from the morgue."

The necromancer frowned thoughtfully, surveying the various tools on the table between us. "You have a similar tattoo, as I recall."

I pulled back the sleeve of my sweatshirt to reveal that

mark. "It's blessed as it's inked, so it's not just a regular tattoo. All Templars have one."

"May I?" He reached out to touch that tattoo at my nod, shuddering as his fingers made contact with my skin. "That might work. Now to decide how to best communicate with this Knight."

"I really need to ask him some questions."

Russell sighed, pulling the Ouija board front and center. "I don't know how clear any responses are going to be. I'm not even sure I'll be able to contact him or not. You've never met him. We don't have anything personal of his that might link to his spirit through the veil. If I can manage a connection using your tattoo, then I'll see what happens."

He arranged the planchette on the board, dimmed the lights and drew the drapes, then walked around the room, lighting candles. I placed my hands palms-up on the table and waited as he sat. Putting one hand on my Templar tattoo, and the other flat on the table, Russell closed his eyes and began to hum.

The air grew thick and warm. The candles flickered. The planchette quivered an inch to the left.

"Bernard D'Angelo, Knight Templar, I reach out to you across the veil and ask that you answer us."

We waited. I stared at the planchette, willing it to move, but nothing happened.

"Bernard D'Angelo, Knight Templar, we call to you. A sister Templar needs help in finding your murderers and bringing them to justice. I call to you through the bond of your mark."

I felt the tattoo on my wrist tingle and warm. The planchette shuddered and slowly moved, letter by letter to spell out a response.

BLOOD.

I waited, but the planchette remained still. Blood. I

assumed the man was telling me that vampires had killed him by drinking his blood.

"Knight D'Angelo, I am Solaria Ainsworth. We know you were killed by vampires. We're trying to track them down and deliver justice. What were you in Baltimore seeking?"

I held my breath as the planchette crept its way across the board.

ROYAL BLOOD

My mind raced, wondering what in the heck D'Angelo was talking about. Royal blood? Had a European prince been kidnapped and the Templars hired to find him? He couldn't be referring to the Holy Grail because we already had that item safely in the Temple. Unless it had somehow been stolen or smuggled out underneath the eye of half a dozen skilled Knights and the Elders were keeping it quiet until it was recovered. Although if we'd lost one of our most holy artifacts, I would have thought the Elders would have sent more than one Knight to retrieve it.

"You were here to retrieve the royal blood?" I asked, trying to keep the question simple. I'd figure out who or what royal blood referred to later, if Russell was able to maintain the connection long enough.

The planchette moved to the "no" word on the board, then once again began to spell out a response.

STOP THEM B4 HE COMES

Okay, *that* raised the hair on the back of my neck. I immediately thought of Chuck's Big Bad, and hoped I wasn't going to have to face whatever the heck that was right now.

"Before who comes?" I asked. "Who is coming?"

I watched the Ouija board, shaking my head slowly as I made note of the letters.

"Marblehead?" What in all that was holy was D'Angelo talking about? Was the connection slipping and the spirit losing control over the planchette? Or was the Knight sent to stop a giant statue of a head?

"A golem?" I asked, trying to think of any stone-like being that might warrant sending a Templar to deal with.

Russell sucked in a deep breath, his hands beginning to shake. Once more the planchette moved.

DEAD SECRETS WILL LIVE STOP ROYAL BLOOD STOP MARBLEHEAD

An icy breeze blew through the room, extinguishing the candles. Russell exhaled, pulling his fingers away from my Templar tattoo and wiping them on the front of his shirt. "I'm amazed by everything you got there. He was very determined to communicate with you, otherwise I doubt I could have even connected with his spirit."

A whole lot of puzzlement is what I had. What the heck was a Marblehead? Royal blood? And what did a group of vampires have to do with any of this? Were the rogue vampires working for a mage who was going to raise a golem using a special type of blood magic?

I'd need to talk to Mom about all this.

"The next one should be easier." Russell moved the Ouija board aside. "You've got a connection with your friend Raven. I might be able to even channel her directly."

"Even if she's in hell?" I asked.

The necromancer nodded. "Yes, although I won't be able to hold the connection for long if she's in hell. If she's in the grasp of that Balsur, I might not be able to get much in the way of communication, but I'll know she's there and be able to get a quick message from her."

That surprised me and I eyed Russell with added respect. If Balsur had Raven, I doubted he'd willingly let her communicate across the veil. That Russell was powerful enough to bypass the demon in his own domain was impressive.

"Do you have the focus item?" Russell asked.

I dug around in my purse and pulled out one of the spell books Raven had given me. The little resin fox that had housed her spirit had been pulverized to dust, but I had lots of things that had belonged to Raven, and I knew how much she'd loved her spell books. This one, with her notes in the margins adding to those of two centuries of mages, would certainly call to her spirit even if my presence alone was insufficient to link to her.

Russell took the book, caressing the spine and paging through it before carefully setting it in the middle of the table. Then he stood, replaced the candles in their holders, and once more set them alight. Taking a small bundle of herbs from the table, he walked around, whispering under his breath. Touching a few sticks to the flames, he placed the smoldering herbs on metal at the base of each candle.

The room filled with a woodsy scent. Russell returned to the table, sat, and placed his hands flat on the surface. I mimicked him, closing my eyes and thinking of Raven.

Russell chanted in an unfamiliar language for what seemed like forever. Finally I opened my eyes to sneak a peek at him, and saw the sweat beading on his forehead. Why was this so difficult? My heart sped up with fear. Was Raven okay? What had happened to her that Russell couldn't manage to establish a connection?

"Hear my call," Russell muttered in English. "Answer my call, Raven. Aria wishes to speak with you. She wants to know if you're safe."

The necromancer scowled.

"What?" I whispered, desperate to know what was going on.

He ignored my question. "Are you safe, Raven? Where do you reside on the other side of the veil?"

What was happening? Why wasn't she answering? At least he'd made contact with her, though—that meant her soul hadn't been destroyed. There was still hope, although hope for what I didn't know.

What the heck was I going to do if Raven was in trouble? If Russell was struggling to communicate with her, I had no hope of his being able to…I don't know, summon her across the veil, relocate her from hell or wherever she was to a better zip code. She'd saved me—saved my life, saved my soul. I couldn't just let her suffer, if indeed she was suffering.

Russell let out a breath, opened his eyes, and shook his head as he removed his hands from the table. I stared at him, feeling as if I were on the verge of a panic attack.

"That was…that was difficult," the necromancer admitted. "She didn't answer my call, so I had to follow the trail to her."

"She couldn't answer your call? Does that mean something horrible has control over her?"

He shook his head. "I got the impression that she was purposefully not answering my call."

I swallowed hard. Was she angry with me? Refusing to talk to me just as Reynard refused to answer my calls? Did she think I should have made the deal with Balsur and had her brought back to life in a human body—assuming the demon wasn't lying about his ability to do that? I couldn't believe Raven would go to all the trouble, losing her life in an attempt to rid me of my demon mark, only to change her mind.

"She was…busy," Russell added.

I wasn't sure if that was better than her not answering because she was mad at me.

"Busy with what? With whom?"

"I don't know. I got the impression there was fighting, like everyone was trying to knock each other out of the way and grab something. Raven was determined, but scared. She's not somewhere good, Aria. I'm sorry, but that's what I felt."

I tried to steady my breathing, to force back the tears.

"What can I do to help her? What can I do? There has to be something I can do."

Russell shook his head. "Not that I'm aware of, Aria. One thing she said to tell you before she cut the connection, though: she said she's coming back. She said the time has to be right. When the time is right, she's coming back, and not in a dog or a piece of resin this time."

I sucked in a breath. "Can she do that? Is it even possible for her to do that? Raven could bring a demon across the veil, maybe she has the ability to bring herself somehow? Or there's a mage that can do that?"

"Bringing a spirit fully across the veil isn't like summoning a demon. It's a very different process, and not easy. Throughout history there have been powerful mages whose diaries are filled with the attempts to bring a deceased spirit fully across the veil, to bring them into an empty vessel as if they were reborn again. It's not something we do."

"But isn't that a necromantic skill?" I asked. "Surely if you can raise the dead, communicate with spirits, summon them back into their bodies, then you have the base talents to perform a resurrection?"

"Necromancy is not resurrection," Russell argued. "We call spirits back on a temporary basis, and often not the entirety of the spirit but just a shadow of their former selves —most likely the portion with anger over how they died. The only magic we do that is permanent is to create zombies, or wraiths, or even ghouls. Those sorts of creatures never house the fullness of the deceased spirit, and sometimes do not house the original spirit at all."

"So resurrection isn't a necromantic rite?" I was so confused.

"No. It's a field unto itself, one that requires a lifetime of study to get right—and even then, as I've said, many spend their lives devoted to the study and never succeed. Resurrection rites actually have more in common with blood magic and demonology than necromancy."

Blood. It always seemed to be about blood lately. Poor Melbourne Cassidy lured from Philadelphia to his death. Bernard D'Angelo drained by a group of rogue vampires, his spirit saying something about a marble golem and royal blood.

"From the limited amount I know, a resurrection spell works best right after someone had died, before the body has time to decompose to the point where it would reject the spirit. And even if a mage manages to perform a resurrection within moments of death," Russell continued, "the price of failure is steep."

"How steep?" I asked, my curiosity getting the better of me.

"A life for a life. And if it fails, you've committed a murder for nothing."

For all that was sacred, the ritual involved killing someone? This was clearly the territory where these spells overlapped with death magic and I was far more shocked than I probably should have been.

"So it's a balance thing?" I asked, swallowing my horror at the thought of sacrificing an innocent person just to bring a loved one back to their body. "Is there always the price of another life to bring someone back from the dead?"

"Fully back from the dead? As in a resurrection? Yes. There is always a price to magic, Aria. The most powerful magic requires the steepest price."

I shook my head, imagining something akin to a horror movie. "And the person has to be recently dead to resurrect them? How recently? Hours? Days?"

Russell eyed me for a moment then let out a long breath. "Not...not always. A resurrection ritual back to the original body is ideal, but there is an alternative."

"Alternative?"

"Alternative." He shot me a stern look. "There have been occasions in the last five centuries where a mage has attempted to resurrect a long dead spirit into another body. They have always failed. Either two spirits have ended up inhabiting the body and the subject went insane, or the intended spirit bounced back across the veil and the subject was never the same."

All this was purely academic. I'd never have the ability to do that sort of thing, and as much as I wanted Raven back, I would never sacrifice someone for that to happen. No, if I wanted to help Raven, I'd need to figure out some other way —some way of getting her to a better afterlife at the very least.

Maybe I needed to be talking to a priest. I picked up the book and stood, thanking Russell for the tea and for his help today.

"I owe you big time," I told him.

He chuckled. "Don't worry. There will come a time when I need a Templar, and then I'll be calling on you."

"And I'll be happy to help."

I put the book into my oversized purse and headed out, wondering if I would have time for a quick nap before my mother got home. I'd given her one of the spare keys before I'd left, but I got the feeling she'd not be back until closer to four or five, and it was barely after noon.

My hopes for a nap faded as I turned the corner and noticed a man loitering around my front stoop.

# CHAPTER 16

Two unexpected visitors in one day was more than odd. Admittedly, there was a convenience store on my block, but it was across the street. They generally didn't encourage loiterers, and most of their customers didn't seem inclined to hang out, so this man was more than a little suspicious. And why my house? There were a dozen boarded up houses on this street where he could have sat on the front steps and not gotten a second glance. But *my* house?

Parking in my usual spot, I grabbed my sword off the passenger seat, and instead of putting it over my shoulder, I kept it out as I walked to my front door.

"Can I help you with something?"

The man jumped, backing a few steps away from me and staring at me with wide eyes. He looked vaguely familiar, and I tilted my head trying to remember where I'd seen him before.

"Are you the Templar? The Knight?" he asked.

I was "a" Templar, not "the" Templar and I wasn't a Knight, but it didn't seem to matter enough to warrant a correction.

"Doctor Tremelay gave me your name and address?" He continued.

This must be the guy Kyra had come to talk to me about —the one who thought he'd been kidnapped by aliens and possessed by a demon or something. Great. Kyra was supposed to give the guy my number, not send him over to my house. I could hear Fulk barking inside, and I did have my sword in hand, so I figured I was reasonably safe. Unless the guy had a gun in his pocket, that is.

"You're not carrying a pistol or anything, are you?" I asked, just to be sure, still trying to remember how I knew him. A coffee shop customer? No, Kyra had said he was from out of town, here in Baltimore for business.

Suddenly everything tumbled into place.

"Rick?" It was the guy from the club Tuesday night, the one who'd gone off drunk with some blonde and stranded his worried sister. Liz hadn't called Tremelay, so I'd just assumed Rick had stumbled back to the hotel in the early morning hours. But judging from what Kyra had told me about this guy, there was plenty about Rick Dimond that I hadn't sensed in the ten minutes I'd spent talking to him at the club.

Now it was his turn to squint and look closely at me.

"It's Aria," I reminded him, realizing that I probably didn't look at all the same as I had with makeup and in the dim flattering lighting of the club. "From the Ottobar Tuesday night?"

He frowned. "You look familiar, but I don't remember going to a bar. Or Tuesday."

I snorted. "You were pretty lit, at least by the end of the evening. You probably had the world's worst hangover for that seminar Wednesday. Why did you decide to stay over the holiday?"

I suddenly realized that's when he must have "indulged"

in some smack and had his really bad trip involving alien probes and demonic possession. Ugh, poor Liz. I wondered if she knew how serious her brother's alcohol and drug problem was?

"I...I don't remember a seminar, or the holiday. And the last time I remember seeing Liz was at home." He frowned. "I guess it was last weekend?"

"You didn't call her from the hospital?" Sheesh, the poor woman must be frantic.

"Of course I did." Rick's indignation was real, as was the sudden loss of balance and the quick hand that darted out to catch himself on my rickety railing before he fell.

I reached out to steady him, concerned the railing wouldn't hold the guy. "You better come in and sit down. Hope you don't mind dogs. Or are allergic to cats."

"Left a message for Liz," he mumbled. "But I checked out of the hospital this morning and I don't have a cell phone, so there's no way for her to call me back. I wanted to see you before I tried to call her again. I don't have any money, no ID and no cell phone, so I was hoping... But you're not a Templar, are you? I vaguely remember you worked in a coffee shop?"

"Good thing, because you look like you really could use a coffee." I edged past him, and opened the door. Fulk shot out like a rocket and began sniffing the guy.

I waited for Rick to get his balance and whistled for Fulk to come back inside before helping the man in. Gaia was sitting patiently on the table, queen that she was. She took one disgusted look at Rick, then meowed and strutted off to the kitchen.

"Sit." I eased him down on the couch, then hauled Fulk into the kitchen with me so he wouldn't keep pestering the poor guy.

Putting on a fresh pot of coffee, I got out a couple of

mugs and thought. He'd obviously returned early Wednesday morning, gone to the seminar, then stayed while Liz headed home. I was assuming he'd gone on a bender Wednesday, then been in a flop house somewhere until waking up and staggering to the hospital a few days later. Whatever he told Liz he was doing, it must have been something where he wasn't expected to check in for a few days, or she would have filed a police report. And Kyra had intimated that he didn't appear to be a habitual drug user—at with least IV drugs.

Had he hooked up again with the blonde woman, who'd talked him into shooting up, only to rob him blind and leave him passed out for days? That was the scenario I was thinking about. And if so, then I needed to hear him out, and let the police know that it wasn't alien scientists and demons we were looking for, but a blonde thief.

And then I'd help him get in touch with Liz, have her wire him some money, and maybe get him on a bus home—hopefully all before Mom got back.

I poured us each a mug of coffee, grabbed the milk out of the fridge, a couple of spoons, and the box with little packets of sugar and headed into the living room. Fulk had dashed back in while I was making coffee. I found Rick sitting as I'd left him on the couch, mindlessly petting the dog who was curled up next to him. I shooed Fulk off the sofa, and handed the man a mug of coffee.

"Cream? Sugar?"

He blinked up at me for a few seconds. "A splash of cream. I don't normally take cream, but I feel like I want it in my coffee now, like that's the way the other drinks it."

Okaaaay. I handed him the milk and a spoon and watched him doctor up his coffee.

"Can I see the marks?" I wasn't sure what to call them. Track marks might set him off. Needle marks? Luckily I didn't have to specify because he rolled up his sleeves and showed me. There were two marks on each inner arm, and they all looked as if they'd occurred at about the same time. I couldn't see any other, older, scars, but maybe he used to shoot up in his feet like Tremelay had said some addicts did. Or perhaps this was his first time doing heroin, or whatever the heck it was he'd taken. Four times.

"You're lucky you're alive," I told him. He nodded, probably thinking I meant the medical experiments, when I actually meant the drugs.

He stared down at his coffee. "They knew who I was. Said I was special. Lucky. I passed out, and when I came to, I was possessed. I felt him in me. *Felt* him."

I sat down in a chair and leaned back. "Let's start with what happened before. What's the last thing you remember before the 'medical experiments'?"

He thought for a moment. "I was home. The Miller funeral, so that was Sunday. There was…you're right. There was a seminar or something. Yes. Facial and bodily reconstruction for difficult cases."

I nodded. "Do you remember traveling to Baltimore?"

"Flew. We flew. Liz was with me because she had an invitation as well. We might not get many clients needing that sort of restoration in our funeral home, but the idea was that we could hire out to other mortuaries if needed. One of us could remain, and the other act as a consultant, or do the reconstruction on a for-hire basis."

His voice was stronger, and I could tell the memories were starting to fall into place. I remained silent, not wanting to disrupt his mental process.

"I rented a car." He lifted a hand and rubbed his head. "Where is the car? Did I return it? Did Liz return it? I can't remember."

He was getting agitated again, so I held out a hand to

touch his arm. "It's okay. Stay with what you remember. What happened after you rented the car?"

"We got settled in. Went to dinner." He tilted his head. "Then the rest is a blurry mishmash. Flashing colored lights? Really loud music? Jasmine. The smell of jasmine was almost overpowering."

That was probably the bar. And I was assuming the smell of jasmine was the blonde's perfume. She'd been all over him on the dance floor and lip-locked with him by the bathrooms, so it stands to reason that he would have remembered her scent even if he didn't remember her.

"Take a sip of your coffee and think for a moment," I instructed him. "Then tell me the next thing you remember."

He complied, frowning in thought. "More weird blurry stuff. People in masks bending over me. I couldn't move. Pain, but not horrible pain. I was so cold. Then I was blazing hot and I felt like I was dying. There were more people in masks and it was dark except for some flickering light, like candles. I smelled jasmine, but also something spicy, and something that kinda smelled like pot."

I grimaced, immediately thinking flop house. Except at a flop house, I would have assumed the odor of unwashed people and garbage would have overpowered any drug smell.

"Then there was a horrible pain from deep inside me and I felt like I was being ripped apart. I don't remember anything else for a while after that." Rick's voice shook and his hands began to tremble.

I let Rick pull himself together, drinking my coffee in silence. Fulk whined and again climbed up on the couch next to him, curling up close.

"My eyes were closed, but I remember that it seemed much brighter. I heard voices saying that I was special, important. Some were arguing over whether something had worked or not and about whether someone was who he was supposed to be. I don't know. It really didn't make sense. I kinda came and went and I'm not sure how much time passed. Sometimes I felt like I was seeing myself through a long tube, or like I was watching myself on TV or something. Then more arguing. The only real thing I remember was waking up freezing cold propped up against a parking meter in what looked like a bad section of town. Some cop was tapping my shoe, telling me I needed to get a move on to the shelter, and that I was lucky I hadn't froze to death overnight. I couldn't get up and was trying to tell him about the people in masks. I guess he realized something was wrong because next thing I knew I was in an ambulance and on my way to the hospital."

I would call to double check at the hotel, but from what Rick said, it sounded like he hadn't been back since Tuesday night. If that was the case, why hadn't Liz contacted the police? Maybe in a drunken or drug-induced stupor Rick had texted her and hadn't remembered? Maybe he was missing all day Wednesday as well as Tuesday night, and this had all happened Thursday? We'd need to talk to Liz to figure out that end of the story, but first I wanted to know more about his alleged possession.

I was ninety-nine percent convinced this guy had been roofied, shot up with drugs, and rolled for everything he had on him, then dumped on the street, but just in case I wanted to hear the rest of his story. Something about him being propped up against a parking meter in a bad section of town sounded too much like the guy I'd stumbled over Tuesday morning for my comfort. And the track marks on his arms looked an awful lot like the ones Tremelay had shown me on that dead man's autopsy photos.

The only real difference was that Rick wasn't dead. And he still had all his blood inside him.

"So tell me more about this demon that's possessing you."

He looked up at me, despair written all across his face. "You don't believe me. The police don't believe me. I don't even think that doctor believes me."

I grimaced, because he was right. Although Kyra had believed him enough that she'd bothered to come to me, and to send him to me.

"Go ahead. I promise I'll keep an open mind."

"I don't know if it's a demon or not. Whatever it is, it felt evil, like it was trying to take me over, to kill me or beat me down and lock me into a little corner of my mind. It was inside me. There was someone else inside of me. I think…I think he's still there."

I leaned forward. "Do you know what the being inside you wanted? Did the others command him to perform some task?"

He shook his head. "I don't remember what the masked people were saying. They might have been speaking some other language. And I don't know what the thing inside me wanted other than to stay and not return."

A demon summoned into a human body would most likely *want* to leave. Most demons were pissed about being summoned. Well, some acted pissed but secretly liked being this side of the veil. And they all longed to get free and harm or kill their summoner along with having unrestrained access to spreading their evil among humanity. Maybe this was a lesser Goetic demon and he was happy to just be summoned outside the confines of a circle? Perhaps giving him a body to possess was part of the offering the mages made?

If they *were* mages and this wasn't just some drug-fueled psychotic break.

"He wanted to stay? You feel like he's still there inside you? How did you manage to get control over the possession?"

"I think something went wrong. The thing inside me… only a shadow remains. I feel it. I still feel him, but it's like he's not enough there to take over. He wants to, but he can't." Rick sighed and lowered his head to his hands. "I lied to get out of the hospital so they wouldn't lock me in the nutty bin or anything, but I want this thing out. I want it gone. I know I sound like a crazy, like I should be wearing a pie plate as a hat muttering about people putting chips in my head, but I swear that's really how I feel. It's true. I'm not a drug user. I'm not crazy. I'm a mortician from Massachusetts and the most daring things I've done in my life is drive over the speed limit and eat some questionable oysters from a shack on the wharf. Oh, and that one girlfriend in college, but I try not to think about that."

A failed demon possession? I'd never heard of a demon being partially across the veil. And why summon one into a person? Why not just get them into a circle, detail the terms of their summoning contract, and let them go. If this was a ritual gone wrong, then there would be a whole lot of bodies on the floor, including Rick's, and a demon terrorizing the city. There wouldn't be a demon "partially possessing" someone. That was…unheard of.

"The guys in masks—what sort of masks were they? Kyra, I mean Doctor Tremelay said you'd claimed these people did medical experiments on you?"

"I wasn't sure what to call it," he confessed. "Like I said, I was tied down with needles and tubes in my arms. There was blood. It was dark sometimes in the room, but they had masks like you see on doctors in surgery. They had things that looked like robes or surgeon gowns, and things over their hair, and masks, and gloves. It was like a bunch of doctors."

"Not Halloween masks, or anything?" I was a little weirded out about his mention of blood. That plus the marks in his arms, plus the fact that he'd been dumped on the street were eerily close to Tremelay's suspected blood-for-money victim. It was too close to be a coincidence, or was it?

"What's your blood type?" I asked, as a long shot.

"O-positive."

"Anything unusual or rare about it?"

He shook his head. "Not that I've ever been told. I've given blood a few times, and they didn't seem any more excited over getting mine than anyone else at the blood drives."

So it was a coincidence then. I wondered what they'd done to him besides stolen his ID, money, and cell phone, and kept him a drugged up captive for two days?"

"Did the hospital say anything else about your physical condition? Dehydration? Anemia? A microchip in your brain?"

He shook his head again. "Not that they told me. Whatever they did to me, it wasn't anything major. Maybe they gave me some drugs that wore off quickly and the hospital couldn't detect them? Maybe they just took some blood from me for whatever reason? I don't have any enemies or anyone who would want to do this to freak me out in revenge for anything. I honestly don't know why, or even really what they did to me."

"But you have something else inside you. A spirit?" It had to be a spirit, because I couldn't figure out how it *could* be a demon.

His eyes lit up with hope. "You do believe me?"

"I don't know," I confessed. "I think you honestly believe this happened, but whether it's some sort of hallucination or not, I can't be sure. Demon possession does occur, although it's far rarer than people think, and what you're describing doesn't sound like demons. Spirit possession occurs, although I'd think that would happen only among the sensitive. If this thing inside you is a spirit, then the memories of medical testing and losing two days of awareness could be attributed to the spirit that was communicating or possessing you. I don't know, that isn't my area of expertise. I do know someone we can consult if you're going to be in town another few days."

He shrugged. "Until I can get in touch with my sister, I don't have any identification, credit cards, money, or anything to even pawn. I won't be going anywhere but the shelter to sleep tonight."

I grimaced, realizing that was a priority. I didn't want the poor guy sleeping in the shelter, but I wasn't putting him up here in my house, and I certainly didn't have enough money to go loaning the guy for airfare home or a hotel room. I grabbed my cell phone and he gave me Liz's number, but once again all I got was her message machine. I left my number and sat back to think, not really wanting to wait around for Liz to call back. For all I knew she'd booked the soonest flight down to Baltimore after hearing Rick's message and finding he was checked out from the hospital.

"Is there someone else that might be able to help you out?" I asked him. "Other family? Someone at the funeral home?"

Well, not a client, obviously. I was hoping maybe there was an employee there besides his sister. There had to have been if they were both down here for that seminar.

"We don't have any other family that I know of. I guess I can call Maria at the home. She's the one who handles the administrative end of things."

This time I just handed him my cell phone and listened as he instructed Maria where to find his passport and one of the credit cards he'd left behind, and instructed her to send that and some cash overnight to him."

He turned to me and I stared at him for a moment, then

realized he didn't know where to tell her to send it. I motioned for the phone and gave Maria my address, then hesitated.

"Wait. Tomorrow is Sunday. I'm off, but I wasn't exactly going to wait around all day for the FedEx guy, and this isn't the sort of neighborhood you'd want to leave a package at the door."

"Can I book Rick a room at the Sheraton?" she asked. "I can put your name on the reservation as well. You'd need to sign in and hold the guarantee until the FedEx packet came with his ID and credit card, then he can pay for it."

I barely knew this guy, but I couldn't exactly let him stay in a homeless shelter, and this was a better option than putting him up here. I agreed and gave Maria my name. She said she'd take care of everything, thanked me, then said something that made my blood chill.

"Is Liz with him? Paul and I were worried sick when we came in Friday. I figured maybe they stayed in Baltimore to see the sights, but it's not like one of them to not at least call us and let us know. She must have been going crazy looking for Rick these last few days."

I glanced over at Rick who went pale at the expression on my face.

"No, she's not with him. Liz didn't go back home? You haven't seen her since Monday? Or heard from her?"

"No."

I thanked her and hung up, shooting a panicked look Rick's way.

"I need to take you to the Sheraton anyway to get you checked in. We need to find out what time Liz checked out, and if she left any word where she was going because none of your employees have heard from her since you both left on Monday."

left a note for my mom in case she returned before I did, then I called Tremelay on his cell phone and somehow managed to explain the whole thing, letting him know we not only had a missing person's case, but the missing person was related to a guy who'd at best case been kidnapped, drugged, and robbed, and worst case had someone summon a spirit into him through some weird medical experiment/occult ceremony.

"Not the weirdest thing I've heard in the last four months, Ainsworth," he'd told me before instructing me to wait with Rick outside the hotel as he wanted to question the guy before we went in and asked the front desk manager very nicely about Liz's stay.

Even though the hotel had been in Rick's name, without any ID I was fairly certain they wouldn't give him any information at all. Nor me. But Tremelay just had to wave a badge and hopefully they'd comply. Hopefully, because I hated to think what might happen to Liz while we waited around to jump through legal hoops.

Worst case scenario, we'd need to wait until tomorrow when Rick's ID arrived.

Rick was a nervous wreck and I wasn't much better as we drove to the hotel. He kept bouncing his legs and staring out the window intently, as if he expected to see Liz dragged down a back alley at any moment.

"She'll be okay." I was trying to reassure the both of us. "Maybe she left a message at the funeral home and it didn't go through. Maybe her phone's on the fritz or broken, or she lost the charger. She probably just stayed and is frantically looking for you. We'll probably find her at the hotel in her room, and she'll smack you around for worrying her half to death."

That got a brief chuckle out of him before the tense expression returned to his face. I knew as well as he did that what I'd suggested was improbable at best. Liz would have money, ID, credit cards. If her phone had broken, she would have called from the hotel, and probably gone to the nearest store to pick up a replacement. There was no reason for her to have gone dark for four days—well, no reason beyond things I didn't want to contemplate.

Rick had turned up alive, and pretty much okay. I was holding on to that and hoping for the same for Liz. But hope aside, Baltimore wasn't the safest city, and someone who didn't know their way around could easily wander into the wrong part of town and find themselves beaten and mugged. But not murdered. Yes, there were a whole lot of murders in Baltimore, but I felt certain that if Liz were a Jane Doe, a victim of a drive by or an angry robber, then the police would have been able to identify her by now and have notified...someone.

I felt sick at the thought. If her only relative were Rick and he didn't have his cell phone, who would they have notified? And it was entirely possible with the holiday that a Jane Doe might still be sitting, waiting.

I hoped for Rick's sake that wasn't the case. I prayed with all my might that she'd be found unharmed, and that this would all be some horrible, terrible trip for the pair of them, but that they could go home and get on with their lives.

We pulled into the front parking area of the hotel and managed to find a free spot. Tremelay showed up about ten minutes later, just when I was about ready to jump out and run into the hotel to see if Liz was there. He introduced himself to Rick, and we all stood outside my car in the cold, blocked in by his unmarked sedan, while Rick went over his story again.

"Could she still be in the hotel?" Tremelay asked.

I shrugged. "We called, but they won't verify guests over the phone for security reasons. I'm assuming not since she hasn't been in contact with their employees since Monday, but it's a possibility."

"Do you think her disappearance has anything to do with what you went through?"

Rick twisted his hands together. "I don't know. I don't know who did this to me, what exactly happened, or why. I just assumed I was a random grab, the guy who was in the wrong place at the wrong time. But if they got Liz as well…"

"Dario and I drove her back to the hotel Tuesday night— well actually it was early Wednesday morning," I told the detective. "We made sure she went inside before we left. I don't know for sure, but I'm thinking Rick never came back that night, which means Liz would have vanished sometime after we dropped her off. She was planning on calling you the next morning if Rick didn't show up."

"And she didn't." Tremelay scowled. "Which means either Rick returned, or contacted her before morning, and she vanished later, or she went missing soon after you dropped her off."

"Which is why we wanted the hotel to give us information on when and if she checked out. When they'd seen her last. When she'd last used her pass key to the room."

I crossed my fingers inside my coat pocket and hoped we'd find Liz still in the room, unharmed. But I knew that probably wasn't going to be the case.

Tremelay finished his notes, then motioned for us to follow him into the hotel. Once inside, he flashed his badge, asked for the manager, then introduced Rick and explained the man's lack of identification.

The manager nodded. "I don't recognize you, but I do know the name. Rick and Elizabeth Dimond were registered guests here this week."

"Can you let us know when Miss Dimond checked out?" Tremelay had his nicest smile on, and even I was charmed. Janice was right. The guy was good-looking, and pretty bangable when he smiled liked that. Of course, I was already with the hottest guy in the city, probably the whole world, as far as I was concerned.

I wondered if he liked smart, tall, leggy women? Although given Janice's profession and what a pain she'd been in Tremelay's side, I doubted I'd ever be able to make a match between those two.

The manager hesitated for a moment. "I recognize the name because she didn't check out. Thursday we auto-checked the room out as Wednesday night was the last reservation date, but when housekeeping went in, all the belongings were still there. We contacted both numbers on file, and when we didn't get a response, we charged the room for another day. When housekeeping went in Friday, the belongings were still there, but there was no sign that the beds were slept in or that any towels or washcloths were used, so we left messages that we would be removing the belongings and storing them."

Rick swayed and put out a hand to the wall. I sucked in a breath, thinking the worst. Tremelay didn't bat an eye.

"Did housekeeping make any notes as to whether the beds were slept in when they cleaned Wednesday morning?"

"Let me look at the records, just to check." The manager went behind the front desk at typed away. "It doesn't say. They didn't note anything for Thursday either, but that's not unusual. Sometimes guests don't sleep in their rooms, if you know what I mean. They only noted it for Friday because we'd flagged the room as an overstay."

Tremelay nodded. "Do you have any record of the house-keeping staff that serviced the room Wednesday and Thursday mornings? I'd like to see if they remember."

The man wrote down a few names on a piece of paper. "Sasha and Dee. I can ask them, but they might not remem-ber. They're cleaning dozens of rooms a day."

"I appreciate it." Tremelay pointed to the computer. "Can you see if there were any phone calls made in or out of the room anytime Wednesday through Friday?"

The manager typed again, then shook his head. "No, but that's not unusual. People have cell phones and most of their friends or business associates don't use the room phone."

Tremelay nodded. "Is there a way we can see the items left in the room?"

The manager hesitated. "I hate to release them without consent." He turned to Rick. "When your ID gets here, I can let you have them since you were on the prior reservation."

"Can we just see them?" Tremelay had on his charming smile again. "You can watch to make sure we don't take anything. I just want to check and see if there's anything that might let us know where Elizabeth Dimond might be."

The manager nodded. "Of course. If the poor woman is

missing…I mean, I know it's urgent that you find her if no one's heard from her for days."

He pulled out a pass key and led us to a back room, then went through several old-fashioned, metal keys before inserting one into what looked like a bunch of stacked, locked, wire dog cages and opening the door. There were two carry-on sized suitcases, then a huge black construction sized trash bag full of stuff. Tremelay and Rick went through the suitcases, which held only clothing and some receipts, while I went through the trash bag.

Make up. Toiletries. Phone chargers. A pair of men's shoes and a pair of women's heels. A stack of printed e-mails. I turned to Rick.

"Let me look through her clothes. Unless you know what she packed and what she was probably wearing when she went missing?"

Rick shook his head. "I barely know what I packed. I don't really pay much attention to Liz's clothes or shoes or purses or anything."

I didn't know what she packed in her suitcase, but I did remember what she was wearing Tuesday night. The super cute cowboy boots weren't in the bag or the suitcase, but the short black skirt and silky t-shirt were.

"She changed clothes." I held up the t-shirt. "So Tuesday she went into the room and changed. Her nightclothes are in the suitcase, so I'm going to assume she spent the night in the room Tuesday, got up Wednesday for the seminar, and disappeared sometime after that."

Rick frowned. "How do you figure that?"

"If she was taken from her room, she'd either be wearing the club clothes or her night clothes," Tremelay told the man. "And if she got an emergency call and quickly threw on some clothes, she wouldn't have bothered to fold and pack the pajamas in her suitcase. She'd have tossed them on the bed and they would have been in the trash bag with the toiletries and other things."

"You don't have any information about that seminar, do you?" I asked Rick, thinking if we could confirm Liz's attendance or absence, that might narrow down the timeline a bit.

Rick rattled off the name of another hotel.

"I'll follow up on that," Tremelay said before turning to the manager. "Do you mind if we take these receipts? And these e-mail print outs? I can sign something if you need."

The manager nodded. "I've got a voucher up front you can sign saying you took them. I hope you find her. It's horrible to think that something might have happened to her."

Tremelay went off with the manager to sign for the papers while I went up front with Rick and got him checked into his room.

"Get some sleep," I told the man. "You've got my number and the detective's number. Call either of us if anything comes up. I'll call my friend and meet you tomorrow morning to go see him about this spirit possessing you."

The man chewed on his lip. "I'm so worried about Liz. She's been gone for days, and I didn't even know it. What if she's…?"

"You were gone for days and you're okay." I reached out to squeeze his arm. "Detective Tremelay is a good cop. He'll contact you as soon as he knows anything."

I watched the man take the elevator up to his room, then turned to see Tremelay coming toward me, papers in hand. We walked out to our cars, both of us lost in thought.

"What if she got a text from her brother asking her to meet him somewhere?" I conjectured as I pulled my keys out of my pocket.

"I was thinking that too, but I want to check up on this seminar first." Tremelay frowned. "I would think they would have contacted the funeral home if two of their registered attendees just didn't show. I'll also pull a picture from Elizabeth Dimond's driver's license and get it out there. I'll need to take Rick down to the station for a formal missing person's report as well as the report for the possible kidnapping, assault, and theft of his belongings. I wonder if the Ottobar has cameras?"

I let out a breath and felt my shoulders relax, knowing that Tremelay was on the case.

"Thank you for coming so quickly," I said as I unlocked my car.

A tired smile creased his face. "That's my job, Ainsworth. You take care of the supernatural stuff, and I'll take care of this sort of thing."

I would. And if I hurried back, I could grab a quick hour or two of sleep before I figured out what the heck sort of spell was on this wand fragment and had to attend what would no doubt be a very tense meeting between my boyfriend and my mother.

# CHAPTER 18

"Royal blood," Mom mused as we sat in my basement behind a protection ring, the broken piece of wand safely within a two-by-two null space we'd created.

"The rogue vampires kidnapped a prince?" I shrugged, as I threw the idea out there.

Mom slowly shook her head. "You know, I'm beginning to think you were right about a mage. If Marblehead means a golem, then perhaps Knight D'Angelo was sent to stop the golem, and thus the mage."

"And the rogue vampires are just hired thugs." It made sense. They help protect a mage while she raises a golem, then she rewards them by ousting the *Balaj* and giving them the city. Or paying them with either money, blood donors, and/or magical items.

"I still can't figure out what a golem would have to do with royal blood," Mom said.

"Maybe the mage is the royal? It sounded as if Knight D'Angelo was saying that the Marblehead wasn't the only thing that needed to be stopped, but the 'royal blood' as well."

"Possibly." Mom waved a hand toward the wand. "Well, if we're going to be going up against a mage or a group of mages, let's get an idea of what she and her buddies are capable of."

I stepped forward to dismiss the null space while Mom readied her sword, angling herself to protect me from any magic that might come my way. The null spell dropped and I jumped back behind the protective circle of runes as Mom stepped forward.

Nothing happened. I let out a breath and Mom sheathed her sword.

"See the safeguard magic?" I pointed at the faint aura around the broken wand. "It reminds me of one of our Templar blessings."

"That's because it is." Mom's smile held a sharp edge. "A Templar's blessing broke this wand."

Holy crap, she was right. "The Walk With Me blessing." Now that I had the wand in decent light and could see the magic properly, I realized exactly what D'Angelo had done.

It was a powerful blessing, but not normally powerful enough to destroy a magical item. The amount of energy Knight D'Angelo expended to do this must have left him weak and vulnerable. He'd put everything into destroying that wand—energy and effort he could have otherwise used to escape his captors.

"What did the wand do?" I asked, moving past the protective circle to peer closely at the symbols etched along the sides of the magical item.

Mom moved up beside me. "I'm more of a kill-the-bad-thing Knight, so I'm not really sure. Looks like there's quite a bit of Mercury symbols, though."

Dad wouldn't know either. He was more knowledgeable about magical spells than Mom, but he'd still need to research this and we needed answers fast.

Too bad Reynard wasn't returning my calls. That left me with two choices for fast information, and I wasn't about to risk summoning a Goetic demon again after what happened last time.

"Wait here," I told Mom before running upstairs.

Seconds later I was back, thrusting a spoon in front of the broken piece of wand. "What do you think?"

"Nice." Chuck's voice was clear and loud, as if he were standing right next to us. "Inflicts pain without leaving a mark, and pulls the truth out. Basically whoever was at the business end of this wand would be in agony and telling every secret they ever had from the candy bar they'd stolen in second grade to the married woman they'd had an affair with last year."

Mom scowled at the spoon, clearly not happy with my use of Chuck for information, but too bad. I delivered caramel popcorn to the guy every month, I was entitled to some free consultation as far as I was concerned.

"Like a truth spell?" I asked the mage. "The spellcaster asks a question and the subject is compelled to answer truthfully?"

"More. There's no way to prevaricate or dance around this spell. Whatever information the mage wants, they get. I've mainly seen these used with fae, who are notoriously tricky about answering truthfully. They can't lie, but the bull they spin is just as bad as a lie."

I frowned. "It's powerful then. The wand would have been an expensive magical item to purchase? Because we're not sure if a mage was wielding it or some rogue vampires."

Chuck laughed. "There is no way in seven hells a vampire or any non-practitioner was using that wand. It's not beginner stuff, and anyone who went to the trouble of making one wouldn't sell it for a price that a bunch of rogue vampires could afford. Either this was in the hand of a very powerful mage, or a mage who had one heck of a trust fund."

"Then it's a mage, or mages, with a cadre of hired rogue vampires," Mom mused from behind me.

I felt the spoon vibrate. "Who is with you?" Chuck asked.

"My mother, Knight Mavia Ainsworth." I turned the spoon so Chuck could see my mother.

There was a second of hesitation where the spoon grew hot in my hands before the mage spoke. "Ah, the beautiful woman who threw me across your kitchen earlier today."

I bit back a laugh, but my mother's face hardened, one eyebrow rising. "Do not harm my daughter, mage. I'm rather occupied at the moment, but I can easily spare a few hours to drive to Jessup and put my sword through your skull."

The spoon warmed once more. "Promises, promises," Chuck teased. "Yes, Knight Ainsworth, a mage held this wand. And one more thing, since I'm inspired by your beauty to share all I know—whatever broke this wand caused damage. The caster of the counter spell, which isn't one that is familiar to me, would have been protected but not the others. If vampires were nearby, they would have suffered magical wounds that would take days to heal. The mage, unless he or she were particularly skilled in the healing arts, would bear scars. Burns. Probably on the arms, although possibly on the face and body as well depending on what the mage was wearing."

"Enough of an injury to go to the emergency room?" I asked.

"Maybe. Maybe not. It depends on the mage. One that had good reflexes might have been able to throw up a protective shield in time to avoid the worst of the blast. And some people are more knowledgeable about home medical care and able to tolerate pain better than others."

I looked over to my mother, who was gazing at the broken wand, a thoughtful expression on her face.

Turning the spoon to face me, I spoke. "Thanks, Chuck. I appreciate the help."

He nodded. "Let me know if I can help further. I'm intrigued that there might have been a powerful mage in Baltimore that I was unaware of. Keep me in the loop."

It was more of a command than a request, but I let it slide because right now I needed Chuck more than he needed me. Taking the spoon back upstairs, I shoved it in a cabinet before heading back down to see my mother holding the broken piece of wand.

"When I was out today, I searched the garage where you found this and walked around asking residents and business owners about the incident."

"And?"

"No one heard anything that night, although that's to be expected given the silence spell you found in the garage. The man who found the body early in the morning was upset and worried. He claimed there was an elderly Italian man who had been in the neighborhood quite a bit the last month, and that this man gave him a scary vibe. He referred me to a corner grocery where he said the evening clerk was friendly with the man."

"Fidel," I told her. "He's one of Dario's and not involved. That's his favorite...neighborhood." I didn't want to say hunting grounds because that sounded a little more predatory than I wanted.

"The residents are concerned. They said they've taken to locking their doors at night. One woman had sprinkled holy water around her house, claiming she'd seen a gang dragging a man down the street after midnight Thursday. She said this gang is well known around Franklin Square and that her hairdresser claims they are demons who suck the life out of people."

Franklin Square. Everything seemed to be pointing to that neighborhood.

"I spoke to the hairdresser, and she gave me several contacts among the locals who knew where this 'gang' was hanging out. I went there, but didn't find any vampires at the time. It's clearly not their daytime resting place. Depending on what your boyfriend has to tell us tonight, I'm thinking that's the area I need to search this evening."

"Need a backup sword?" I asked. "And possibly a few vampires on our side?"

"You have other commitments," Mom said. "That man who was kidnapped and possessed by a spirit, and his missing sister. Your boyfriend's struggle to retain his territory. Your job at the coffee shop. I can handle this on my own."

Templar enforcers tended to work alone, unlike back in the days of the Crusades when we were part of an army, fighting for God and His Kingdom. That didn't mean I liked the idea of my mother doing this solo. Not because I thought she was incapable of handling anything she came up against, but because this was *my* city, and *my* responsibility, and anything that went down here as far as supernatural crimes, needed to be under my eye.

"It wouldn't be the first time I've gone a week or two on little to no sleep," I insisted. "It wouldn't be the first time I've juggled three of four competing priorities and responsibilities and managed to get them all done. I'm Baltimore's Templar, Knight Mavia Ainsworth. And if you're hunting rogue vampires and a mage who have killed a Knight, then I need to be involved."

She shot me a quick smile. "It's almost sunset. Send a follow-up text to your vampire boyfriend. Order dinner.

Take that poor dog for a much needed walk. I'll be up in a moment."

I headed upstairs, texted Dario, ordered Chinese, fed Gaia and Fulk. And I felt the surge of Templar magic the moment my mother snapped the splintered wand in her hand.

# CHAPTER 19

"**I** can assure you that the killers are not part of my family," Dario snapped.

We were sitting in my living room with containers of Chinese food spread all over my coffee table. Gaia was curled up in Dario's lap snoozing, and Fulk was sitting at my feet, hoping I would drop some food on the floor for him to snatch up. Dario was the only one not eating, and I didn't blame him given the circumstances.

He'd called me back so soon after sunset that I wasn't sure he'd even fed yet. I knew he probably had a million things to do, but he'd arrived right about the same time as our food delivery and immediately sat down to discuss the situation.

Mom lifted an eyebrow. "No offense, but if the killers were part of your family, I'm pretty sure you'd work to protect them, given the decimation your *Balaj* just suffered this past month and the challenges you're facing in trying to hold your territory."

"I completely understand your skepticism." Dario reached into his back pocket and pulled one of those foldable maps that people used to get at the gas station before everyone had cell phones and GPS in their cars. He moved aside the food containers under Fulk's watchful eye, and spread the map out. "Aria was with me and two of my family last night as we investigated this man's murder. At the time, none of us knew he was a Templar. Where I agree that it could be possible for a member of my family to take advantage of the situation and feed beyond what is safe, *none* of us would be so foolish as to murder a Templar—especially now. And we would certainly not be partnering with a mage when we have Aria willing to assist and protect us."

Mom eyed the map. "Given what I've found out today as well as what Aria has discovered, I'm less inclined to think any of your *Balaj* was involved, but I still need you to be aware of what will happen should that be the case."

"Understood." Dario pointed to sections of the map. "Here are the areas where we've been dealing with incursions from rogue vampires over the last month."

Mom and I both leaned forward, noting the areas outlined in blue, mostly to the north and west of the city.

"And here are the areas where, based on recent information, we believe this group is hunting." He pointed to a section outlined in red. "They're organized and working under leadership, but they are not part of our *Balaj*. From what our allies have gathered, they're a mercenary group out of Virginia—a splinter faction of a *Balaj* in Richmond."

"How large do you think this faction is?" Mom asked.

"We're guessing twenty to thirty."

I sucked in a breath. That was the same size or slightly larger than Dario's family, which meant there was about to be a serious fight for the Baltimore territory—a fight that Dario might not win.

"And they're smack in the middle of your territory," my mother mused.

Dario grimaced. "Yes, they are. We have yet to find out

who hired them, and for what purpose. We also don't know if they have plans to challenge us for the Baltimore territory or not. Normally I'd say no, but we're in a vulnerable position right now, and these mercenaries might decide to make a play for the city once their job is done—that is, if the city isn't part of their pay."

"I checked this area today." Mom pointed to the map. "There's a building that may or may not be one of their bases of operations. There are no magical traps, and no vampires were bedded down at the time I was there, but residents have seen them come and go."

Dario frowned. "This could be their hunting territory and they're using the building for that purpose. If they're using the addict population as a food source, then they'd want to take them somewhere to feed and for the human to shoot up afterward."

"That makes sense. We found that broken vial of heroin in the garage," I added.

"But why be so stealthy?" Mom asked. "If your *Balaj* is stretched so thin, they could feed on whomever they wanted. Instead they're basically paying off their prey with drugs for their silence. If they hadn't killed Knight D'Angelo and left his body on the street with clear signs of vampire predation on him, then we would never have known they were here."

"Clearly Knight D'Angelo knew they were here and was trying to stop them," I said. "I think they meant for his body to point to Dario's family and leave them undiscovered."

Dario nodded. "Whoever is paying them wouldn't want to bring attention to their activities. I'm sure they felt the Order would target my *Balaj*, and kill two birds with one stone. We've been so busy dealing with rogues to the north, that we wouldn't have realized the Templars had targeted us until too late. And after wiping us out, you would have gone home, leaving them to operate without any real chance of detection."

And that's exactly what might have happened if I hadn't fallen over Melbourne Cassidy's body while jogging, if Janice hadn't gotten those morgue videos, if Detective Tremelay hadn't gone and checked for similar crimes, and if the Enforcer the Elders sent hadn't been my mother.

Mom tapped a finger against her lips. "We still don't know what Marblehead or royal blood has to do with any of this, but clearly a mage was involved in Knight D'Angelo's death as well as this group of vampires. My job is clear—I just wish I knew if I was going to be facing a golem or rescuing a prince, or what."

"How about the artifact angle?" I asked. "You said it was possible Knight D'Angelo was here to collect an artifact. Perhaps Marblehead refers to that? And 'royal blood' as well?"

We both looked at Dario.

"You took the only artifact we had," he told me. "I'm not aware of any others in the city."

"Me either." I turned to my mother. "Do you think if you called one of the Elders and put some pressure on them, they'd tell you exactly what the heck Bernard D'Angelo was doing in Baltimore?"

She shook her head. "I wish. You know how they are. They said it's need to know and that I didn't need to know. The Elders and Knight D'Angelo were the only ones aware of his mission. In the meantime, I'm going to nose around this area where the vampire faction may be holed up and see if I can find out what's going on."

I glanced outside at the street. It was dark tonight, not even the light of the moon to help the dim streetlights out. A perfect night to hunt—for both vampires and Templars.

"I can send a few of my family to accompany you," Dario offered.

Mom shook her head. "No. I don't want to spook them. If they smell your vampires, they'll go underground and I'll never find them."

"Or they'll all band together and jump the two of us," I added. Mom was more than capable of taking out a handful of vampires on her own, but this was my city and I was determined to go with her tonight.

Thankfully it wasn't Dario's family we'd be hunting—at least not tonight.

# CHAPTER 20

"I want at least one vampire with you," Dario said. I was pretty sure the unsaid implication was that he wanted to be that vampire.

"Absolutely not," Mom told him. "Aria and I can sense vampires, so none are likely to be sneaking up on us. Plus they'll scent any vampire we're with and be on guard. It would ruin any element of surprise we might have."

"We know our territory better than either of you, and we've been taking out rogues for the last month. They won't know we're there until we're on top of them."

"Templars fight alone," Mom shot back.

"This Templar doesn't," I drawled. "And we can only sense vampires if they're still in the vicinity. Having one of Dario's family along means we can scent track them. It will save us time."

"And that way you don't accidently lop the head off one of our family," Dario added.

That was definitely a risk. I knew most of the *Balaj* but not all of them, and a vampire moving toward me at speed was pretty indistinguishable from another. I'd swing first and ask questions later in that sort of scenario, and I knew my mother would do the same.

Mom scowled. "They need to do as I say. If I want them to back up, or stay outside, or do the hokey-pokey, then it better happen."

Dario shot me a questioning glance and I nodded. Mom was in charge of this. She was a Knight. She was the senior Templar. And she was my mother.

"Opal will go with you," Dario announced. "I'll have Balen and Madeline take two of the younger vampires and work from the outside in herding any vampires toward a central place."

Mom reluctantly nodded. "All right. But the goal is to take one alive to question. If that can't happen, then kill them. I don't want any alive to go back and report on what happened tonight."

Dario pulled out his phone and sent a quick text. "Opal will be here in just a minute."

I bit back a smile, knowing he'd probably had her waiting outside, just in case this happened. He was sending Opal with us instead of going himself because he couldn't be in a position where he was taking orders unquestioningly from my mother. Opal was young, and she trusted me. She'd not do anything that would harm her family, but it would be no issue for her to sit or stay or do the hokey-pokey if my mother told her to.

And unlike most of the older vampires, I was pretty sure Opal knew what the hokey-pokey was.

Once Dario was done texting the others in his family, we hovered over the map. Dario let Mom indicate where she planned on searching, then he texted the areas to each of his teams, asking them all to start three to five miles from us and move inward.

Opal was waiting on my front porch stoop and was oddly silent as she followed us, climbing into the back of my mother's enormous Mercedes sedan.

"Hi Mrs. Ainsworth," she squeaked once we got moving. "It's so nice to meet you. I'm a friend of your daughter's. I helped her with some magical stuff a few months ago, and she's really good. She didn't burn my hair off or kill me or anything."

Mom's eyebrows knitted together. "That's good to hear."

"This is a very nice car." Opal began pushing the buttons to open and close the windows, adjust the climate control, change the speakers and audio settings in the rear of the car. "It's very nice."

I choked back a laugh, feeling like when I was ten and Mom was driving a bunch of my friends to a birthday party at the duckpin bowling alley. They'd all been a bit in awe of her too—and whatever luxury car she'd been driving at the time.

"I'm really good at tracking," Opal babbled on. "You've got no idea how stoked I am that the boss entrusted his girl-friend to me. And you too, Mrs. Ainsworth. I'll take good care of both of you, and I'll find these mercenary candyasses, and I'll kick their butts. And rip their heads off."

"You do the tracking and stay out of the way," Mom told her. "We'll take care of the butt kicking."

Opal nodded enthusiastically. Her hair today was in an amazingly huge afro, her eyeliner winging out from the outer corners of her eyes. In keeping with the stealth nature of our mission, she'd put aside the psychedelic prints and bell-bottom jeans and was dressed in black leggings and a black leather corset that looked as though it had been resurrected from the days of Leonora's reign.

"Yes, ma'am. I'll do whatever you say because you're like the boss' mother-in-law or something. But I need to protect you because if anything happened, the boss would have my head. Especially Aria. It's hard for us when we care about a human. We want to lock them in our house and keep them safe and cherish them for every moment of their short lives."

Mom sent me another worried glance.

"Don't worry. Dario is not locking me in his house like a fragile vase. We've discussed this. I've stayed over at his place once, but normally he comes to my house—a house I'm renting and completely responsible for. Dario's not at all involved with my house or my car or my finances."

I knew that my parents were concerned about a conflict of interest, and not just me having a vampire for a boyfriend. If he started giving me money, paying for my housing or my car, then I'd owe him. And where I was beginning to think that Dario would never take advantage of a situation like that, I knew my parents didn't know him as well and feared I'd fall under his spell, become enthralled with him, let him take my blood and become nothing more than a shell of who I was.

Mom pulled over and parked on a residential side street. The Mercedes stuck out like a diamond in a pile of coal. Every other car on the block was at least ten years old, although they seemed to be well maintained.

We hopped out and my mother didn't even bother to lock the car. I stared at the vehicle, imagining returning to find it gone, or stripped, and my mother perplexed about what had happened. With a quick glance at the two, I placed my hand on the car and said the words to perform a quick illusion. It wasn't much, but it would make the car look less like Cal Ripken Jr. had pulled up into the neighborhood.

"This is the building I checked earlier today," Mom told Opal. "There were no vampires sheltering there, but I got the impression this was a place they often brought their meals for the evening."

Opal nodded, her eyes focusing on something in the distance as she lifted her head to scent the air. With the smooth easy stride of a predator, she circled the building as we followed.

"There are six vampires who frequent here—four as recently as last night. There were also six humans here and all of them frequently used heroin." She turned to my mother with an embarrassed smile. "Addicts make up the majority of our blood donors. They're willing and eager, and it's easy for us to pay them with their drug of choice. Over time, we've come to enjoy the flavor heroin gives their blood. It's like comfort food. Like mac and cheese, or mashed potatoes and gravy."

Mom hid it well, but I could tell the idea revolted her. "Do you think you can track them?"

Opal grinned, her teeth perfectly white including a set of intimidating fangs. "I'll do my best, Mrs. Ainsworth. If they go in different directions, is there one vampire in particular you want to track?"

I was now wondering if we should have had more than one of Dario's family accompany us. It had never crossed my mind that the rogues wouldn't have all gone back to wherever they stayed en masse.

"Can you tell if any of these vampires is more senior than the other? Older, or more powerful?"

Opal tilted her head, her lips pursing as she thought. "They are all very similar in age, and most are equal in power. I'll pick two, and if the paths diverge, I'll make a decision. We can always double back. If we move fast, we'll have more time to search."

"We can run," Mom told her. "Not at your speed, but I know Aria is fit and I'm able to maintain a quick pace for three or four hours."

Opal took off and we jogged after her. I'll admit we got

quite a few odd looks being two women with swords strapped to our backs running after a lanky young woman with an afro dressed all in black, but from the lack of patrol cars descending on us no one must have bothered calling the police.

After an hour of crisscrossing back and forth for endless blocks, we slowed. Opal took out her phone and sent a few texts as she walked. "Balen's group found three vampires to the west that they're herding toward us. None of the others have sensed any vampires in their areas, so they're spreading out a bit."

"Where and when can we expect to intersect with these vampires being sent our way?" Mom asked.

"Half an hour. I'm not exactly sure where they're going to be here, but I'll get us within a few blocks."

Opal led us six blocks down and we stood waiting as she texted, getting updates from Balen about the vampires coming our way.

"They've split up. One is coming right for us down this street here. Balen and his team are taking the other two."

Opal pocketed the phone and we each took a position. When our quarry appeared, he didn't seem to be in any particular hurry. The vampire looked to be in his twenties, although from the static feel of his energy, I knew he was far older. He was dressed in dark pants and a white button-down shirt with a dark jacket. His blond hair was long and straight, tied at the neck in a low ponytail. He tensed when he drew even with us, his head swiveling to look right at Opal.

That's when he bolted.

Opal shot past us, cutting him off at the next street while Mom and I circled around. He was less afraid of us than Opal, and fell into the trap. Mom swung her sword just as he saw the weapon and dropped. With a quick reverse, my mother's sword sliced along his calf, cutting through the dark pants and skin, leaving a line of dark blood.

The vampire shrieked in pain, but jumped up and away from my mother, keeping an eye on the pair of us as he quickly glanced behind for options.

Opal appeared behind me, nodding for us to move forward. I went left and Mom went right, each of us carefully blocking the vampire's escape and slowly edging him down the street. He darted back and forth, trying to get find an opening. Opal dashed around with a blur of speed, making sure he didn't take any of the side streets. As we headed toward a line of huge buildings, she fell in behind us.

We maneuvered the vampire across Route 40 and between two huge buildings that backed up to a ten-foot brick wall. He slowed his frantic attempts at escape, and eyed us, tense and ready to take advantage of any opening.

"You're trespassing," Opal called out. "You know the penalty."

"I've been hired to do a job that requires I be in the city," he countered. "I'm no rogue. I haven't attacked any of the local *Balaj*, nor killed prey. I've only taken what I need and left them unharmed."

"You know protocol," Opal countered. "You never presented yourself to the *Balaj*. You never requested permission to enter the city."

The vampire eyed my mother and me. "And your *Balaj* is so weak that you need to rely on humans with magical weaponry to help?"

"Actually, the *Balaj* is helping *us*," Mom chimed in. "A Templar Knight was murdered, and I'm here to find the killer."

The vampire's eyes widened and he looked around,

judging the height of the wall and clearly evaluating whether he'd have time to scale it before we caught him. "It wasn't me. I had nothing to do with killing any human—Templar or not."

Opal edged around me, putting herself closer to the wall. "Your group killed the Knight—your group of vampires, and the mage."

He caught his breath. "I don't know anything about that. Nothing."

"Well that's a shame." Opal took a few steps forward. "Since you don't know anything, then you're just a trespasser. If you knew anything about those who killed the Knight, then you would have gotten a swift death at the hands of these Templars. If not, then you're ours to kill."

The vampire moved to the wall, springing upward to grip the top edge. Opal leapt up and sideways to head him off, but instead of trying to go over as we'd thought, he launched himself off the wall, straight toward us.

Opal was now on the other side of him, ineffective as backup. I closed in, thinking that if I missed the vampire, Mom would be right behind me to stop him. He moved so fast, he was a blur, but this guy wasn't nearly as old or as powerful as Simon had been, and with a quick pivot and thrust, I cut along the front of his right thigh.

The vampire screamed, stumbling forward. Mom swung her blade in an upward arc, aiming not for the head or torso as she normally would have done, but for his arm.

With a clean slice, his left hand hit the ground. I heard Opal shout "Ewww" as the vampire shrieked once more, clutching his stump at the wrist and limping around the back of one building with far more speed than I would have managed if I'd had my leg cut twice and my hand sliced off.

"Stay here," Mom instructed Opal. "If he comes back around the building, grab him. Aria, you circle around the block and come up from behind. He's hurt and that makes him dangerous, especially if he's cornered. I'm going around the other building, then up along the front."

I nodded and ran to the next cross street, barely hearing Opal's cry of "wait". The static feel of vampire overwhelmed me, so I slowed down as I turned the corner. More. There were more. I tried to sort out Opal from the vampire I was chasing and couldn't tell if there were more than the two or not.

Behind me. I could feel a vampire behind me and I had to assume it was Opal who was obeying Dario's instructions to protect me over my mother's orders because I couldn't freak out about being flanked by a bunch of mercenary vampires.

I moved slowly along the side of the building, hugging the wall. The static feel of vampire hung at the edge of my awareness. He hadn't run far, and he was clearly too injured to move at his usual speed.

A black blob of blood caught my notice. I traced the trail, barely visible in the moonless night, to an overhang at a loading dock. Holding my breath, I waited and watched the shadows, rewarded when I saw a faint movement in the corner next to the loading dock door.

I eased closer, feeling a twinge of sympathy as the vampire hiding in the shadows shivered and drew himself into a ball.

"Come out." My voice didn't sound anywhere near as commanding as my mother's, and in all honesty I wasn't sure I could lop the guy's head off with the amount of conviction she could either. Yes, I'd cut his leg, but executing a hurt vampire cowering in a loading dock bay seemed wrong.

"I didn't do it."

His voice was filled with pain and I felt another twinge of guilt. I really wasn't cut out for this stuff. Killing psychos like

Simon and Dark Iron were one thing. Killing a hurt vampire who was pleading innocence was another.

"Then tell me who did. Tell me where your mercenaries are, and where the mage is."

"I didn't do it." The vampire panted. "I can't tell you where they are. They're my family. They're all I have. And I can't tell you about our client. You have to understand."

I wouldn't give up my family either, but these vampires and mages had killed a Templar, and Knight D'Angelo deserved justice.

The feel of vampire behind me grew stronger and I shifted, glancing along the side of the building. If this was Opal, then she had a few others with her. It was either three or four vampires, or one really strong vampire.

I'd already battled one strong Master vampire, and I really didn't want to have to face another right now.

I took a step forward and eyed the loading dock bay, wondering what the best approach would be. Should I jump up on the opposite end and approach him across the narrow ledge? Or approach from below and risk having to fight an opponent who was basically over my head?

"It will be easier on you if you talk. Just tell me where they are. They killed a Templar Knight." I held back from promising to let him go, although I was leaning that way. Not that the poor guy would bounce back from his injuries. Wounds from a blessed weapon didn't exactly heal like those from a sword bought at a local pawn shop.

"No. I'll die before I give up my family. They're all I have. When I was alone in the world, they took me in. They gave me a home, a purpose."

I hopped up on the loading dock ledge, a bit worried about the feel of vampire behind me. If I was being trapped, it would be better to be up high with the door at my back.

"Aria. Stop."

I froze, because the voice was Dario's. Suddenly the static vampire feel made sense. It wasn't a group coming up behind me, it was a powerful vampire whose energy signature was oh-so familiar to me, but in the adrenaline fueled stress of the moment, I hadn't recognized it.

Irritation and anger flared through me. Did he really think I needed help in taking down an injured vampire? Had Opal called him? Had he been stalking behind us the whole time?

Suddenly Dario was on the ledge between me and the other vampire. "Hold back. I'll deal with him."

"Because you don't think I can manage to defend myself against an injured vampire? Seriously? You've watched me fight before. I killed a master vampire, for crying out loud. I've got a blessed sword, a spelled butter knife, and a crucifix on my keychain. I think I'm good here."

Dario reached out to touch my arm. "I know you are. It's not your skill I doubt, I just…you have enough blood on your hands and this isn't your fight. It's your mother's job to avenge the murdered Templar, and it's mine and my family's job to protect our territory. Hold back and let me do it instead of you."

He was right. I wouldn't have been able to kill this vampire. What the heck was I planning on doing with him? He was clearly not going to answer my questions. I would have been faced with having to put down a cowering, injured vampire, and I was pretty sure that wasn't something I would have been able to do.

Now that Dario was here, his fate was in the hands of the *Balaj* as a trespasser.

"Okay," I said, hoping he made this quick.

Dario turned and took a step forward.

The injured vampire snarled, then froze, a look of

surprise crossing his face. "Adeyemi?" he whispered. "Is that you?"

Dario stopped abruptly. "James?"

I raised my sword, pivoting slightly so I could see around Dario and keep the injured vampire in my sights. "You know him?"

And who the hell was Adeyemi? The name sounded vaguely familiar to me. Had that been Dario's name before he'd come to Baltimore? Before he'd even been turned? Maybe he'd mentioned it to me at one point, and I'd forgotten.

The injured vampire held out his hand. "Adeyemi. I didn't know this was *your* family here in Baltimore. If I had, I would have given you the courtesy of a visit." The vampire's voice faltered. "I would have not come, if I had known this was your *Balaj*. Please forgive me. If I must die tonight, let me at least know there is no ill feeling between us."

Dario waved for me to lower my sword. "James, how did you get involved with this group of mercenaries? The last time I saw you it was in Atlanta nearly two hundred years ago."

The vampire stood and swayed against the loading dock door, clutching his wrist. "Perry was killed along with half our *Balaj* when the city burned during the war. Wilhelm took over."

Dario grimaced. "So you went rogue."

James nodded. "It was that or face death. Wilhelm always hated me. I made my way to Richmond and they were not welcoming, but a subset of their *Balaj* had formed a mercenary group, and offered me protection if I joined. I'd been on my own for thirty years, so I jumped at the chance. Anything to have a family again and not be living in fear of starvation or being discovered."

"What sort of mercenary work does this group do?"

James looked down at his feet. "Security and protection for humans. We guard gangsters from the law, kill for hire, do security detail for some political people, make sure really long magical ceremonies go uninterrupted. That sort of thing."

"And what are you doing in Baltimore."

The vampire sucked in a deep breath, then looked up at Dario. "I don't know the details, really I don't. We're just supposed to make sure everyone stays away from certain assigned areas, catalogue who is coming and going from certain buildings, follow assigned individuals and note where they go and who they talk to. We take shifts, because we've got to feed."

I glanced over at Dario, hoping he could read my unspoken plea because I didn't want to interrupt and risk that James might clam up and refuse to talk further if he remembered a Templar who'd sliced open his leg was standing right near him, sword in hand.

"Who killed the Knight, James?" Dario's voice was soft and kind. "It's put us in a real bind here in Baltimore. I know whoever killed him was trying to pin it on us, but that back-fired because, as you can see, our *Balaj* has a close relation-ship with the Order. They know it wasn't us. We just need to find out who, so the Templars can get justice, and we can get them the heck out of our town."

"I don't know." His voice was anguished. "There are twenty-six of us here in the city on this job. All I heard was that there was a human snooping around, and we were told to take care of the problem. I wasn't involved and no one told me anything about killing a Templar."

I held back, my sword at my side. Dario was doing a far better job of getting information from this guy that any of us had been able to do, and if the vampire ran for it, I was posi-tive Dario could stop him.

"So you don't know what the mages are doing?"

"No. And I'm not sure exactly what building they're in or street they're on. My assignments so far have been to watch a place in the Inner Harbor, and another on Fulton and let Martin know if the police or other vampires are nosing around."

Dario's eyes met mine and I knew we were both thinking the same thing.

"We'll let you go if you find out where the mages are and where they're doing whatever they're doing, and tell me," I told James.

His gaze darted from Dario to me and back again. "You'll slaughter them. I don't care about the mages, but Martin and the others…they're a bunch of niffynaffy rufflers, but they're all I've got. Without them I'll be a rogue again, I'll be wandering without a family."

Dario took a step forward. "I've never known you to be anything but loyal and honorable, James. You were kind to my family and me when no one else was, when we had nowhere to turn. If you find out where the mages are and what they're doing, if you help us, then I'll offer you a place in our *Balaj*."

James nodded eagerly. "I'll do it. Tomorrow at sunset, I'll have the information for you. I won't be able to deliver it myself, but I'll send a human I trust with it. Just tell me where."

I gave the man my address. With a hopeful smile at Dario, and a wary glance my way, he hopped off the loading dock ledge, stumbling as he landed. I watched as he limped off into the shadows the way I'd come.

"You do realize my mother is going to kill me for letting him go?" I told Dario once James was out of sight.

"He didn't know anything. This is a better solution than

killing him and trying to hunt down another mercenary who might or might not have the same lack of knowledge."

Dario jumped down with far more grace than poor James had, then held out a hand for me. I landed beside him, not needing the assistance, but taking his hand anyway because I appreciated the gesture.

I appreciated the other gesture as well—him intervening so I wouldn't have to make a decision on whether or not to kill an injured vampire who was huddled in pain against a loading dock door.

"Did you mean it about letting James into your *Balaj*?" I didn't think Dario would lie about something like that, but I was surprised. I knew vampires occasionally allowed non-family into their groups, but I also knew Dario was very selective and didn't trust easily when it came to vampires or humans.

"Absolutely. If I had known what had happened with Perry in Atlanta, I would have intervened and asked to have him brought in. We owe them. We owe him. It's the least I can do."

We headed around the other side of the building where we met Mom and Opal. I confessed what had happened, and after a somewhat heated discussion with Dario about whether he could trust James not to rat us out and send a bunch of vampires or human hitmen to my door, Mom calmed down.

The walk back to the car was a bit frosty. Opal decided she'd make her own way back home, and Mom and I drove in silence. I wasn't sure if I was happy or not to see Dario's SUV parked outside my house as we pulled up.

"So he's spending the night?" Mom's tone of voice dripped with displeasure.

"He often spends the night, Mom. And he's especially going to spend the night after you put all sorts of worries in his head about vampires attacking us. I wouldn't be surprised if he decided to shelter in my basement during the day just to be close by."

It was my house and I wanted him there. If Mom didn't like it, she could go find a hotel room.

Dario was inside, a pot of coffee on, Gaia curling around his legs. Mom announced she was going to bed and headed upstairs to where I'd made a makeshift sleeping area in one of the spare rooms using an air mattress and some extra sheets and blankets. Dario and I drank coffee and sat at the kitchen table until we heard the bedroom door close, then went up ourselves.

I was exhausted and I knew tomorrow was going to be hectic, but more than sleep, I wanted to talk.

"Tell me about the Atlanta *Balaj*, about James and this Perry and what happened when you and your family were there."

He sighed and pulled me close. "A handful of our *Balaj* had come from France, but a good number of us were from Saint Dominigue. It was difficult to hunt as a dark-skinned black man during a time of slavery. We were very limited in who we could safely feed from, and we were constantly under scrutiny. If a human caught us hunting, we were presumed to be escaped slaves. It put us in a bind where we either needed to kill the human, or flee the area to stay safe." Dario shook his head. "The hunter became the hunted. We were constantly on the move, always near starvation. I met James when we were rogues outside of Atlanta, and rather than run us off with threats, he took us to the Master. We were allowed to remain as guests for two weeks. It gave us time to regain our strength."

I curled up against him and listened to him continue to talk about what happened two hundred years ago. I listened to him tell me about James, about Atlanta during those two weeks. I listened to him talk about the treacherous journey they'd made north from the city, the time their daytime resting place had nearly been found out by a mob looking for escaped slaves. I listened to him tell me of how it felt to be hungry, to be desperate.

I listened, because tonight, I was his sanctuary.

"How did yesterday go?" Tremelay smeared a thick coating of mustard on his egg, cheese, and ham croissant.

I snort-laughed. "Oh, peachy. My mother's in town because the dead guy with the vampire bites was a Templar. I spent the entirety of yesterday and last night working with her and Dario trying to figure out who killed him and why, and doing reconnaissance. The few hours I got to curl up with my man were completely cock-blocked because my mother was sleeping in the bedroom right next to mine and I felt a little weird doing the nasty with her listening in."

"So no sex?" Tremelay grinned. "One night out of…what? A month? One night out of a month you don't get any and you're complaining. Otherwise it sounds like a normal day for a Templar, or a police detective, in the glorious city of Baltimore."

"To think I was complaining about being bored. I've got a group of vampires led by a mage who murdered a Knight, *and* I've got a kidnapping/robbery that might or might not involve possession by a ghost coupled with a missing person."

"No rest, or sex evidently, for you." Tremelay grinned. "At least that vampire killing got yanked right out from under me once someone higher up got word of the tattoo on his wrist. Can't say I'm sad about one less case on our murder board. I spent the night working on that blood-for-money murder, and following up with another detective on the missing person's case for Liz Dimond."

"That's not your case?" I asked, surprised.

"Homicide, Ainsworth. Baltimore is a big city and I only do homicide. But lately it seems my job has changed and now I'm in charge of 'All The Weird Shit'."

"Who recognized Knight D'Angelo's tattoo and called the Order?" I asked, curious about who in the city police department would recognize a Templar tattoo, or have contact information for one of the Elders.

Tremelay shrugged. "I've got no idea. All I know is that by noon, it was off the board and there was a note in the system that said it was being investigated outside the department. I assumed the dead guy was with a federal agency or active military until you told me."

I thought for a second while I ate my bagel. We'd made progress last night, and I felt like we were narrowing in on the vampires if not the mysterious mage who they were working for. It worried me not knowing who she was, how powerful she was, if she was working alone or with a group of mages, or what she wanted to achieve in Baltimore with a group of vampire flunkies.

"So what do you have on Rick?" I asked, deciding to move on to the other issue.

"Hotel records showed that the room was accessed by a key card at one thirty Wednesday morning."

I nodded. "That's about when we dropped Liz off."

"After that, the only access is through the housekeeping keys. I reviewed security footage—and let me tell you that made for a very long night last night. The hotel security footage shows someone matching Liz's description leaving the hotel at seven the next morning, and I don't see her returning."

"She was probably heading to that seminar," I mused.

"A seminar that didn't exist," Tremelay informed me.

I stared at him. "Seriously? That means someone went to a lot of trouble to set that up and get Rick and Liz to Baltimore."

"That also means this wasn't random, or an attack of opportunity. Whoever grabbed Rick, and I'm assuming Liz, wanted *them* for some reason—them specifically."

I thought back to Liz, leaving the hotel at seven o'clock and either being waylaid in route to the seminar, or possibly at the seminar location itself.

"Did the place where the seminar was supposed to be have security footage? Did anyone see Liz enter or exit?" I asked.

Tremelay shook his head. "No footage that I've been able to find, although we're checking neighboring buildings. No one saw her enter or exit that they remember. The doorman at the Marriott remembered Liz and said he'd offered to call her a taxi, but she said she'd called for an Uber. I'm hoping to have the information on who drove her and where she was dropped off by this afternoon."

The detective had been just as busy last night as I had—and probably had gotten even less sleep.

"But why wouldn't she have called you if Rick hadn't been back by morning?" I mused. "Why the heck did she head to a seminar with her brother missing and not call the police?"

"There are no records of a missing person's report for Rick Dimond," Tremelay said. "I didn't see any sign of him in the hotel security footage. I reviewed the Ottobar security cameras outside the back fire door exit and the one in the front, and clearly saw you and your vampire boyfriend leaving with a woman I assume to be Liz. There's also some footage of Rick staggering down the street with a woman. At least I think it's him. It's kind of grainy and he's not really in frame, so it's hard to tell. It was at the eleven twelve mark."

"That's about when I saw him making out with some blonde woman by the bathrooms," I told Tremelay. "Liz said she couldn't find him soon after that, and none of us saw him again. We figured he'd left with the blonde and would show up back at the hotel early in the morning."

"Well he didn't take his car. We found it down the street from the club, and it looks like it's been there since Tuesday night from the amount of tickets it's got and the boot attached to one tire."

"So the blonde drove." Which was probably a good thing given how out of it Rick had seemed.

"I'm hoping you can come down to the station sometime today and work with a sketch artist given that you're the only one who got a good look at the woman Rick left with."

I grimaced, thinking about how my day was getting overwhelmed with things I needed to do. Good thing I didn't have to be at the coffee shop until tomorrow, but I hardly expected to spend my weekend off doing everything but relaxing.

"Okay. I'm picking up Rick in an hour or so and taking him to see Russell. Hopefully we can get some information from whatever spirit is possessing him before we banish the thing."

Tremelay nodded, nonplussed by the idea of getting

investigative information from the dead via a necromancer. How far he'd come from months ago when he thought I was crazy with my talk of magical rituals and demons.

"Oh, and one more thing. Whoever has Liz is definitely the same person or people who grabbed Rick."

I shrugged. "Well, we kinda figured that. It would be a weird coincidence for a guy to go missing for days, and his sister to also go missing not twenty-four hours later."

"We're not just assuming anymore. I ran by Walmart last night and picked up a new phone for Rick, then went back by the hotel. We spent a few hours on the phone with Verizon, getting it onto his account and getting all his data downloaded. It seems he, or someone with his phone and access to his thumbprint, sent Liz a text message at six ten Wednesday morning asking her to meet him and bring a clean shirt."

I could imagine how irritated she would have been by that. Her brother stays out all night with some pickup from a club, and the morning of their seminar wants her to drop off a change of clothes.

"Did she reply?" I asked

Tremelay grimaced. "It was a bit snappy, but she agreed. I went to the address in the text message on my way here and it's a house up in Woodberry. The woman who lives there is off on vacation according to the neighbors. Homeowner's name is Sarah Brunner. They said a few people have come and gone—the cleaning service, the lawn maintenance people, and a woman they figured was a relative bringing in the mail and watering the plants. Nice nosy neighbors, just the sort we cops like."

"Please tell me the woman bringing in the mail was a younger, attractive, blonde?"

"Yes, but so was one of the cleaning service. The lawn maintenance people were all 'Mexican guys' according to the neighbors."

I rolled my eyes at that. "So what's next?"

"Sleep, because I haven't done much of that in the last few days. We're trying to see if we can get the towers the text message came from and try to pin down a general location to search. We're also going to see if we've got enough for a warrant to search Sarah Brunner's house and dust for prints —if we can't get a hold of her and get her permission to have a friend or someone let us in that is. We're hoping she can also tell us the lawn and housekeeping service she uses, along with if she was in fact having someone come in to water the plants. We'll track down from those angles and see what we can get. The sketch of the woman Rick was last seen with will help as well. I'll run the sketch by vice and see if any of them recognize her. She may have been a prostitute hired to slip Rick something and entice him away from the club to the kidnappers, or whatever they are."

"What do you think our chances are of finding Liz alive?"

"Normally I'd say not good with her missing four days, but Rick came out of this alive. If it's the same people, there's a good chance they'll do to her whatever freaky thing they did to him and let her go."

"I get the feeling they let Rick go because whatever it is they wanted to do, it didn't work. Or it only partially worked. I'm worried they might succeed with Liz."

"Let's hope they're just a bunch of nutjobs, and not actual mages or murderers who think Liz is a replacement for Rick." Tremelay slugged down his coffee. "And after I do all that, I still need to track down who drained Melbourne Cassidy of blood and left his body out on the street. *And* investigate dozens of attacks and murders that might or might not be done by vampires."

I smiled up at him as he stood. "Go get some sleep. I'll text you if I find anything out, and let you know what Russell says."

"Just make sure you let me know before you talk to that reporter." He scowled, but there was a hint of a smile around his mouth as he waved a finger at me.

I held up my hands. "Hey, Janice has had some good information for us in the past. Sharing a little is well worth access to that information. Besides, she's always held back on stories if it's really important. She's good people, Tremelay."

"I just don't want to find out about something by reading it in the paper."

"I promise I'll give you at least a few hours head start."

I waved at him and watched him leave, then I sat and finished my coffee and bagel until it was time to drive over to the hotel to pick up Rick.

He met me down in the lobby and I noticed that in addition to a new cell phone compliments of the Baltimore Police Department, Rick had new clothing.

"My overnight package got here." He did a little pirouette with arms outstretched. "Maria grabbed the spare set of clothes I keep at the funeral home and sent them along with my passport, cash, and credit card."

"I'm sure it's a relief not to be wearing the only clothes you've had for the last five days."

"Now that I have ID I was able to get our suitcases out of the hotel lockup. Luckily the hotel had shaving stuff and a toothbrush as well as their complimentary toiletries."

These are the things you never really think about. What would happen if suddenly you found yourself in a city with nothing but the clothing on your back?

"How are you feeling?" I asked. "I mean, do you still feel like there's someone else inside you, or with a good night's sleep and a shower has that feeling passed?"

Rick's mouth thinned into a grim line. "Oh, I always feel it. Or him. Or whatever. It's like a splinter that you just can't manage to get out no matter how much you dig. I try to ignore it, but it's there eating away at my concentration. I don't know if I'd eventually get used to it, or if it would drive me crazy, but I'm worried it will be the latter."

I hoped Russell could help. The man had really impressed me with his ability, but I knew every mage had their limits.

It wasn't a long drive to Russell's house, but Rick remained silent, gazing out the window at the buildings we passed. It reminded me of when Dario and I drove Liz back to the hotel and she'd worried the whole way about Rick. I shouldn't have brushed off her concerns. I should have taken her word for it that Rick wouldn't have gotten drunk and run off to have sex with a woman he'd just met, stranding his sister and not even letting her know where he was going. Maybe if I'd taken her to Tremelay that night, Rick wouldn't have been jabbed with needles and been possessed by a spirit. Maybe Liz wouldn't have been taken and possibly be suffering the same fate—or worse.

Had they killed her? Sacrificed her like the Fiore Noir mages had done so they could bring some powerful spirit or demon fully across the veil? Was Rick spared because of a fault in their ritual, or because there was something not quite right about his physiology? I glanced over at the man, and knew that as concerned as I was, he worried even more. If this were Athena, or Roman, I'd be frantic. I had no idea how the man was managing to hold himself together.

Although panic did no one any good. Rick was strong. He'd prevailed against whatever these people had done to him, and was managing to keep his sanity with whatever spirit was possessing him. He was remaining calm and doing all he could to cooperate and help get his sister back safe and sound.

I parked outside of Russell's rowhouse, waving to the

neighbor woman rocking on her tiny front porch as Rick and I climbed the stairs. Russell ushered us in and told us to take a seat, informing the pair of us that he would bring tea before vanishing into the kitchen.

"It's not what I expected," Rick whispered. "I thought he'd be some dude with eyeliner and a head scarf, and his place would be full of incense with silk curtains everywhere."

"He's got a Ouija board. And tarot cards. And bones. And I think he's got a crystal ball somewhere." I sat on the beige sofa that I was pretty sure Russell had gotten at Ikea and motioned for Rick to do the same. "There are a lot of different levels when it comes to magic that specializes in spirits, the dead, and the world beyond the veil. There are those who use spirits to divine the future and reveal the past, and those who can actually command those spirits and the bodies that used to house them. A high-level necromancer can raise the dead. A very high-level necromancer can manipulate undead such as wraiths and vampires. There are even legends of necromancers in history who walked among an enemy's army and ripped the souls from their bodies, killing them with a wave of their hand."

Rick shivered and I suddenly regretted my little lecture. I'd been brought up with a Templar Librarian as a father, and was just as fascinated with lore and the supernatural as he was. Rick was less fascinated, and more terrified. He looked as if he were about ready to pass out on Russell's Ikea couch.

"Russell is a good guy," I assured him, even though there was a time in the not-so-distant past when I wasn't sure whether Russell was a good guy or not. "He'll do everything he can to help you. I wouldn't have brought you here if I didn't think he could, or if there was any chance at all that he'd hurt you."

Rick leaned his head back against the couch cushions and took a few deep breaths. "If you'd told me a week ago that I'd be possessed by a spirit or a demon or something and visiting an occult practitioner to perform some sort of exorcism, I would have laughed my head off. I don't believe in this stuff—well, I didn't believe in this stuff. I was the pragmatic guy, the one who didn't believe in luck or God or anything. I didn't play the lottery. I didn't go to church. I'd never had my fortune told at a county fair or flipped a coin to make a decision. Logic. I was all about logic and what I could see before my very own eyes. But here I am."

I reached out and patted his arm. "I'm all about logic and what I can see before my very own eyes as well, but the things I've seen in my lifetime are very different than what you've seen. There's more to this world than what you've experienced, Rick. Just because you've never traveled to Japan doesn't mean it doesn't exist. Likewise, there are things of legend that truly walk this earth."

He closed his eyes and took a few more deep breaths. I wasn't helping. I needed to just shut up and let him live in his own world, like so many humans did. I was trying to help him make sense of all this, but instead all I was doing was scaring the guy. Templars and demons and ghosts and vampires and necromancers...it was all too much and too soon for him. Actually, it might always be too soon for Rick. I got the impression that he was one of those people who truly wanted to turn a blind eye to the supernatural and live their life unaware.

I'd lived my whole life with this as my reality, but Rick hadn't. Tremelay had been able to accept all this and work it into his life. So had Janice. Rick...I got the feeling he wouldn't. After all this was over, he'd probably push it all to the back of his mind and maybe even deny it had ever happened. He'd probably treat it all as if it had been a bad dream.

Zac was struggling with all of this. It's no surprise that

Rick would as well. And I couldn't fault him for that. Realizing everything you'd thought was just a fantasy, was only metaphorical mythology, was actually real? That was a reality many people just didn't want to acknowledge.

Russell walked in with a plastic tray holding three glasses of iced tea, looking like a middle-aged, blue-collar man serving beverages to his church group. Rick took the tea and drank, his eyes bugging out as he swallowed. I almost laughed.

"Russell likes his tea sweet," I commented.

"There's no other way to drink tea," the necromancer announced, picking up his own glass and motioning for us to follow him. "Let's go into the dining room. That's where I have everything set up."

Rick eyed me nervously but followed. The dining room was more of what Rick had imagined when I'd told him we were going to consult a spirit-worker. There weren't colorful scarves hanging everywhere, but the faint odor of sage and myrrh hung in the air. The oak farmhouse table with captain's-style chairs around it held the tarot cards, bones, Ouija board, and a whole host of other occult paraphernalia.

We took chairs across from Russell, who was not wearing robes or a head-scarf, but some rather worn jeans and a t-shirt with a picture of a black bear and two cubs climbing a tree. As he sat, the necromancer took a swig from his ultra-sweetened tea and ran a hand over his thinning hair.

"Now, Mr. Dimond, what can you tell me about the spirit that possesses you?"

Rick's eyes grew huge. "You believe me?"

Russell waved the hand that wasn't holding his iced tea. "I sense its presence, but you've managed to push the spirit into the far reaches of your physical form. That either means that you're a very strong individual psychically, or that the spirit is very weak, or that he, or she, was not fully brought across the veil. You'll excuse me if I believe the latter is the reason. I'm open to considering one of the other options though. I'll know more once we begin and I make contact, but I'd like to hear your take on things beforehand."

Rick swallowed a few times and looked at his hands wrapped around the glass of tea. He told Russell the story he'd told me, from coming to Baltimore for a seminar, to his hazy recollections of medical experimentation, to finding himself on the streets, confused and feeling as if his body was being wrested out of his control. He went on to tell Russell of his experience in the hospital, his coming to see me, and the disappearance of his sister.

Russell listened intently, his hands steepled before him, nodding occasionally. At the end of Rick's story he waited a few moments before speaking.

"I believe I can help you, but it will involve you placing your trust in me. In order to remove the spirit from your body, I'll need you to allow it to come forth, which means giving up control. Is this something you're willing to do?"

Rick grimaced. "What's my choice?"

"You can live the rest of your life with a spirit who is fighting to fully cross the veil and take your physical form for his own. There are times during the year when the veil between the worlds is thin, and those are the times the spirit will fight hard to gain control. He may succeed. And even if he doesn't, you may go insane fighting him."

Rick eyed his tea. "What are the risks in relinquishing control and letting you attempt to send the spirit back?"

"I need to widen the gap in the veil to send the spirit through. If he is especially powerful, he may overcome me and be able to fully slip through the veil and into this world. If that happens, you might not be able to fight him off and regain control of your physical form. You could spend the rest of your life under the control of this spirit."

Rick breathed deeply and exhaled. "Can you tell me what that would be like? Would it be like the biblical stories of hell? Tortured and confined?"

"Confined surely, but not tortured. It would be as if you were watching a movie of your life, but unable to control what you were doing or what choices you made. When your body dies, both you and the spirit would be released to whatever afterlife you were destined to."

I saw a muscle twitch in Rick's jaw. "Would the choices the spirit made reflect on me as far as where I went in my afterlife? I've never believed in an afterlife before, but I suddenly find myself re-evaluating my beliefs and I want to make sure if the worst happens I won't be condemned to an eternity in hell because some asshole of a spirit decides to go do a bunch of horrific shit in my body."

Russell eyed Rick with an odd intensity. "I'm not a priest, nor am I privy to the criteria for judgement, but I believe that you would not be held accountable for actions you had no control over. I'm sure Aria would know better than I would about that sort of thing."

My eyebrows shot up. I wasn't a priest, I was a weapon of God. "I'm not in a position to comment authoritatively on that sort of thing. I'm a Templar. Redemption and forgiveness and judgement are between you and God, but a priest or reverend may be able to guide you in that."

Rick looked at the table, tracing a line of grain with a fingernail as he thought. "Okay. I'll risk it. I don't want to be a powerless observer of my own life. I'd rather take the chance of eternal damnation and at least know I made an effort to be a master of my own destiny."

"Then we'll proceed." Russell put a little metal pot on the table and placed a chunk of resin in it along with a piece of charcoal, then set it alight. Instantly the room was filled with the scent of pine and eucalyptus. The necromancer placed his hands on the table and began to chant in a language that wasn't familiar to me, and I knew six languages in addition to smatterings of twelve others typically used in magical dealings. The smoke from the resin coalesced and spiraled upward in a circling line of white. The room darkened, backlit with a dim golden-red glow.

Suddenly Rick's eyes widened, his head tilting to the side.

"My name is Edward Kelley and I have knowledge and gifts to present to the world." Rick's voice took on a higher-pitched and a British accent.

My mind raced through all the texts I'd read. My father's teachings had mainly been with supernatural creatures and their habitats and behaviors, but at an early age I'd been intrigued with magic and had studied not just the Templar blessings and banishments, but illusions, charms, and hexes. And my short time with Haul Du had brought in increased knowledge of demonology and summoning,

I recognized the name Edward Kelley, but couldn't quite place it.

"If you allow me in, I will grant you the knowledge of alchemy as well as a connection with the divine and inter-pretation of the Enochian language."

I rolled my eyes and Russell shook his head.

"Why have you crossed the veil and attempted to take possession of this body?" Russell asked.

The spirit laughed. "Because the opportunity presented itself. A doorway opened, a pathway to this vessel was made clear. Many spirits hovered near, sensing the doorway was about to open, but I was the fortunate one who made it through first."

Russell frowned. "Spirit workers call forth a specific being, and normally they channel it through their own bodies. I don't understand this, unless the mages knew that this man had sympathetic energies aligned in such a way that would make him an appropriate vessel. But why go to all that trouble and not limit which spirit could use the doorway?"

I shrugged. "Maybe they screwed up?"

"If so, then they're not skilled in the magics of the spirit world," Russell scoffed. "That's basic stuff."

Maybe they weren't. Chuck had been a member of Fiore Noir, but was more than just a death mage. Many higher-level mages crossed disciplines, and magical disciplines often had overlap. The Goetic mages of Haul Du had some rituals in common with necromancers, and blood magic had cross-over with death magic. Perhaps these mages were generalists, and didn't have the skill to draw only their intended spirit through the veil.

If so, then what they were doing was even more dangerous than I'd originally thought. Anyone could come through and possess a body, and maybe not just human spirits either. The thought of a high-level demon given human form and unfettered access to this world made me shiver.

"Bring me across and I will show you the future and the past. I speak with the angels, and can deliver word of the divine. Just let me complete my journey and take this body."

I turned to Russell, my eyebrows raised.

"Edward Kelley, you have no claim to this body. Your possession is only temporary."

The spirit laughed. "I've been summoned before to give my wisdom and direction to rank practitioners. I've been allowed to talk through a medium, a channel. This is different. A door opened, and this body was prepared to receive a spirit as a host. Permanently. For as long as this body shall live."

"Then why are you and Rick both in this body?" I asked.

"Why is this host able to overcome your possession and retain autonomy?"

The spirit scowled. "They didn't kill him first. If his spirit had left his form, then I would have had full access to the body."

A chill swept through me at his words. Did these mages realize their mistake? Would they kill Liz and try again with her? Why the Dimonds? And who were they trying to resurrect if not this guy who was residing in Rick's body?

Suddenly I remembered who Edward Kelley was. "Weren't you the sixteenth century occultist who proclaimed that swinging and sharing wives was some sort of divine proclamation? And didn't you end up in jail because you couldn't or wouldn't reveal your divine mysteries to your patron, the Pope?"

Rick, aka Edward Kelley, squirmed. "He was not suitable to receive divine proclamations."

"The *Pope* was not suitable to receive divine proclamations?" I scoffed. "You're a hack. How you managed to squeeze through the veil and into this physical form is beyond me."

Kelley shifted angrily in his chair. "There is a gap, and a beam of light. Many of us were drawn to it, knowing it was an opportunity to cross the veil and live life anew. If those stupid mages hadn't screwed it up, I would have taken this body. They weren't specific enough in their ritual and the physical form was available to whoever could cross the veil and assume ownership. I was first. I pushed my way to the forefront, but those fools didn't widen the gap sufficiently. I have gifts to give this world. I can grant you knowledge and abilities, if only you allow me to fully cross the veil."

I struggled to keep from scoffing. This guy was an idiot. And from what I'd learned in my lessons, he was far from skilled. Snake oil. Charlatan. The dude had nothing but smoke and mirrors to share.

"Can you send him back across the veil?" I asked Russell. "Can you get him to leave Rick's body and never return?"

"No!" Kelley howled.

Russell nodded. "Thankfully, I can. If he had been fully across the veil, then I wouldn't have been able to send him back, or to even oust him from Rick's body."

The necromancer began pulling crystals from a box, setting amethyst, hematite, tourmaline, and citrine on the table. Kelley shoved back his chair, trying to flee the room, but I was ready for him. Grabbing him from behind, I kicked his legs out in front of him one at a time and used my weight to force him back down into the chair.

Russell rearranged the crystals removing a few more hematite stones and placing them in a line.

"Can you hurry a little?" I grunted as Kelley thrashed around and landed a sharp elbow in my stomach.

The necromancer seemed satisfied with the crystals because he took a sage bundle from the table and lit it on the charcoal, waving the smoke toward Kelley with a feather as the smudge stick burned.

Kelley fought harder and we both fell to the floor, the chair wedged between us. My shoulder hit hard, the arm going slightly numb. Kelley took advantage and squirmed free, so I jumped on top of him, trying to pin him to the floor.

Russell chanted something that sounded like "Gaaan swortie moo." I took another elbow to the stomach and strongly considered bashing Kelley's head against the floor. The only thing stopping me was that it was actually Rick's head and the poor guy had been through enough without my having to beat the snot out of him while he was being possessed by a psycho spirit.

"Moo. Moo. Mooooo."

I laughed, because the oddity of cow noises being used to banish a possessing spirit back across the veil was pretty darned funny. Either the cow noises, or the heavy odor of sage was working because Kelley stilled, his protests growing fainter. The body beneath me convulsed and I got up, positioning myself near the door just in case Kelley was faking it.

"What…what happened?" Rick moaned, reaching a hand to his forehead. "Why am I on the floor? And what is that smell? Is that pot? Is someone smoking pot?"

"Sage." Russell put the smudge stick in the black metal pot and clamped a lid over top of it, waving his hands around to dispel the smoke. "The spirit of Edward Kelley is no longer in you and has been returned to the other side of the veil."

Rick staggered to his feet, righting the chair as I rubbed where he, or rather Kelley, had elbowed me.

"I feel… I don't feel his presence any longer, but I still don't feel right."

I shot Russell a warning glance. "I'm sure you'll feel better soon. You must be exhausted from this whole thing. Why don't I drive you back to the hotel, and I'll check in on you later?"

Rick nodded, rubbing his forehead again. "I…I'll wait in the car for you."

He wasn't walking steady, so I helped him out, got him settled, then came back in to grab my purse and have a quick word with Russell.

"He's going to have dreams," the necromancer immediately informed me. "That Edward Kelley was in far deeper than any possession I've ever seen before. There will be an imprint, and that will never go away."

"He won't go crazy though, will he?" I glanced out the door to where Rick sat in my car.

Russell lifted his hands. "I don't know. His friends and family will think he's different, changed."

The man had been kidnapped, drugged, subjected to medical procedures, and possessed. Even without the possession, I didn't think anyone could go through that and still be the same.

"Is there anything I can do to help him?" I asked.

Russell looked at me, his expression grim. "Pray."

# CHAPTER 22

"Can I have a copy of that?"

After a few revisions, the police sketch artist had a rendition that I felt looked somewhat like the blonde woman I'd seen Rick with at the Ottobar. Of course, I'd been pretty tipsy, it had been dark in the club, and I'd only caught a few glimpses of her when she wasn't plastered to Rick dancing, or trying to swallow his tongue by the bathrooms.

"Sure." Tremelay nodded to the sketch artist who went off to make copies. "I'm going to send one over to Janice."

I bit back a smile. "Actually cooperating with the press for once? Goodness, is hell freezing over? Pigs swooping down Lombard Street with the pigeons?"

He ignored my teasing comment. "We're going to put out that this woman is a possible witness, just to encourage people to come forward."

It made sense. All we really knew right now was that she was probably the last person to have been with Rick before his kidnapping. Whether she was involved or not was specu-lation—although I couldn't believe the woman would be innocent in all this. Rick wasn't a heavy drinker. I was positive someone had drugged him, and this blonde was top of my suspect list. At best, she'd been paid to drug Rick and lure him out. At worst, she was actually in league with these people.

"We got the homeowner's permission to search that house in Woodberry," Tremelay went on, handing me the copy of the sketch and walking me out of the station. "We're meeting her sister in a few hours to let us in. Seems that the lawn service was legit, but she didn't have cleaners nor someone coming to water the plants, and she's upset that someone may have used her house for criminal activity. Not concerned enough to fly back from St. Thomas, but concerned."

"I'm heading over to the hospital to see Kyra now that I've got Rick's permission and see if there's anything medically from his hospital stay that might yield some clues," I told him. "I'll call you if I find anything out."

"Likewise." Tremelay touched his forehead in a salute and headed toward his car as I went the opposite direction to where I'd parked.

It didn't take long to drive to the hospital, park, and make my way up the elevator to the floor where Kyra said she was making rounds today. After asking a few people for directions, I found her coming out of a patient's room, discussing something with one of the nurses.

I held back until she was done, then waved to get her attention. With a smile, she motioned me into a sitting area, closing the door behind her.

"I'm hoping you've got more on Rick Dimond," I commented. "Your dad is making some progress on finding who may have kidnapped the man, but if there's something in his medical records that can give us a hint of why these people targeted him and his sister, it would help.

"There's really not much beyond what I already told you."

Kyra sat down and pulled up the files on her tablet. "He was disoriented in the emergency room, so we took vitals and drew blood. First thought was a potential overdose or possible psychiatric case. He freaked about the needles, which is unusual for addicts, but could have been due to drugs. Pupils were normal and responsive. Blood pressure and pulse was a little high but nothing alarming. There was some bruising on his chest, wrists, and legs. Needle marks on the inside of both arms. Patient denied drug use or prior psychiatric history. Patient claims he was kidnapped and subjected to medical experimentation by people in surgical masks. Patient says they put a ghost inside him and that he's currently possessed by this ghost."

I grimaced, surprised that Kyra had taken the man seriously enough to come see me.

"He was dehydrated, so we administered fluids. After the initial panic over the needles, the patient calmed down and was cooperative. At the one hour check, the patient was lucid but continued to claim possession. Possible psychiatric hold pending assessment." Kyra scrolled a few pages on her tablet. "General assessment shows patient is not a risk to himself or others and is okay to be released. Oh—bloodwork came in. Hmm, this is odd."

"What?" I leaned toward Kyra, eyeing the tablet although I was pretty sure I wouldn't understand any of the medicalese on the report.

"Patient history shows blood type is O-positive, but the bloodwork revealed what we call a mixed field. There was O-positive, but with significant traces of another blood type. I wonder if he'd had a recent transfusion? Needle transfer wouldn't show up like this, so it would have to be significant. But a transfusion of enough blood to show up on the test would usually be because the patient was a trauma case, and this man wasn't."

"Medical experimentation," I mused. Rick had been right, only the transfusion wasn't medical experimentation, it was most likely to facilitate a magical rite. Did resurrection involve a blood transfusion? Was there significance to the type of blood, or who it came from? And did there need to be something specific about the host body/recipient?

Russell didn't know but Chuck might. I took a deep breath, thinking that I might need to once again pick up that spoon in my kitchen drawer.

"O-null." Kyra shook her head. "That's an incredibly rare blood type. There's a databank of donors that we call on for emergencies because these rare types aren't readily available in blood banks. I wonder how they got O-null and why he received a transfusion?"

I knew. And I could barely speak from the shock of puzzle pieces snapping together in my brain. "Call your dad. Tell him the cases are connected. The O-null homicide and Rick. Tell him what you told me. They're connected, and I might know why. I just have to talk to a spoon first."

"What?" Kyra wrinkled her nose.

"Call your dad and tell him." I grabbed my coat and dashed for the doorway. "And thanks, Kyra. Thanks."

"Okay."

Her voice trailed after me as I ran down the hall, thinking furiously. O-null blood. And something about Rick and Liz Dimond. Rick said he'd heard them talking, that they'd botched it somehow, and Edward Kelley had agreed. They'd gotten the wrong spirit, and Kelley hadn't come all the way across the veil.

Who were they trying to resurrect? And would we be too late to save Liz?

I tore around a corner, dodging a cart and nearly colliding with a woman wearing a pantsuit, a stethoscope around her neck and a tablet in her hand.

"Ooo, sorry. I'm so sorry." I held up both hands, taking a step backward before looking up at her face.

I might not have recognized her had I not just spent an hour with a sketch artist trying to recollect her face. It was the blonde woman who'd been making out with Rick at the club Tuesday night—the one who I suspected might have been involved in his drugging and abduction.

Her somewhat irritated expression made it clear that she hadn't recognized me. I saw her eyes narrow as she stepped to the side.

"Slow it down. This isn't a racetrack," she snapped before continuing briskly down the hall.

I turned to follow her, lagging behind far enough to hopefully seem just another hospital visitor. I wasn't sure what to do. I could hardly confront her and end up tossed out by security. There were hundreds of doctors here, though. There was no way if I lost her that we'd be able to find out who she was. She might not even work at the hospital, but could be here for some sort of consult.

I had to find out who she was. Liz's life depended on it.

The woman entered an elevator, and I hesitated. I'd practically run her over. If I darted into the elevator with her, she'd know I was following her and I was pretty sure my next move would be getting thrown out by security. Frustrated, I watched the doors close.

"Who was that woman? The blonde? The doctor that just got into the elevator?" I asked a man in a polyester uniform who was emptying one of the garbage bins.

The janitor stared at me blankly.

"The doctor," I urged. "Blonde hair. Pretty. Late thirties, maybe?" The woman had looked younger in the club, but hey, we all look younger in that sort of lighting.

"I don't know the doctors' names," he confessed. "I just clean. Not like I talk to them or anything."

I nearly pulled my hair in frustration, turning again to the elevator. It had stopped on the third floor, but I didn't know if the woman was getting out on that floor, or the elevator was stopping to allow someone else in. I waited and saw the elevator begin to descend.

Walking over to the elevator, I looked at the map. This hospital was freaking huge and the third floor had a myriad of wards and hallways. Determined to figure out who this woman was, I headed up the stairs, texting Tremelay that the blonde from the Ottobar was currently at Hopkins and was either a doctor, or was dressed as one.

*Was* she a doctor? I'd seen the badge around her neck, but had been so shocked to see her that I hadn't had time to read the name on it or even get a few numbers of her ID.

On the third floor I worked my way through Urology, feeling like a total idiot as I showed every nurse I passed the sketch and asking if they knew this blonde doctor. I went through the outpatient cancer center and the oncology wing before turning back, feeling a bit defeated as I headed to the elevator. Tremelay's team was better suited to canvas the hospital than me. I needed to get home and talk to Chuck about this ritual and maybe get in a nap before tonight, not spend the day roaming the halls of the hospital trying to find one doctor in thousands of staff, patients, and visitors.

Entering the elevator with two nurses, I pushed the button for the level that would take me to the parking garage, looking down at the sketch in my hands.

"Did you draw that?" one of the nurses asked, looking over my shoulder. "That's really great. It looks just like her."

I froze, gaping up at the nurse like an idiot.

"What do you think, Jeff?" she asked the other nurse.

He glanced at the drawing. "Doctor Hendricks? Looks more like her younger sister, though."

"Does Doctor Hendricks have a younger sister?" I asked, stunned at my odd luck.

Jeff shrugged. "Heck if I know."

"Where does she work?" I glanced at the lighted numbers indicating the floor in anxiety. "Do you know her first name?"

The female nurse eyed me and took a step away. "Um, neurology. Doctor Ellen Hendricks."

She and Jeff exchanged one of those knowing glances that made me realize I was one weird comment away from meeting security.

"Thanks," I told them. "My mother drew this. My late mother. I never knew the doctor's name, and we're so grateful for the care my mother received here. She was so fond of Doctor Hendricks. Now I can write her with our gratitude. Thank you."

It was the worst lie ever, but the two nurses seemed to believe it. I sent a quick silent apology to my mother about her fictional untimely death, and breathed in relief when the elevator doors opened.

"I'm so sorry for your loss," Jeff told me as I stepped out. "Glad we could help."

Keeping my pace to a walk until the elevator doors closed, I pulled out my phone and sent a quick text to Tremelay. Then I broke into a run.

I sat at my kitchen table, talking to a spoon with my mother sitting across from me in pajamas, holding a sword across her lap. She wasn't happy that I was dealing with Chuck. Worse, she wasn't happy with the payment the death mage had asked for in return for his assistance this time.

"One visit in the next two weeks," The mage repeated. "Bring your sword."

"You're not touching my sword." My mom's eyes narrowed. "You're not touching me either unless you want to be known as Chuck the One Handed."

What was it with Mom and cutting off hands lately?

"They won't let you bring your sword in anyway," I told her. "I always have to leave mine behind."

Mom sighed. "They'll let me bring it in. I'm not happy about this, Solaria. Not happy at all."

But she didn't decline to do it, which meant the deal was made and Chuck would tell me everything he knew about the resurrection ritual or whatever the heck it was these mages were trying to do.

I only hoped Chuck actually knew something, because my mother was going to have to pay a prison visit that she really didn't want to make.

"Agreed," Mom said with a sigh.

"Good." I imagined Chuck rubbing his hands together, even though all I could see in the spoon was his face. "So what do you need to know?"

I told him everything I knew, from the Dimonds' abduction and the spirit possessing Rick to Knight D'Angelo's communications at the séance.

"Edward Kelley is a hack." Chuck made a disgusted noise. "He's been trying to get across the veil for hundreds of years. He promises all kinds of things—which of course he never delivers on."

I hid a smile. "Sounds like the disgruntled voice of personal experience."

Chuck shrugged. "I'm not one to seek guidance from dead mages. I'll read their grimoires, I'll study their essays and texts. But in my opinion, a spirit is going to always tell you what you want to hear as long as it will get them out of hell."

"Evidently the mage trying to resurrect someone thinks otherwise," I drawled.

"Sounds like it. They must want someone pretty bad to attempt a resurrection ritual not just once, but twice." Chuck sniffed. "Idiots. One little thing goes wrong and you can wind up with half of hell on your doorstep."

"So the ritual requires O-null blood? Does it have to be from a specific person? And what about the host body?" I asked, knowing time was not on our side here.

"These rituals were written down long before people knew how to type blood. They specify 'blood most royal, golden, and precious in its rarity' for the spell. No one has ever figured out exactly what that meant, so although your mages might be idiots, they're persistent idiots. I'm guessing they ran a whole lot of test cases to determine the blood type needed."

"So they killed a lot of people figuring that out?"

Chuck shrugged. "Probably. Personally, I would have used at-risk individuals. They wouldn't have made suitable hosts for a resurrection, but at least you could determine the appropriate blood qualities without much notice of their deaths. Still, with all the differences in blood beyond type, it would have taken hundreds of experiments. These people are as much scientists as they are mages."

"And what's the ideal host?" I felt sick just thinking about all this.

"Well, the original body is the ideal host, but usually there's a reason the person died, and that makes the physical body no longer suitable. A close relative has the best chance of non-rejection. Identical twin is perfect, of course."

I frowned. "So whoever these mages are trying to resurrect is a relative of Rick and Liz Dimond, then."

Chuck's surprise vibrated through the spoon. "Dimond? You said Dimond? As in the Mage of Marblehead, Dimond?"

Mom's hands tightened on her sword.

Marblehead. Royal blood. O-null blood. Dimond. Resurrection. It wasn't just the dead man I'd tripped over Tuesday and Rick's kidnapping that were connected, but Knight D'Angelo's murder and the mercenary vampire group as well. A female mage. A female doctor who drugged Rick and hauled him away to an occult ritual.

"There's a guy named Dimond that was called the Mage of Marblehead?" I asked in a shaky voice.

"You need to learn more than the Crusades." Chuck made a tsk noise. "Edward Dimond was commonly called 'John'. He was born in 1641, and lived in Massachusetts, but was far too powerful to be targeted in the witch trials of the time. The man had eleven children and lived to ninety-one years old, although there are records that he lived quite a few decades beyond that before he passed. The man was one of the most powerful mages who'd ever lived, although he's not widely known because he tended to keep to himself and wasn't quite as controversial or flashy as other individuals in history."

"Like Edward Kelley?" I asked.

"Him, Crowley, and others. Dimond was a bit of a generalist in the occult world. He could find lost objects, divine the future, identify who stole something or murdered someone, or slandered a person. The locals found his talents quite useful, which is probably one of the reasons he was never persecuted."

"He didn't leave a grimoire? I'm assuming these mages want to resurrect him so that he'll reward them with his spells and magical knowledge?"

"If Dimond kept a grimoire, one was never found," Chuck said. "I don't know if he's eager to regain a physical existence or not. Unlike Kelley, Dimond doesn't jump to every spirit-worker's call. He's not easy to communicate with. And I can assume he wouldn't be easy to bring across the veil—either partially or fully."

"So why not try another mage?" I asked. "Surely there are mages all throughout history who have skills in divining the future and the past who would be easier to bring across. Heck, I know a dozen Goetic demons who would share information without the need to collect special blood or kidnap a relative off the street."

"Oh, but the Mage of Marblehead is special." Chuck's face distorted as he leaned close and the curves of the spoon acted like a funhouse mirror. "There is documentation that he had control over the weather. Not just within a small geographic area, but for hundreds of miles. He could control the wind and the storms according to several accounts and often led sailors to safety, shielding their ships from the squalls. Of course, those ships had captains who'd paid for such protections. Those who'd refused, or those who had angered him found themselves suddenly beset by gale-force winds, broken up on the rocks after being driven off course."

I stared in astonishment. The man had been running a seventeenth-century protection racket using the weather instead of a sword or a gun.

"As you can see," Chuck continued, "that would be a very valuable skill to have in today's world—especially with global climate change."

There were all sorts of magical specialties, but none that I knew of made any claim to be able to influence the weather. This Mage of Marblehead had been powerful indeed. And he was clearly a distant ancestor to Liz and Rick for the pair of them to have been considered appropriate host bodies.

Tremelay was hunting down Doctor Hendricks and whoever might have been responsible for Rick and Liz's abduction. Dario and Mom and I would need to take the other approach and search for the mercenary vampires and the mage, or mages, involved—which might include Doctor Hendricks. The mage at the garage who'd tortured and ordered the killing of Knight D'Angelo, the one who we were assuming had hired the vampire mercenaries, was a woman. I was willing to bet that woman and Doctor Hendricks were one and the same, because that's the way things seemed to be going in this mishmash of interconnected cases, but I wasn't going to rule out that there might be more than one woman involved in this thing, and that several of them could be mages.

Going up against one mage who'd been powerful enough to craft that wand, or wealthy enough to buy it, was enough to make me exercise caution. Going up against a group? That was worrisome, even with my mother and Dario by my side.

These people might have screwed up the one resurrection ritual with Rick, but they were clearly skilled and ruthless. And if the attempt with Liz failed, how many other descendants of the Mage of Marblehead would be kidnapped to potentially die in these resurrection attempts? How many others with the rare O-null blood would die?

"Tell me everything you know about this resurrection ritual," my mother commanded. "Please." She grimaced at the last word, as if it pained her.

"Of course, Knight Ainsworth." Chuck's grin was a little unsettling. "There are six mages throughout history who are considered to be the experts when it comes to resurrection. It's tricky—not really necromancy, not really death magic, not really blood magic, not really demonology. It's a mix of all four."

I remembered Russell saying much the same thing.

"You need a special sort of blood, which I assume your mages have determined to be O-null. A direct descendant or someone with close family ties is needed for the host. It's a very complex ritual. From what I've read, a magical wedge must be placed through the veil during Halloween. The strain on this wedge increases as the year goes on, so the resurrection ritual should take place within three months. Ideally, if the mages are powerful enough, it should be timed with the winter solstice to minimize host body rejection."

"So there's a lot that could go wrong," Mom commented.

"Absolutely. That they had partial success with the brother is commendable. Usually the wedge opening the veil doesn't hold, or allows a ton of spirits and demons to flood through. The wrong spirit can come through, as happened with the brother. The spirit may not completely cross the veil. The host can reject the spirit. The original spirit in the host can refuse to leave, or not cross over, or snap back into the body. There are too many variables for me to list."

"What if it does succeed?" I asked.

"There is a period of disorientation for the resurrected. They may not be aware of who they are for a few months. They may not be the same or have the same skills and abilities as they did in their first life. No one has ever documented a successful resurrection, so I really wouldn't know what to expect."

Mom's eyes met mine and she adjusted her grip on the sword. "We'll get them, Solaria."

We might, but would we be in time? I doubted it.

"Liz is probably dead by now." I felt sick at the thought. "They took Rick Tuesday night and released him on Friday morning. If they grabbed Liz on Wednesday morning, they would have done the ritual by now. She hasn't been found, so I'm assuming it worked and she's now possessed by this Dimond mage ancestor of hers."

"I doubt it. They most likely waited until Thursday to do the ritual on the brother because there's some prep time involved. The sister was obviously kidnapped as a backup plan, and held until they saw what happened with the brother. When that failed, I'm sure they took the time to do some additional research. They wouldn't want to rush into the ritual and risk using another potential host. The null blood is good for four weeks if properly stored. It's better to wait and do it right, than try to find another potential host with the clock ticking on the blood."

It made sense. "So how long do you think we have?"

Chuck shrugged, which looked really odd in the spoon. "If it were me, I'd keep the woman in a cell for a few weeks, just to perfect everything. Of course, that would depend on how cooperative she was being as well as the risks of detection. If these mages think you or the police are closing in on them, they may just go ahead and proceed."

We were closing in on them. I was sure by now that Dr.

Hendricks knew we were onto her. Which meant we had to find and stop them tonight.

"When is the ideal time to do this ritual?" I asked Chuck. "Midnight? Dawn?"

"Between midnight and moonrise is ideal."

Mom and I exchanged puzzled looks. I'll admit I pulled out my phone to look it up. What a crappy novice mage I was that I didn't have the moon cycles memorized.

"Moonrise is at 4:30 in the morning." No wonder it had been so dark at night this week.

"And sunset is around 5:00." Mom grimaced. "If we want your *Balaj's* help, we'll only have a window of seven hours to find this mage and the mercenary vampires."

"More like six, since Dario and his family will need to feed and take care of any pressing issues." I looked down at the spoon once more. "Thanks Chuck. I appreciate it."

"Remember our bargain, and feel free to call on me anytime."

I shoved the spoon back into the cabinet, not replying with either an affirmative or a negative. It was clear that Chuck would require his pound of flesh for any future assistance. The wand had been a freebie, and this request wasn't bothersome for anyone besides my mother, but there could come a time when Chuck's help would carry a price that would be too dear for me to consider.

I really needed to find a way to make nice with Reynard, because I'd so much rather deal with him than an incarcerated death mage.

# CHAPTER 24

Sunset came and went. Dario had come over to wait with us for James's message, sending out teams to patrol not only the Franklin Square area, but Druid Hill and the surrounding areas.

I was going crazy with the inaction, pacing and worrying that every minute we sat in this house was another minute we might be too late to save Liz.

"Look, we know they've got to be using some sort of surgery center or office with an outpatient surgical wing. It's a small or private practice since they'd draw notice in a larger one. Plus a small practice might be closed for the week due to the holidays where a larger practice wouldn't."

"Does this Doctor Hendricks have an office?" Mom asked. "I can head over there while you wait for our informant."

"Tremelay has patrol watching both her office and her residence, but he can't search them because he doesn't have probable cause to get a warrant yet. She's just a person of interest."

"I don't need a warrant." Mom's mouth was set in a determined line.

"It's a tiny office with nothing beyond a receptionist and waiting area, and two patient rooms. She's a neurologist. She wouldn't do surgery. According to Kyra, she would need to refer patients to a neurosurgeon."

"She still might be using her office. Or her house," Mom insisted.

"I'll go over to her office," Dario said. "And I'll send Madeline over to her house. We don't need a warrant either, and if she's not involved in any of this, we won't be facing any liability for breaking and entering."

"Can you do that?" I asked. "The breaking and entering thing? I thought you all needed permission to enter someone's house."

"There are ways around that." Dario waved away the question, and I knew he didn't want me, or my mother to know exactly what sort of ways he was referring to.

"The doctor I saw looked just like the woman at the Ottobar," I told Mom. "But it was dark in there, and I only saw her for a few moments. I'd hate for us to have made a mistake based on my memory and the identification of two nurses in an elevator."

Mom bit her lip in thought then nodded. "Okay. Go. We'll research likely surgical centers while we're waiting for the informant, but if he doesn't get here by midnight, we're heading out."

Mom was just as frustrated with the inaction as I was, but I knew we both realized that wandering the streets of Baltimore wasn't the best use of the limited time we had. Hopefully Dario or Madeline would find something—or James's messenger would get here before we went out of our minds with worry.

Dario left and Mom and I got to work. It quickly became evident that there were way too many surgical centers and doctors' offices that had an outpatient surgery suite.

"There are a whole bunch of them on West Belvedere," I commented. "And Quarry Lake Drive, and Saint Paul Place, and Loch Raven Boulevard, and Patterson Avenue."

"The ones on Quarry Lake Drive are in a huge building," Mom said. "I don't think they'd risk dragging kidnapped, drugged people through a medical complex then back out again. It's got to be something smaller. How about this one on Joppa Road?"

I looked over at her phone. "That's in Towson. It's got to be close enough to Franklin Square that any vampires who are out hunting can get back quickly if they're needed, but far enough away that any 'oops' deaths won't draw attention to the area."

"That rules out the one on Loch Raven Boulevard then." Mom kept scrolling on her phone.

"The ones on Belvedere and a few of the side streets are right near Sinai Hospital. That's north of Woodberry where the home was that they lured Liz to."

"Isn't that too far from Franklin Square?" Mom asked.

I waggled my hand back and forth. "For vampires? I don't know. They move really fast. And I've seen Dario drive when he's in a hurry. Mario Andretti has nothing on the guy."

Mom nodded and marked down Belvedere with a question mark. "If that's where they are, then we'll need to leave fairly soon. Looks like a bit of a drive."

"It's only fifteen minutes if we hop on 83," I told her.

We continued writing down possible areas of town, the list growing longer as the clock approached midnight. Just when I was ready to suggest we give it up and head up to Belvedere Avenue, there was a knock at the door.

Fulk went nuts, barking and dancing around. I used my body to keep him from rushing whoever had arrived, and opened the door. A woman stood on my stoop, bundled up against the cold with a North Face jacket, a knitted scarf, and a hat pulled low over her head. She had glasses on, and that was about all I could see of her.

"Are you…" She looked around nervously, then dropped her voice to a dramatic whisper. "Are you the Templar?"

I opened the door wider. "Come in. I hope you don't mind dogs. He'll settle down once he sniffs your feet and gets a pat or two."

She walked over the threshold, her gaze taking in my house and my mother who stood in the kitchen doorway with a sword in her hand.

"I can't stay. James asked me to come by and give you this." She thrust a piece of paper into my hand. "Is he gonna be okay?"

As she asked, the woman unwound the scarf from her neck, revealing a thick mass of curly red hair and two small marks on her neck.

Well. It seems James might have some added incentive to accept Dario's offer.

"I hope so," I told her. "Do you have a place to stay tonight?"

She nodded. "If you see James, tell him to call me. Or text me. Something, anything before sunrise so I know he's okay. I don't want to be worried all day."

"I will." I wasn't sure I'd see the vampire. Hopefully not. The best case scenario would be if he'd sent me this information, then got the heck out of town until the air cleared, but I had a sick feeling that wouldn't be the case.

I saw the woman out, then opened the paper, reading the address out to my mother.

"Downtown." I shook my head. "Practically under our noses."

Mom sheathed her sword. "Let's go."

I grabbed mine off the table, quickly shoving my phone in

my back pocket. "You drive. I need to text this to Dario and to Tremelay."

"They need to know I'm handling this," Mom warned as I locked up behind us. "This is my job. It's justice for the murder of a Knight, and that supersedes both police procedure and whatever issues the local *Balaj* might have to do with this group."

One look at the expression on her face told me all I needed to know. My mother was going to lay waste to twenty-five vampires and one mage tonight, and no one better get in her way.

 om drew her sword. *Do you feel them?* she mouthed silently.

We'd parked a few blocks down and walked north, the downtown area feeling strangely deserted this time of day, as if we'd suddenly found ourselves in a post-apocalyptic movie.

I held up a fist, spreading my fingers wide four times, then wiggling it back and forth before spreading the fingers wide one more time. Twenty or twenty-five vampires. That's what I sensed. They were all here—or at least most of them were here. If the mage wanted all her mercenaries standing guard inside this building, that meant the ritual she planned to do with Liz was most likely going down tonight.

Mom nodded, pointed to me and to the right, then pointed to herself and to the left. I understood. We were to canvas the area. I pointed down the block to where the car was and Mom nodded, indicating we'd meet there afterward.

I drew my sword as I headed to the right around the building to the back before looping around the neighboring one and returning to the car.

It wasn't the one-story, private practice I'd expected, but a four-story office building which, from my quick internet search on the way over, housed four doctors' offices and an outpatient surgical center on the bottom floor. None of the listings said Doctor Ellen Hendricks, and none of the specialties had anything to do with neurology. This medical building housed gastroenterology folks, and I could only assume that the surgical center was for things like colonoscopies and not transfusions for resurrection rituals.

If Dr. Hendricks was involved, then she must have known the owners of the surgical center and been able to somehow get private use of it over the holidays and the weekend. And since the surgical center was on the first floor, I was pretty sure we'd be neck-deep in vampires the moment we entered.

We had three choices. There was the front-door—locked, but nothing my spelled key couldn't take care of. There was also a back entrance where I assumed they discharged patients who might not want to walk through the lobby with other patients gawking at them. The third entrance was a fire door, no doubt to meet code for emergency exits. I was pretty sure we wouldn't have to deal with any alarms since there were a group of vampires and at least one mage in the building, but I pulled my keychain out, unwilling to take any chances. The magic I'd done on the one key might not work on an alarm system, but it was all we had outside of yanking wires or stabbing the console with a sword.

"Let's take the front door," Mom decided, walking up next to me. "There's an atrium with lots of room to maneuver. There will most likely be three or four there, but first let's take out the two watching the building."

"Did they see you?" I asked, concerned that they may have raised the alarm.

"Of course, but your spell worked because they clearly didn't see my sword." She sniffed. "I was just a bag of blood, looking for a place to shoot up as far as they were concerned. They were both on the left side of the building down the service driveway, although they may have separated to do rounds by this point."

"Want me to go right and circle the building while you go left?" I asked.

She nodded, pulling her sword out once more. "Think you can actually kill one this time?"

I winced at the jab, but she was right. "I'll do what I need to do to hopefully get Liz out of there alive and with one spirit in her body."

Mom smiled. "That's my girl."

It was stupidly easy. The vampire patrolling around the building watched me with narrowed eyes until I smiled at him and asked him if he had a twenty to spare for a date. He licked his lips and nodded, motioning for me to follow him behind a dumpster. I did, and plunged my blade through his heart, scooting him farther back behind the dumpster out of sight.

I met Mom at the front right corner of the medical complex.

*Ready?* she mouthed silently. I nodded.

We'd fight back-to-back, making sure there was no way a supernaturally fast vampire could catch either of us on our blind side. But first we had to get inside the building. Mom held back as I sauntered up to the glass entrance, pulling my key out and magically opening the doors. There were three vampires in the lobby. They hesitated, my casual confidence in entering no doubt making them wonder if I was supposed to be here or not.

That hesitation cost them their lives.

Before they could reach me, Mom was at my side. The vampires were insanely fast, but there were two of us, and our swords gave us a reach they lacked. They were obviously used to fighting against other vampires or humans armed with guns. Where bullets wouldn't do much to stop a vampire, our Templar weapons did, and they quickly realized their error, backing up and trying to circle around us.

I put my back to my mother's and we pivoted, swords at the ready. The vampires were injured, shaken that these wounds pained them and weren't healing with their normal speed. We hadn't come through the first scuffle unscathed, though. Both Mom and I had cuts from the vampires' knives, and I had one particularly painful bruise where one had punched me in the shoulder, trying to knock the sword from my hand. He'd have done it too, if Mom hadn't nearly taken his arm off.

One lunged for me, and I swung. He ducked, but I reversed, and as he went to avoid the blade, I smacked him on the cheek with my gold keychain crucifix.

"*Ansurb*," I shouted as his flesh sizzled. "*Jesu, pashtpanel indz bolor ansurb eakneri.*"

The long form version of the Templar incantation was more for show as the first word had done the job. Pulling my keychain from the vampire's face, I drove my sword into his heart.

Mom had already dispatched one, and in the time it took me to turn, she'd killed the remaining vampire. A surge of magic rolled through the building and I eyed the door to the outpatient surgical office just as it opened and over a dozen vampires poured out toward us.

My stomach twisted. This was going to hurt, and I wasn't sure we were going to make it out of this one alive. Even if we did, I wasn't sure we were going to make it to Liz in time.

I didn't have a moment to think before the vampires mobbed us, coming so fast it was all I could do to parry and duck trying to keep from getting stabbed.

Shifting to the side to counter their attack, I realized two things. One—this group was far better at fighting strategy than the others had been. And two—they had managed to separate me from my mother, meaning each of us needed to cover three-hundred-and-sixty degrees around us as opposed to one-eighty.

With a shout of warning to Mom, I spun, taking several slices to my arm as I worked my way to the center of the atrium where a bank of elevators stood. I heard glass breaking, but didn't have time to register what that sound might mean. I planted my back firmly against the wall next to the elevator, swinging wildly and hoping to connect with one of the vampires rushing me. I heard screams, felt my sword impact, but there were just too many of them. They pressed forward, getting inside my range and hindering my ability to use the sword. I reversed my grip, using the less effective pommel and trying to burn every vampire I could reach with my keychain. They pushed against me, and I found myself with my arms pinned, two vampires holding me tight to the wall. Desperate, I tried to head-butt one, but he laughed and grabbed my jaw in an iron grip, fangs glistening as he leaned toward my neck.

Before I could feel the sharp slide of fangs through my flesh, his hand suddenly loosened, and his head rolled unnaturally to the side, sliding from his neck and bouncing across the floor. I had a second to note the sluggish ooze of black blood from the stump where his head had been then I felt the other vampire being ripped away from me, his head joining the other one on the ground.

I looked up to see Dario in front of me, his clothing covered in vampire blood, kukri in hand.

"No one else bites you," he informed me as he wiped the blade on his pants. "Except me. Maybe. In the future if we decide we both truly want that. No one but me bites you ever again."

I smiled, thinking that was one of the sexiest, most romantic things anyone had ever said to me.

"Help Mom." I turned him around and gave him a quick pat on the ass. "I need to go find a mage."

There was a clear pathway to the outpatient center door with the remaining vampires concentrating on fighting my Mom, Dario, and the others of his *Balaj* that were beginning to arrive. And thankfully, the door was already open and off its hinges, so I didn't need to waste time using my magical key.

Magic surged through the air again, and I followed the faint sound of chanting, trying to hurry but also very aware of the fact that there were most likely more vampires guarding the room where the mage had chosen to do her ritual.

Sure enough, I rounded a corner and nearly ran smack into one of them. With all the blood dripping from my various cuts, I couldn't believe he didn't scent me coming, but I still managed to catch him by enough surprise to run my sword through his chest, twisting and angling it upward to make sure I got his heart before pushing him off the blade.

A knife sank deep into my shoulder and an arm came around my neck. My arm went semi-numb, and I barely managed to keep a hold on my sword, gripping the keychain tight with my other hand. His arm around my neck tightened, and time slowed as I realized he intended to snap my neck. Without a second for even a quick prayer, I plunged the long end of my crucifix keychain up and over my head, feeling it sink keep into something soft.

Flesh smoked and sizzled. The vampire screamed and let go. I pivoted to see him clutching his face, a black hole where an eye had once been. Swinging my sword in an upward arc, I tried to aim for his neck, but my arm was numb and I'd lost more blood than I wanted to admit.

Instead of taking off his head, the blade lodged between his tenth and eleventh rib.

Yeah. Nowhere near his head.

Kicking him off the blade, I stumbled a bit, then gripped my sword with two hands to try again. This time I did manage to take the vampire's head off. Breathing heavy and staggering a little, I ran toward the door of the surgical room, praying that there wouldn't be any more vampires to fight, because I was pretty close to tapped out and I still had a mage to deal with.

I flung open the door. The surgical room was big and bright with white walls, white floors, and tons of eye-wincing lights bouncing off the stainless steel equipment, beds, and tables. A woman in surgical scrubs held a ritual knife toward the sky as she stood next to a bed where a dark haired woman was strapped down. Both looked over at me.

The dark haired woman on the table was Liz. Recognition flared in her eyes, and she struggled against the restraints that bound her to the table.

"Help me," she shouted.

"*Portae fores objicere.*" The doctor dropped the ritual knife onto the table and threw a biohazard box toward me. I batted it out of the way with my sword and it exploded in a burst of magical energy, sending blood soaked pads and syringes at me with unerring accuracy.

I grimaced, trying not to think about Hepatitis B as I yanked three needles from my legs and moved cautiously toward the mage. Liz was still between the two of us, and I was very aware that this woman could use her as a hostage.

Instead the mage leaned down as Liz struggled. "Is it you? Is it truly you?"

Panicked that the woman might kill Liz if she didn't give an appropriate response, I rushed her, throwing the keychain. I didn't play much baseball as I kid, but I did joust and had a decent arm. The keychain smacked the mage in the head and she staggered backward, throwing her hands upward.

I used a half-sword grip and thrust forward, stabbing at the mage over the top of the table and Liz. My aim was true, but the blade hit a magical barrier and stopped, the force jarring through my arms and sending me down onto my rear.

As I scrambled to my feet I saw the mage look down at Liz for a split second of decision-making before she darted for the door.

I ran before I was fully upright, using my momentum to launch myself in front of her before she reached the exit. Predictably, I bounced off her force field and slammed into the door frame, knocking the breath out of me for a brief second.

Things got a little fuzzy and dark, but I shook my head and readied my sword. I couldn't hurt her with the magical force field up, but she couldn't exactly walk through me to leave either. It would be my physical strength against her magic in a sort of reverse tug-of-war, and as powerful as she was, I was betting I'd win that contest.

The mage stepped back and ripped the surgical mask and hat from her face and head, gasping in air. It was the doctor I'd seen in the hospital hallway. And on her hands were red, angry welts—burns from having a magical wand break in her hands.

I bent my knees and prepared to hold my position. "We know who you are, Doctor Ellen Hendricks. Your vampire mercenaries are all dead by now. Even if the police manage to get to you first, you murdered a Templar Knight, and you'll answer to God for that crime before dawn."

"I did it." She laughed. "I did it, and no one can stop me

now—not the police, not the vampires, not the Templars. I did it."

I glanced over at Liz, a little worried at the confidence in her voice. Rick's sister was struggling against the bindings, muttering what I was pretty sure were curse words under her breath.

"You failed. Again," I told the mage. "No one has successfully done a resurrection spell. You failed the first time and you've failed this time as well."

She stepped forward, testing me. I felt the pressure of her force field scooting me back a few inches until I dug in and leaned forward.

"You're wrong. John Dimond was successful in resurrecting at least three people. I've been in contact with him. He told me how to do it, promised me if I let him live again, that he'd show me where he'd hidden his grimoire, that he'd teach me his spells. And I'll resurrect other mages too. No one will be able to touch me. No one."

Lord, please save me from the villain monologue. I heard a faint clink and out of the corner of my vision, I saw the bindings fall away from the upper part of Liz's body. She leaned forward, the ritual knife in her hand as she worked the clasp on the ones holding her legs to the table.

I turned my attention back to the mage, determined not to let her know Liz was freeing herself. Better to keep her attention on me, than let her decide to use Liz as a hostage.

"You can't keep this up forever," I told Hendricks. "You'll weaken before I do."

I saw Liz slide off the table and stumble down to one knee.

The mage laughed. "Think again. You're covered in wounds. Your hands are shaking. You can't even hold the sword in one hand anymore. There's blood running down your shoulder."

To illustrate her point, she pushed forward again, and I slid back, stopping only when I braced my foot against the door jamb.

"You might get past me, but I'm not the only Templar here. And if she doesn't manage to get you, my boyfriend will."

She snorted, pushing harder. I breathed evenly through my nose and concentrated, my legs shaking as I tried to keep her from knocking me over and getting past me through the doorway. I had to hang in there. I had to outlast her. Then, once she was dead on the floor, I could lay down and take a nice nap, maybe on one of those surgical tables over there.

I saw Liz struggle to her feet, but needed to immediately shift my attention as the mage pushed even harder. Turning my sword sideways so it locked against the door frame, I hung on for dear life, my feet scrabbling for purchase.

*Sorry Trusty, this isn't the most dignified use of a blessed Templar weapon,* I silently told my sword.

She pushed harder, and I struggled to breathe, my grip slipping on the sword. I could hear footsteps in the hallway, and hoped they were my mother's, or Dario's.

If it was one of the mercenary vampires, I was done for.

Gritting my teeth, I put every bit of effort into holding on to the sword. Suddenly the tension dropped and I fell forward onto my knees. The mage's eyes widened. I looked up and saw Liz standing behind the woman, a grim expression on her face. She was holding the ritual knife, its blade coated with blood, and as I watched, she plunged it into the mage's back again.

And again. And again.

The mage spun and raised her hands, trying to fend off the attack, but Liz was like a fury, stabbing the other woman with a speed and determination that seemed almost otherworldly. Even as the mage fell to the ground, Liz kept stabbing her.

Then she began to sob, the bloody knife falling from her hands.

I stood and went to her, helping her to her feet and holding her tight as she cried.

A pair of strong arms came around me, and I smiled, because this time I'd recognized Dario's energy signature. I welcomed his cinnamon and spice scent, welcomed the way he fussed over my injuries.

And I really welcomed when he discretely licked the horrible wound on my shoulder, clotting the blood and sending a happy wave of pain relieving euphoria through me —along with some other feelings.

"Later," I muttered, guessing that he probably had the world's biggest hard-on right now. Heck knows I would have been ready to do it on one of these surgical beds if I wasn't consoling a traumatized woman.

I was injured, covered in blood, and exhausted as the adrenaline drained away from me, but it wasn't just the vampire saliva that made me want to get busy with Dario. Life was short. Anything could happen to either of us. And at this moment, I wanted nothing more than to lose myself in a frenzy of hot sweaty sex with a guy I loved.

"Oh my." My mother entered the room, took one look at the carnage and went to Liz. "Are you all right, dear?"

Was she all right? She seemed like Liz, but Hendricks had been so insistent that the ritual had worked. Was there the spirit of John Dimond in this woman who clung to me, crying? Was it still Liz?

"I don't feel well, but I don't think I'm seriously hurt." Liz took a step away from me with a sniff and a watery smile.

I took her hands to inspect the needle marks on the inside of her arms and she grimaced.

"They gave me a transfusion or something. It wasn't too bad. It wasn't much worse than giving blood, really."

I frowned. Rick had seemed far more shaken, but from my brief acquaintance with the two, Liz had come across as the stronger and more stoic of the pair.

"Rick is okay and has been staying at the hotel while we searched for you. He'll be thrilled to see you," I told her. "He's been worried sick. And I know you're probably frantic over where he is."

For a brief second she seemed confused, then she smiled, her face lighting up. "I'm so glad he's okay! I was pissed that he'd stayed out all night with that girl and texted me to bring him a shirt after his hookup. Had the same thing happened to him? Things got fuzzy after I left the hotel…"

Oh. She hadn't realized her brother had been kidnapped and gone through the same ordeal. I patted her on the shoulder, deciding I'd let Rick tell her the story because I was seriously thinking about taking a nap on one of those beds over there.

A siren wailed outside, close enough that I imagined the police car pulling right up in front of the building.

Dario grimaced. "Time for us to leave. Do you two have this?"

Mom waved a hand at him. "Yes, we've got this. Thank you for your help by the way. I do appreciate the assistance."

I blinked at her in surprise, unsuccessfully trying to bite back a grin.

Dario gave me a quick hug. "Should I wait at your house for you?"

The grin turned into a grimace. "I'll probably be at the hospital getting stitches for a few hours, then off to the police station to give a statement. I'm thinking it will probably be close to dawn before I get home."

"Tomorrow night then." He kissed my forehead. "I'll bring

dinner and you can lay on the couch while I feed you and kiss all your boo-boos."

Hopefully he'd be kissing more than my boo-boos. I watched him leave, then waited while the police made their way through the carnage of dead vampires to where Mom, Liz, and I stood over the body of a dead mage. It had been a long night, and I got the feeling I wouldn't be seeing my bed for quite a few hours.

Worse, I needed to open at work tomorrow. Hopefully I'd have time to shower off the blood before I need to clock in and start making lattes.

# CHAPTER 26

I sat across from Janice, feeling that weirdly energetic hyperness that comes when you've had no sleep and spent the last eight hours making caffeinated beverages. Normally I would have asked for a rain check on our meeting, but the reporter was buying me a late lunch, and I did feel like I owed her a story after she'd patiently waited all weekend for her scoop.

"You look like you got run over by a truck," she commented as she nibbled on a slice of pizza.

I felt like I'd been run over by a truck—or by a dozen or so vampires and a psychotic mage. All total, I had a dozen wounds requiring stitches, and a couple of nasty bruises. Mom had begged me to take the day off work and relax, but I couldn't call in at the last minute like that. Sean needed me, and I knew he wouldn't be able to find someone to cover with such short notice. I was totally taking Dario up on his feed-and-kiss-my-boo-boo plan tonight, and hopefully I wouldn't fall asleep during either activity.

"Vampires are fast, and they like these stabby little

knives," I told Janice. "It could have been worse. I'm happy I walked out of there alive."

"Why don't they use guns?" The reporter shook her head. "Idiots. They could kill a heck of a lot more people if they'd stop stabbing and start shooting. Same goes for you and your sword."

She had a point, although my sword worked a whole lot better against supernatural beings than bullets—unless they were silver bullets, that is. Or magic bullets.

"I'm surprised they didn't keep you at the police station longer," Janice said with an incredulous shake of her head. "Two women with swords, and a victim with a knife kill twenty-some vampires and a crazy-ass mage. That should have sent up all sorts of red flags."

I took a sip of my soda. "It did until Mom made a call. It was all red-carpet treatment after that. Suddenly all they needed was a basic statement and it was yes Knight Ainsworth, ma'am and no Knight Ainsworth, ma'am from then on out. Within half an hour an attorney showed up from the Order, put us in a limo, and took us back to my house.

"So you guys are like the Illuminati?" She wiggled her fingers. "Connections everywhere? All the world's leaders like puppets on your strings?"

"Hardly, but the Elders know people and they're not afraid to call in favors." I pointed heavenward just to show her I was teasing. Maybe.

Janice picked at her pizza, pulling a piece of pepperoni off and popping it into her mouth. "You know what Tremelay found out about Sarah Brunner, the woman who owned the place in Woodberry where Liz was supposed to meet Rick? Turns out she knows Ellen Hendricks. They're friends. Evidently Sarah had given Ellen the code to her house one time or another, and didn't think anything about it. She was completely shocked when she heard the news about her friend. I have an interview with her tomorrow morning when she gets back from her vacation."

I narrowed my eyes as I took a bite of my pizza and chewed.

"Really? I didn't know that. When did you speak to Tremelay?"

The reporter flushed. "First thing this morning. He actually called me. He said he didn't want me printing a bunch of rumors and innuendos and that he wanted to let me know the real story."

"Huh. How about that." I took another bite of my pizza. Tremelay had called her. I couldn't wait to see him again and give him a whole raft of shit about this. I wondered if this would go anywhere. Hopefully so. I knew the detective still mourned his wife, but if he was ready to date, then I'd love to see him and my friend get together.

"Do you think Liz is really okay? I mean, do you think that crazy mage doctor actually…did it?"

That was the question of the day. It was probably the question of the year.

"That mage was a hack. Liz is totally okay," I lied, just as I'd lied to Rick, and Mom, and Tremelay. I didn't know if she was okay or not, but maybe if I said so, it would be true.

Because I wasn't sure what I was going to do if it wasn't true.

Janice and I finished our late lunch and I headed home to find my mother ready to head out, showered and refreshed after a long sleep. She had almost as many stitches as I had, and that seemed to add to the bond that had developed between us the last few days. Things had been strained between us since I'd refused to take my oath, but lately…well, lately I got the idea that she saw me less as an obstinate child and more as an independent woman who deserved respect.

"I expect to hear that you're scheduled to take your Oath in the next few months, Solaria," she told me as she gave me a quick kiss on the cheek.

Well, an independent woman who *sometimes* deserved respect.

"Not today, Mom. We'll argue about this at Christmas."

Strangely that got a laugh from her instead of a scowl. "Okay. You still need to send me your list. And Dario's, too."

My eyes widened at that.

"I still don't like that you're dating a vampire, but he seems very dedicated to you. Please let him know he's welcome at family weekends, and any of the holidays."

Before I could find my voice to reply she'd given me another quick kiss on the cheek and left, bounding down the stairs with far more energy and athleticism than I felt capable of right now.

My mother had accepted Dario. With a few grudging words, she'd given our relationship as much a seal of approval as she was capable of. That was the best early Christmas gift I could imagine.

Rick and Liz were both alive, and hopefully they'd be okay. Dario's *Balaj* had secured their territory—for now. A psychotic mage was no longer murdering and kidnapping people. James...well, I hadn't heard anything about James, but he'd not been among the vampires who'd attacked us at the medical center, and he wasn't among the dead there either. Hopefully he'd taken Dario's advice and hidden himself safely away. Hopefully come nightfall, he'd emerge and join his new *Balaj*.

In the meantime, I was going to take a nap. I had a vampire coming over with dinner in a few hours and I wanted to be somewhat refreshed for the kissing of boo-boos. And the kissing of a whole lot more.

* * *

WANT MORE? Read on for Chapter 1 of Dark Crossroads, book 6 in The Templar Series.

# DARK CROSSROADS

## CHAPTER 1

I was in my basement, staring at a spoon.

"The candles are lit. What's next?" I asked.

"Place the object in the center of your circle by walking the east-to-west line of the pentagram."

Thankfully the candles meant I could actually *see* the pentagram. Before I'd lit them, the basement had been dark as I imagined the grave to be—if a grave had a faintly luminescent outline of stones around a magical circle, a giant furnaced, and some broken furniture and rusty paint cans, that is. Weirdly enough, even in the darkness I could see Chuck's face in the spoon. Let me tell you, that was one of the creepiest things I'd seen outside a horror movie, and as a Templar, I'd seen lots of creepy things.

"There." I was now at the west quarter candle of my magical space, eyeing a smooth river stone at the center of the circle.

"A quick review," Chuck said, sounding an awful lot like one of my college professors. "Why six candles?"

I wanted to be a smart ass and reply "because that's what the ritual calls for," but I held back. When I'd been with Haul

Du, they'd only taught me to follow the ritual as outlined in various grimoires. They did encourage further study of symbolism and structure of a ritual with the more advanced mages, but with novices the idea was to get them to follow directions down to the last letter, and get used to channeling energy and controlling Goetic demons.

Chuck was making me deconstruct each ritual before I even attempted it, which meant there was a frustratingly long time before I got to actually try magic. I persevered because I understood why Chuck was taking this approach. After he'd met my mother and eyeballed her sword, he believed my Templar gifts would sometimes counteract a magical spell—or send it off in an unpredictable and possibly fatal direction.

I also persevered because Chuck was the only mage who would teach me. I'd been kicked out of Haul Du the moment they'd discovered I was a Templar and blacklisted from any registered magical group—which was basically any magical group. If I wanted to level up my magical skills, then I had no choice but to do it Chuck's way.

"The four corners anchor the magical space, but candles at the pentagram capture and hold. Using both sets a strong barrier, and holds the spell tightly inside, concentrating it. That's useful when the energy you're trying to read, or what you're trying to divine is faint. Six is also the number for harmony."

"And as a Templar…" Chuck prompted.

I glanced at my candles, glad that I'd bought long-burning ones because this lecture in the middle of my ritual was really slowing things down.

"Three is the most sacred of our numbers. It's the symbol of creation. It's the beginning, the middle, and the end. It's the Father, the Son, and the Holy Spirit. It's also a masculine number. Usually feminine numbers are considered Satanic, hence the symbolism of 666, but six on its own escapes the darkness of other female numbers. It's the first perfect number, therefore it is balanced. Two trinities. It is the only number that is both of the light and the dark."

"Good."

I squinted at Chuck, wishing he'd been able to perform this magical Skype spell on a larger utensil. I guess people serving time in prison couldn't be picky about what dinnerware they had access to.

"And you have the herbs?"

"Birch bark, rosehips, goldenrod, and raven's bread."

All those had been easy except for the raven's bread—otherwise known as Amanita muscaria or fly agaric. First, it wasn't an herb, it was a fungus. Second, even though it was supposedly common in North America—a large, bright red toadstool that grows in birch and evergreen forests—finding any in the wild was pretty much akin to that whole needle in a haystack thing. Most mushrooms could be easily bought over the internet, but given that this one was lethally poisonous in some doses, and intensely hallucinogenic in others, it was illegal—as in "Class A Drug" illegal. Chuck had finally needed to step in and help out by giving me the name of someone who sold the stuff over the dark web. I had purchased the raven's bread and hoped I wasn't on any FBI or DEA watchlist.

"And the ritual?"

This was where things got tricky. The usual words hadn't worked the first time we'd tried this, so Chuck had made me modify them to mimic a Templar blessing. In addition, I was using my sword as an aid instead of the athame I'd purchased that had never felt right in my hand.

"Light incense at the west quarter. Sprinkle on the crushed herb mixture, which you hopefully measured correctly, then build your energy. When you feel it peak, recite your incantation and direct both energy and intent in the words toward the object using your sword as an aid."

I knew all this since I'd practiced the ritual a few times, and memorized the heck out of it. I also had been meticulous in measuring and crushing the herbs, all while chanting to blend their properties and power. This better work because I'd put a ton of time and effort into it. And it would be an incredibly useful spell. Knowing what human owned something would be awesome. From there it was a small step to modify the spell to know who held something last, or even whose energy was within a radius of an object. I could even work to expand the spell to include whether the owner was human or supernatural. Next time I came across a soul trap, a charm, a bloody crime scene, I would have a spell in my arsenal that would cut mine, and Detective Tremelay's, job in half.

"Showtime." I breathed in for six counts then out for six counts, clearing my mind of all except for the spell I was about to perform.

I was already at the west quarter, so I just had to squat down and light the incense. It took a few minutes for the flame over the fragrant disk to die down, leaving a glowing round ember. Holding tight to my intent, I sprinkled the herbs on top, standing and stepping quickly back so I didn't breathe in anything that might end up with me in the hospital or running naked through the streets babbling about pink unicorns.

Even in the dim light I saw the curl of smoke rising from the incense disk. Suddenly, energy filled the circle, snapping tight to the confines of the barrier I'd established. The lines in the concrete glowed blue, the perimeter stones sparkling like stars. This energy wasn't from within me, it was gathered from the cosmos and held together by a magic I didn't quite understand, no matter how many books I read.

I admired the energy for a brief moment, then stepped forward to stand on the circle, willing my body to become just another conduit to its flow. It felt strange, like I was holding on to the hot wire of a cattle fence with one hand and gripping an icicle with the other. With a ragged breath, I slowly began to draw the energy into myself. There was a point where I wasn't sure I could hold any more, but still energy remained swirling about in the circle. Chuck hadn't covered this in his instructions and I wasn't sure what to do. Would the spell work if I wasn't holding all the energy? Would I explode if I tried to take in more than I felt I could hold? Unfortunately I wouldn't be able to communicate with my bodiless mentor until the spell was over, so I was going to have to make a decision on my own.

Hoping Dario didn't arrive tonight to find me splattered all over the basement, I eased more and more of the energy inside until I held it all.

Bloated was an understatement about how I was feeling at that moment. I'd gorged myself on Thanksgiving dinners before and not felt quite this stuffed.

Raising my sword, which I belatedly realized was the icicle-feeling item, I pointed it toward the stone in the center of the circle. Energy quivered at the edge of my hand, barely held in check and ready to race down the blade.

"Earth is to earth, and stone is to stone. Saint Anthony show me who calls this their own."

I was no poet, so I'd kept it simple and to the point. The original spell had lines of gratitude to everything from the four quarters to the elements, and individually called upon a host of deities. I had no problem performing spells that expressed gratitude to God's creations, but I figured Saint Anthony was the dude I needed for this particular spell, not Celtic goddesses.

I recited the incantation over and over until my vision

blurred and my skin heated, then I sent the energy down the sword in a huge bolt of white. The basement lit up like the sun, then just as quickly went dark. Temporarily blinded, I held still and blinked until my vision slowly adjusted. I was supposed to see something overtop the rock. With the spell modifications, Chuck wasn't sure if I'd see a person's face, or words with their name or both, but he said I should definitely have a sense of who owned the object in the center of the circle.

There was nothing over the smooth river stone—not the face of my beloved great grandmother, not her name, not even a crude stick figure. I was still so hot I felt as if I were in a sauna, but there was no sixth sense of who owned the stone.

"I don't think it worked." Think. There was no doubt in my mind that it hadn't worked. I'd spent so much time on this spell—time, money, effort. And I'd gotten nothing for it. Maybe this just wasn't a spell I would be able to work. Maybe this wasn't a Templar-compatible spell.

"Everything looked spot-on from my viewpoint," Chuck-in-the-spoon said.

I walked forward, thinking that maybe instead of a giant projected image, there would be something so small I couldn't see it from the edge of the circle. When I got close, I saw something flicking around the stone. It was dim, fleeting, and looked sort of like a distorted diamond shaped object that was a bright reddish-orange.

I went to pick up the rock and yelped, dropping it back to the ground and shoving my burned fingers into my mouth. The faint illusion vanished and I saw steam rise off the rock.

"What was that?" Chuck asked.

I took my fingers out of my mouth and flexed them gingerly. "I don't know. Looked like a red-orange butterfly or something. It wasn't very distinct."

"Well, that's clearly a success, but it may not have been the result you were hoping to get," he commented.

"No shit, Sherlock." I waved my fingers around, thinking an ice pack would be nice about now. What the heck had the spell delivered? It was supposed to reveal the owner of the rock, not it's fiery origins. Maybe this could be a useful spell if I wanted hot burning rocks to lob at enemies, but honestly it would be faster to just shove a bunch of stones in the fireplace if that was my intent.

I frowned, thinking about the spell and all the different iterations that could return. Owner. Who last touched the object. Where it was last.

"Remember when you did the identification spell on the soul trap and it initially returned the Argentinian mage instead of Dark Iron because he was the actual owner?" I asked. "Do you think instead of who owned it last, maybe my spell identified the original owner."

There was no mistaking the exasperation in Chuck's sigh. "It's a smooth rock. That's not exactly the sort of thing someone passes down for generations."

"My great grandmother gave it to me," I countered. "Maybe someone gave it to her."

It did sound ridiculous. It was a worry stone, a rock worn smooth by water and decades of oils from Essie's hand. But just as she'd given it to me when I'd gone off to college to soothe a troubled mind, perhaps her great grandmother had done the same to her."

"And the someone who gave it to her is what?" Chuck drawled. "A dragon? A fire elemental? A demon?"

Crap, I hoped not. It was actually better to believe the spell was a dud than think Essie stole, or was given, the stone from a demon.

"It would have been easier to just kill a chicken," Chuck lamented. "That spell works. That spell always works."

"I'm not killing a chicken. Besides you said that *wouldn't* work for a Templar."

Not that Templars were vegetarians and I'm sure at one time we'd killed plenty of chickens to stick in the dinner pot. Chuck felt the problem wasn't in ending the life of an animal, it was doing so for the purpose of a magical spell. I agreed because any sort of ritual killing was a line I wasn't going to cross.

"Let's move on and try something else," I suggested. "I really do want to perfect this spell, but maybe later when I've had a few more successes under my belt."

My confidence had really taken a hit the last few weeks, and I needed a win to show me that this course of study really was something I could do.

Chuck sighed. "Tell me what you've done so far—besides accidently summon a high-level demon and get yourself marked, that is."

Jerk.

"I can create null bags. Templars learn to create null spaces since we might be called upon to bring in an artifact. My keychain is spelled to blister vampires, but that's also a Templar thing since it's a blessing and not really a mage spell. As a Templar I can send wraiths and undead spirits back to their graves. I can create a globe of light. I can also sanctify an object and create a holy space. Oh, and my butter knife!"

Chuck's face in the spoon scowled. "You can conjure a butter knife? Like, if you need to spread some jam on toast or something? What in the world is that spell possibly good for?"

"No, I put a spell on a butter knife. At first it was a spell to harm vampires. Then I spelled it to open locks, which I'm particularly proud of I'll have you know."

Chuck didn't look impressed. "So what's on the top of your list? What spell do you want to try next?"

I thought for a moment. The ownership spell would have been handy, but there was something else that had been bothering me. Yes, I knew how to shoot, but throughout the centuries, our consecrated weapon had always been a sword. That had been pretty handy in the fifteenth century, but in the twenty-first, it was…well, it was bringing a sword to a gunfight.

Although it would be amazing to figure out how to bless a Glock and have the equivalent of a holy hip cannon, I was more concerned about not getting shot again.

"Can I do something to make myself bulletproof? I mean, I'd really love it if the spell could make me invulnerable to any sort of attack, but if that's too ambitious, then I'll take just not getting shot."

I watched the spoon as Chuck's face distorted in thought.

"There's a potion. It's a pain to make, but I think it would be compatible with your Templar alignment."

We discussed the ingredients and the preparations for the spell, then I signed off, which meant I stuck Chuck's spoon into an old Crown Royal bag and stashed him behind a rusty paint can. Then I picked up the worry stone which was now only room temperature, and went upstairs.

Working with Chuck was more difficult than my brief stint with Haul Du, and it wasn't just because he was a pain in the butt. He had a broad knowledge of different magical practices, but his main focus was in death magic. And, of course, that was the one practice I wouldn't do. Even if I was willing to cross that line, Chuck was fairly certain that my being Templar meant death magic wouldn't work for me anyway, so that left us sifting through the others, trying to figure out which spells could be modified, which ones would work as-is, and which ones were a definite "no."

Goetic demonology was compatible, but I wasn't about to go down that path without someone who specialized in that particular practice. Blessings and charms were compatible as were hexes and curses but wouldn't be as helpful as spells that did days of research in a few hours, or ones that could protect both me and others.

I got ready for work and walked to the coffee shop in the Inner Harbor, willing to brave the January cold rather than drive and fork out the exorbitant fees to park within a few blocks of the shop.

There was something about January that always seemed so bleak. The streets were bare of their holiday decorations and cheerful colored lights. The joy on people's faces just last month had been replaced by a grim sort of stoicism. *Just get through this month. Just manage to chisel down the Christmas debt a little. Just keep the heat on and don't get the flu,* seemed to be the silent mantra of everyone inside and outside the coffee shop.

We hadn't had a customer in over an hour. The sun had set, but I still had three hours left on my shift. I was tempted to text Dario and tell him to swing by, but I knew he had stuff to do as the head of his *Balaj*, and I was supposed to go over to his house later. We were doing this balancing game in our relationship, trying to figure out the perfect mix of work time, alone time, and together time. Now that I was on a more regular schedule at the coffee shop, and his small *Balaj* wasn't facing any immediate threats, we'd fallen into a pattern of spending three nights a week together, and at least meeting for dinner or something another one or two nights.

We could spend every night together if I moved in with him, but I wasn't ready for that. I liked being in my own home, with my magical space in the basement and my pets. I didn't want to wake up to a Renfield fixing me breakfast and hanging around the house. Plus, Dario's place had become a sort of home base for the *Balaj*, which meant at nightfall half a dozen vampires or more were in and out of his house until a little before dawn. It wasn't a home, it was a business, and the trade-off of having Dario with me most of his waking hours would be a severe decrease in intimacy in the time we did spend together. I wouldn't be getting just a nice home and a convenient way to see more of Dario if I moved in with him, I'd be getting an entire *Balaj*.

And where I was a little nervous about taking the next step with Dario, I was *really* nervous about becoming some sort of Templar house mom to a group of vampires.

Tired of hashing through all this mentally in the silence of the coffeeshop, I poured Brandi and myself a cup of Ethiopian Blend and leaned my back against the counter.

"So what's up with you?" She asked, sipping the coffee. "Any New Year's resolutions?"

I thought of Chuck and the failed spell this morning. "I'm on a bit of a self-improvement kick. Running with Fulk each morning. Practicing with my sword every day. Studying some...stuff with a mentor."

She nodded. "I enrolled in two courses at Towson this semester. I've been taking college on the ten-year plan, and I figured it was time to get things done, get a real job, and maybe eventually move into a bigger apartment."

I poured some caramel syrup and a dollop of cream into my coffee and stirred it. "What are you studying?"

"Biology. At first I had dreams of being a veterinarian, but then I realized by the time I was out of school I'd be forty. I'll probably end up a lab tech somewhere."

She didn't sound all that enthusiastic about the prospect. "If you could do anything in the world, what would you do?"

Brandi thought on that a moment, looking out the door with a pensive expression on her face.

"I really don't know. There's no job I can think of that sets my heart on fire. I just want something that pays decently, has regular hours and good benefits, something where I can occasionally chat with coworkers without getting yelled at. I want a job that doesn't suck the soul out of me."

"And when you get home?"

The pensive expression was replaced with a dreamy one. "Take off my shoes and my bra. Make plans with friends to go out. Watch TV. Game. LARP. Read comics. Hopefully find a cute guy who likes to do the same and marry him."

It sounded kind of boring to me, but I'm sure my life probably would be equally boring to her—well except for the demons, evil mages, vampires, and monsters part. That would probably scare the pants, or bra, right off Brandi.

"How about you?" she asked. "I mean, you've got this history degree, but you're here. Isn't there something you really want to do with your life? Either work, or in your free time?"

I'd refused to take my Oath of Knighthood for years now, left home and moved to Baltimore in an effort to figure out who I was and what I wanted from life outside of the Templar role I was born into. Ironic that here in this city I'd discovered myself, I'd found what really gave my life meaning was the very thing I was born to do. But my version of a Templar Knight was a bit different from what the Elders and our Order saw it to be.

"Fight the monsters. Protect Pilgrims on the Path. Safeguard the Temple and the artifacts that are held inside. Facilitate the dissemination of knowledge, both sacred and profane, that we've studied, collected, and catalogued for centuries."

"Always the paladin," she teased. "So your ideal life is LARPing and playing RPGs. Huh. We're not so different after all."

Brandi and I were both members of Zac's role-playing game. We met weekly, and next month would be my turn to host the group. I couldn't wait. Unlike my old apartment, my new place had ample street parking, no asshole landlord, and no neighbors who made noise complaints every time I conducted a magical ritual or made out with Dario in the hallway. Plus if any of my gaming buddies had too many beers, I had an air mattress in the spare bedroom, and a comfy couch ready to accommodate an impromptu guest.

"Wouldn't it be nice if we really could LARP and play Anderon for a living?" She sighed.

"Yeah, until you roll a one and the demon you summon isn't Goetic and he marks your soul as his, then your best friend dies twice trying to rid you of the mark."

In real life, you couldn't just roll up a new character and rejoin the game. I felt a sharp twist in my chest as I thought about Raven. Russell, my necromancer friend, had tried several times in the last few months to contact her, but to no avail. She was gone. It was like she'd vanished from every plane of existence. I hoped that meant her soul was at rest, that she'd somehow been lifted up into heaven, but a knot of worry in my gut told me otherwise.

"Yeah, I guess you're right." Brandi sipped more coffee. "With my luck I'd be the dude in the red shirt that was victim number one of the dragon, demon, or whatever Big Bad we had to face."

Big Bad. It reminded me of the unknown horror the death mages had been trying to anesthetize with death magic, then soul magic. Chuck had been giving me little hints each month, but none of them were enough for me to have any idea what might be descending on Baltimore when the weather warmed a bit.

Brandi had been playing these games for far longer than I had, and although there were differences between the monsters in the players' manuals and the ones in the real world, there were also some shocking similarities. It made me wonder if the creators of these games had used research as much as their imagination.

"So what would be the worst Big Bad you'd ever want to encounter?" I asked. "Something that is pretty much immortal, that can be lulled into slumber by magic, but also by cold weather. Something that lives underground."

"Dragons."

I'd played with Brandi long enough to know she really had a thing about dragons. Not that I blamed her given how books and movies had been portraying them for the last century. I'd never personally encountered one, and from what I'd studied about them, I hoped I never did.

"Dragons mostly live in caves," I countered. And although there were a lot of dragons who didn't give two figs about weather, a few of them were definitely your typical reptiles in that they preferred warmer climates.

"Caves are underground," Brandi shot back.

She had a point. I made a mental note. "What besides dragons?"

"Undead. An army of wraiths or banshees or zombies or something."

That would totally suck, but outside of banshees, I think I could manage. Well…maybe. "Like how big of an army?"

Brandy waved the hand not holding the coffee. "Hundreds. Thousands. Everybody up and out of the grave."

"No one has the kind of magical power to raise that many dead," I told her.

"No one that you *know of.*" She tilted her head and gave me a side-eye.

I opened my mouth to argue, then thought. Russell had only been able to raise a couple dozen undead at a time, and he admitted he was a necromancer of middling talent. Would a high-level mage be able to raise hundreds? Would a truly powerful one be able to raise thousands? If so, why was he waiting to do so? What could trigger him to summon an undead army and attack a city? Did the Conclave that governed groups of mages know of any such necromancers? Would such a powerful person be off the grid, or someone even the Conclave was afraid of?

An undead army would definitely fall under the Big Bad heading, but a few things didn't make sense. Chuck had indicated that whatever it was had been contained and kept asleep by others, but that Fiore Noir had taken over the duties recently. If a powerful necromancer had been constantly thwarted for what I assumed to be centuries, then I'd think he'd either level up, or find something else to attack the city with.

"No. Not undead. A creature or a monster or something."

She shrugged. "Well, zombies *are* underground. Although I think they'd probably like cold better since they wouldn't decompose as fast. Unless it's an army of skeletons, then you're screwed at any time of year."

"It can't be undead, unless they're autonomous undead like a lich or ghoul. Think of something else." I mentally added lich and ghoul to my list, although I didn't think one lich or ghoul would be enough to warrant a group of death mages' attention. Plus neither liches nor ghouls liked hanging in packs. They were solitary creatures.

"A demon trapped inside a rock or something that's slowly degrading? A pissed-off demigod? Godzilla—which would be some sort of dinosaur that's been in stasis a gazillion years? Aliens that were cryogenically frozen, whose spaceship crashed here three thousand years ago, and due to global warming, they're thawing out?"

Wow. Brandi should be running her own games. The woman really had an amazing imagination. I'd made a list of potential Big Bads, but never thought to include frozen dinosaurs or aliens.

Dragon. What if it really was a dragon lulled to sleep over the centuries by some varying kind of magic? A dragon that would wake this spring, or earlier. But dragons were primarily in Europe, Asia, the Middle East, and Northern Africa, not in the Americas. They *were* territorial though. It was possible that a few thousand years ago one was forced to migrate here.

A dragon waking up after an abnormally long sleep would be hungry and grumpy. Plus if anyone had raided his treasures while he was dozing, he'd be more than grumpy. There was no way I could handle a dragon on my own. Even if Dario enlisted his *Balaj*, vampires wouldn't be much of a threat to a dragon. I'd need backup, especially since I wasn't about to resort to the techniques Chuck and his buddies in Fiore Noir had used.

If I needed help, I'm sure my family would assist, but the timing might mean some of them were unavailable. Right now, Mom and Dad were off on some Templar business in Italy. Roman and his wife were in France for the next two months with their family teaching at the Academy. Athena and her husband were available, but I hated to risk little Jet losing her parents before she'd even had a chance to really know them.

It wasn't like I could appeal to the Order. I mean, I *could*, but I doubted they'd provide any help. I'd not taken my Oath. I wasn't a Knight, thus they viewed me as a sort of child Templar who'd aged out of the system. Even if I *were* a Knight, I wasn't sure they'd help. I would need to phrase the request very carefully for the Elders to consider an attack on Baltimore to be something that required the Order's attention.

Brandi and I continued to talk about gaming. A grand total of three more customers came in between then and closing. We locked the door promptly at nine, cleaned the few things that hadn't been cleaned hours before, then went home.

The walk to work had been cold, but the walk home was worse. I clutched my coat snug around me, pulling my hat down farther over my face and ears. The wind grabbed my scarf and threatened to sweep it off and into the Patapsco River, so I knotted it again and tried to stuff it into the neckline of my coat.

A few blocks and I'd left the tourist area behind for a sort of no-man's-land area of Baltimore. During the day, this area was busy with people and commerce, but at night the streets were empty and the businesses shuttered. There was a shadowy feel about the place that made me grip my butter knife tight in my hand and wish I'd brought my sword with me. I'd gotten pretty good at the spell that concealed my huge sword from view, but it was still a pain having to find somewhere to stash it back in the storeroom while I was working. And pulling the scabbard straps around a bulky wool coat wasn't any picnic either. Maybe I was an idiot for leaving it at home, but I'd come to rely on my affiliation with the local vampire *Balaj* to keep any human gangs away. It irked me that the other vampires and their affiliates saw me as "The Boss's" property, but it *was* nice knowing I could walk pretty much any Baltimore street and remain unmolested.

In spite of the creepy horror-movie atmosphere, I made it home without incident. Stomping some frozen slush off my boots, I headed up my stairs only to stop abruptly when I saw the envelope on my poinsettia-print doormat. The wind hadn't blown it away. The light snow that had fallen a few hours earlier hadn't touched it. More amazing, no one had stolen it.

I reached down to pick it up, noticing the warm electric

feel I'd grown to recognize since I was practically in the cradle. A Templar blessing had safeguarded this note.

Eyeing my full name on the front I frowned. The handwriting wasn't one that I recognized. What Templar besides my family would be leaving a note on my doorstep?

Deciding this was a mystery best solved inside my warm home, I opened the door, shutting it tight against the cold as I took off my layers of outerwear and tried to avoid being knocked over by an excited dog, or tripped by the cat winding around my legs.

There was no way I could open this note and read it while my fur-babies were demanding my attention, so I set it aside and went about the nightly ritual of welcome with Gaia and Fulk.

It was a fairly brief ritual since both of them were hungry. Once I got them settled and happily munching on dinner, I returned to the note. With trepidation, I slid the card from the envelope and read.

*Solaria Angelique Ainsworth – Elder Emmett Purcell requests an audience with you at your residence Tuesday at four to discuss your upcoming Knighthood ceremony.*

Fuuuuuuuuck. And I really meant that word and not my dog's name, which was Fulk. Had my mother done this? Although she pestered the heck out of me to take my Oath, I couldn't see her stooping so low as to schedule the ceremony without my agreement. None of the others in my family seemed to care overmuch about my Knightless status, seeing it as a phase I was going through that would soon be over. I stared at the note, trying to decipher what was going on. Usually it was the prospective Knight that came to the elders to schedule their ceremony, not the opposite.

Feeling as if an anvil were about to drop on my head, I stuck the note back into the envelope and put it on my coffee table. I was pouring myself a big glass of cheap boxed wine when a knock at my door about gave me a heart attack.

It wasn't Tuesday and it wasn't four in the afternoon, but I still opened the door half expecting to see a stern-faced Elder Purcell standing there.

Instead of a Templar, the man at my door was a mage—a mage who hadn't returned my calls since that fateful Halloween night.

Reynard smiled that sexy, bad-boy smile that had made Raven fall in love with him, and I'll admit I wasn't exactly immune because instead of slamming the door in his face, I opened it wide and invited him in.

DOWNLOAD Dark Crossroads and read on!

ALSO BY DEBRA DUNBAR

## IMP WORLD NOVELS

### The Imp Series

A Demon Bound

Satan's Sword

Elven Blood

Devil's Paw

Imp Forsaken

Angel of Chaos

Kingdom of Lies

Exodus

Queen of the Damned

The Morning Star

With This Ring

* * *

### California Demon Series

California Demon

Sinners on Sunset

Ventura Hellway

* * *

### Half-breed Series

Demons of Desire

Sins of the Flesh

Cornucopia

Unholy Pleasures

City of Lust

* * *

<u>Imp World Novels</u>

No Man's Land

Stolen Souls

Three Wishes

Northern Lights

Far From Center

Penance

* * *

<u>Northern Wolves</u>

Juneau to Kenai

Rogue

Winter Fae

Bad Seed

* * *

<u>The Templar Series</u>

Dead Rising

Last Breath

Bare Bones

Famine's Feast

Royal Blood

Dark Crossroads

* * *

<u>Accidental Witches Series</u>
Brimstone and Broomsticks
Warmongers and Wands
Death and Divination
Hell and Hexes
Minions and Magic
Fiends and Familiars
Devils and the Dead (2021)

* * *

<u>White Lightning Series</u>
Wooden Nickels
Bum's Rush
Clip Joint
Jake Walk
Trouble Boys
Packing Heat (TBD)

# ACKNOWLEDGMENTS

Thanks to my copyeditors Kimberly Cannon and Jennifer Cosham whose eagle eyes catch all the typos and keep my comma problem in line, and to Damonza for cover design.